TOP SHELF

DAVID G. KEITH

Chuck —
Hope you enjoy my latest
novel.
Best Wishes
David Keith

Good Egg Press

Library of Congress Catalog Number: 2019914252

ISBN: 978-0-9863706-6-3 (print)
ISBN: 978-0-9863706-5-6 (ebook)

Top Shelf is a work of fiction. Names, characters, places, and incidents are the products of the author's imagination or are used fictitiously. Any resemblance to actual events, locales, or persons, living or dead, is entirely coincidental.

Cover Design by OMG Media
Interior Design by Lorie DeWorken, MIND*the*MARGINS, LLC

Published in the United States by Good Egg Press
www.goodeggpress.com

CHAPTER 1

Centennial Airport was a relatively small municipal airport located twenty miles south of Denver. No commercial flights were allowed at the airport as the runway was much too short, but it could accommodate small private jets.

It was a twenty minute drive up from Castle Springs and the members of the McCallister family were getting ready for their flight. None of them had been on a Lear jet before and they were excited for the experience.

"Dad, we're ready to go. Are you all packed?"

"I've been packed for two hours, Mia. Just give me the word and I'll take Sasha over to Fern's."

Sasha was the family dog, a Jack Russell/Beagle mix. She was a rescue they had found at a shelter a day before she was scheduled to be put down and she had been part of the family for more than eight years. Chuck spent the most time with Sasha and could swear that she somehow knew how close she had come to the end and was appreciative of what the family had done when they adopted her. He could see it in her eyes.

Fern was the neighbor next door, a sweet, charming woman with roots in Northern Ireland. She loved Sasha and always took great care of her when the family left town. Fern's dog, Oliver, got along great with Sasha.

Mia replied, "Go ahead and take her now. We need to get to the airport and we should leave ASAP."

Chuck scooped up Sasha and grabbed her bag full of toys, food, treats, dishes, bed, and blanket. No, she wasn't spoiled!

It was always difficult for Chuck to hand over his beloved friend. He kissed her face and talked to her quietly as he made his way next door.

"Hi, Chuck. How's my girl today?" asked Fern, standing in her doorway.

"She's doing just fine, but I swear she knows we're leaving."

"Oh, she'll be fine. We've got big plans. We're going to try out that new dog park in town."

"She'll love that, Fern. And it'll wear her out."

Fern took Sasha from Chuck's arms and grabbed the bag of stuff. Sensing Chuck's reticence she smiled at him. "Don't worry, Chuck. I promise to take very good care of her while you're gone."

"I know you will, Fern. You always do."

"You'll be back on Monday?"

"Yeah, the wedding is tomorrow and then we'll stay another couple of days and relax a bit. It's been a crazy few months."

"Yeah, I know. It'll be nice for you guys to have some fun."

Chuck nodded, gave Sasha one more quick kiss, and headed back next door.

As he walked back to the house he saw Mia loading up the family SUV in the driveway.

She and her husband, Mick, had purchased the vehicle following the birth of their son, CJ, three months earlier. Charles Jack McCallister had arrived in the world through very trying circumstances but was now healthy and doing very well. Born seven weeks premature, he weighed barely four pounds and had lungs that were not fully developed. But after three weeks in the hospital he finally came home and was soon thriving. Now at three months, his weight had nearly tripled and his lungs were functioning at a normal level.

"What can I help you with, Mia?"

"There's a few things still to pack. Could you check the living room?"

As Chuck walked up the steps to the front entrance of the house Mick came out, his arms full.

"I can't believe the stuff we need to take for CJ."

It wasn't a complaint; Mick McCallister was thrilled to be a father. CJ's arrival had changed his life.

He looked at his father-in-law and continued, "I can't imagine trying to do this if we were flying commercial. There just wouldn't be enough room for everything."

"Yeah, no kidding. But Mia knows what she's doing and if she thinks we need all this stuff, then we need it."

"There's one more small suitcase inside. If you could grab it, that would be great."

Mick had been careful to pack the heavier items himself. Just three months earlier his father-in-law had experienced a significant heart issue, resulting in a stent being put into one of his arteries. The procedure had been done the day before CJ was born. As Chuck had told Fern, the past three months had been a crazy time for the McCallister family.

"Okay, no problem. Be right out with it."

Once everything was packed, Mick locked up the house and climbed into the car.

He looked at his wife and baby in the back seat and said, "Hope we've got everything."

"I'm sure we've forgotten something but we can always buy it once we get there," responded Mia.

"Okay, off we go."

It was still too early for the heavy Friday-afternoon Denver traffic to start, so the drive to Centennial Airport took less than twenty minutes.

Mick pulled up to the front of the terminal and parked in the loading/ unloading zone. He and Chuck climbed from the vehicle and unloaded items onto the sidewalk while Mia and CJ remained in the car.

It was certainly a different experience flying from a small airport rather than Denver International, thought Mick. DIA was a large and very busy place and the idea of traveling with the baby and all the necessary accoutrement left him wondering how families with small kids ever did it.

Once the car was unpacked, Mick drove over to the long-term lot and parke. A few minutes later they boarded the Lear jet and were soon ready for takeoff.

The jet, a Model 45, was sleek and comfortable. It had room for eight, and while the McCallister family numbered just four, the other seats were covered with things Mia and the baby might need during the two-hour flight. The rest of the luggage had been placed in the cargo hold underneath the plane.

"Wow, I could get used to this!" commented Chuck, settling into his leather-bound captain's chair.

Mia smiled at her dad. "Yeah, well enjoy this, Dad. Because it'll probably be the last time we're ever on a plane like this. Just a bit out of our budget, don't you think?"

"Well, we're coming home on Monday, so I'll have at least one more flight on this baby."

Mick sat next to Mia and watched as she held CJ. She was such a good mom, he thought. She was forty-two and had taken very naturally to motherhood. She was on a three-month maternity leave that was set to end when they returned from their trip. Chuck would be caring for the baby once she returned to work, or at least they were going to give it a shot. Chuck was a young seventy-five, and except for the heart scare three months earlier he was in very good physical shape. Chuck had pleaded with Mick and Mia for the chance to care for his only grandchild, and was sure he could handle it. At three months, CJ still slept a lot during the day. Chuck had watched Mia closely for the three months and was confident he could do it. Mick and Mia had agreed to give it a try, at least until the baby got a little older and became more work. Then they would revisit the arrangement.

The pilot poked his head from the cockpit and greeted the McCallisters.

"Good afternoon, everybody. I'm Pat McCarthy and will serve as your pilot today. We're getting ready for takeoff in a few minutes, so if you could all buckle up, I'd appreciate it. The baby needs to be in his carseat and buckled into a seat."

"No problem," replied Mick, rising from his chair to get the baby settled.

Mia handed CJ to Mick who buckled him in. He went to the cockpit and let the pilot know everything was ready. A minute later the jet was in the air and they were on their way to Puerto Peñasco, Mexico.

CHAPTER 2

Jack Keller had arrived in Mexico a full week before his daughter's wedding. He was off work, still recovering from gunshot wounds he had suffered in a shootout three months earlier. Two bullets had entered his back and a third had lodged in his left hip. During a six-hour surgery, doctors were able to remove the two bullets in his back, but the round in his hip had proven problematic. The decision was made to leave it in and see what kind of range of motion Jack would have in his leg. Additional surgeries were an option if necessary. At this point, his ability to move his left leg was quite limited and Jack was relegated to using a walker.

Now he was getting ready to go to the airport to greet his guests coming in from Colorado and was feeling very frustrated by his physical restrictions Getting up from a sitting position was difficult for him but his pride wouldn't allow him to ask for help. He had learned how to twist his body in such a way as to put most of his weight on his right side as he rose to his feet, but it was still quite painful. Once he was up and moving the pain was manageable.

He was determined to get better and was doing all the exercises that Jeannette, his physical therapist, had taught him. He had gained some mobility, but was still very frustrated that he couldn't do all the things he was able to do before the shooting. Patience wasn't Keller's strong suit.

After a couple of tries, Jack was finally on his feet and moving. He shuffled down the hall from his room at the Marbella Resort and headed to the lobby where he was to meet his daughter, Lisa. The two of them would take the resort's limo to the airport to pick up the McCallisters.

"How you doing today, Dad?" she asked watching her father moving slowly with his walker.

"Can't complain," he lied. "Just ready for my daughter's wedding tomorrow. So the real questions is how are you doing?"

"Pretty calm, actually. Peter and I have just decided that things will go fine tomorrow, and if they don't, then we'll just roll with it."

"Good plan, honey. In the long run, it doesn't matter. Just have fun tomorrow and know you're marrying the man you love."

"Are you ready to go and meet your friends?"

"Yep, let's do it."

Manuel, the Marbella's longtime limo driver, climbed from the car and helped Jack into the middle seat of the stretch SUV. Lisa took the seat next to him while Manuel put the walker in the back.

"So, the airport, correct?"

"That's the plan, Manuel."

The co-pilot left the cockpit and walked back to the cabin area of the jet.

"We're about ten minutes from landing."

Mia peeked out the window and could see the beautiful Sea of Cortez below them. The colors were amazing, with a large coral reef visible just a few hundred yards from shore. Rows of white buildings lined the beach, and two golf courses stood out with their lush green fairways. The courses looked like they spilled right onto the beach.

She had done some research on this Mexican port town before they had left to travel to the wedding. Puerto Peñasco was a relatively new destination spot, one popular with people from the southwest United States. It was a short drive from the Arizona-Mexico border and air travel to Puerto Peñasco was available via a brand new private airport a few miles from town. What was a sleepy fishing village when Peter Donnelly first laid eyes on it was now a thriving vacation destination, thanks in large part to his vision and business savvy.

Peter had instantly seen the potential in the beautiful village, envisioning a place for people from the southwest US to vacation. Californians flocked to Rosarito Beach and Ensenada; Puerto Peñasco could be the playground for those from Phoenix and the surrounding areas. Peter started by buying a small motel and then quickly branched out by offering upscale fishing excursions. He found many Arizonans willing to pay good money for a few days on the Sea of Cortez with an opportunity to land the almighty marlin. More investments were made around town and within a decade Peter Donnelly was the primary landowner in Puerto Peñasco. The Marbella Resort had been a dream of his and his wife, Marbella, but she had died of ovarian cancer before construction was completed. A year later, when the place first opened its doors to its guests, Peter had named it The Marbella, in honor of his late wife.

He met Lisa Sullivan many years later and the attraction between the two was electric. What Peter didn't know was the beautiful Lisa Sullivan was on the run, wanted as an accessory in a murder in Castle Springs, Colorado. Peter was about to propose to her when things fell apart. Lisa, who was using the alias Natalie Summers, had been found and was soon on her way back to Colorado to face charges. A good deal of finagling by a very talented defense attorney named Danny Velasco had allowed Lisa to avoid prison time. The deal made between Velasco and Rocklin County District Attorney Dave Baxter was a difficult one for the RCSO to swallow. They felt strongly that Lisa deserved prison time for her role in the killing. The man who had coerced her into assisting with the homicide was ultimately convicted and was serving twenty-five years to life in a Colorado prison.

The wildcard in all this was that after the plea deal was made, Mia discovered that Lisa was actually the long-lost daughter of her partner, Jack Keller. It became clear that Keller had used his position to secretly protect his daughter and keep her from being arrested by having her hide at his vacation home in Puerto Peñasco. Mia kept that secret from her husband, who was elected sheriff of Rocklin County at around the same time, in an effort to protect him. Ultimately, Mick learned the truth, and it remained a closely-held secret known to just a handful of people.

And now Mick and Mia were about to attend the wedding of the woman they had pursued so vigorously. They would be there at Jack Keller's request.

CHAPTER 3

After touching down, it took a few minutes to gather up everything in the cabin of the jet. CJ had not slept much during the flight, which made his parents hopeful that he might sleep well at the hotel. He wasn't sleeping through the night quite yet, but most nights he only required one feeding.

Mick looked out the window and saw the airport personnel rolling up the portable jet bridge to the plane.

"Looks like the stairway is almost here. We about ready?"

"I think so. Dad, can you grab the diaper bag? And Mick, if you could get the car seat, that would be great."

Mia gathered up CJ in a blanket and held him tight.

The co-pilot came out from the cockpit and started working on the door latch.

"Hope you enjoyed the flight and have a great time in Puerto Peñasco."

"Thanks for everything," replied Mick.

"Will you be taking us back on Monday?" asked Chuck, looking at the young man.

"Yes, sir, we're on full time these days."

"I gotta tell you, I could get used to traveling like this."

The co-pilot smiled. "Yeah, we hear that a lot."

Lisa didn't say anything during the fifteen-minute ride from the Marbella out to the airport.

"You're awfully quiet. Are you concerned about seeing the McCallisters?"

Lisa looked at her father. "Yeah, I'm a little weirded out by it. I mean, a couple of years ago they wanted to put me in prison for life, and now they're here to attend my wedding."

"It'll be fine. Things are all smoothed over and I really think they understand now that you had nothing to do with planning George Lombard's murder. It's water under the bridge."

"Yeah, you say that, but is it really? I know they're forever grateful to you for saving Mia and the baby. But they really wanted to put me away and I'm just not sure that kind of desire goes away so easily."

"Yeah, I know sweetie, but we talked about this. You said you had no problem if I invited them to the wedding. I'm telling you—everything changed in the foyer of that hotel three months ago. You shouldn't be worrying about this."

Lisa looked at her Dad.

"I'm sure it'll be fine. I think I'm just stressing a bit about tomorrow."

"Perfectly normal. Just relax and enjoy the day. That's the plan you and Peter had for tomorrow. Just let it happen."

The limo pulled up in front of the terminal and Jack and Lisa climbed from the back seat and walked toward the tarmac. A few minutes later they watched as the Learjet landed and taxied toward them. After a short delay the McCallisters deplaned, carrying a substantial amount of luggage and baby things.

"Come on, let's go greet our guests," Jack said, walking onto the tarmac. As they approached the McCallisters, Lisa felt the anxiety creeping in. Just stay calm, she told herself.

Lisa smiled warmly, turned to Mia, extended her hand, and said "Welcome to Puerto Peñasco! I'm so glad you all could make it."

Mia looked at Lisa and instead of taking her hand, she reached out and gave her a hug.

"We're happy to be here to share in your big day. Thank you for inviting us."

Lisa felt a wave of relief and gave her a tight hug back. She turned and greeted the others, then offered to help with all the things the McCallisters were carrying.

"No, I think we've got it," said Mick, looking over at his top homicide investigator. He hadn't seen him since the day of the shooting and was surprised to see him using a walker.

"Okay, the car is right over there," responded Jack, pointing toward the terminal.

No one spoke as they walked the hundred yards or so to the car. Manuel helped load all the luggage. It was a good thing he had brought the stretch limo, he thought.

Once everyone was settled into the limo, they headed toward the Marbella and Lisa felt a huge wave of relief.

The rooms at the Marbella were like nothing the McCallisters had ever seen. They were given two connecting rooms, and one was equipped with a crib. Chuck had the other room and was immediately drawn to the big-screen TV on the wall.

"This thing gets like five hundred channels," he said, looking at the cable guide on the desk.

"I'm sure it does, Dad. But we're in Mexico and there are a lot of other things to do."

"Oh, I know Mia. It's just that this TV is top of the line—curved screen, the whole nine yards."

Mick jumped in. "I was thinking of maybe doing some fishing on Sunday. All the brochures talk about the marlin and sailfish they catch off the coast here."

"Dad, you should go with Mick and do some fishing. I don't mind the idea of having some quiet time with the baby. Maybe get out onto the beach a little bit."

"Marlin? Wow, that would be incredible. I'm in."

"Okay, that's settled. I think I'll put CJ down for a little nap and I may join him."

"Want to go explore, Chuck?" asked Mick.

"Yep, let's go."

After settling the McCallisters into their rooms, Jack and Lisa walked toward Peter's office at the Marbella.

"See? That went well. Nothing to worry about."

Lisa smiled at her dad. "Yeah, Mia was really sweet. The sheriff didn't say much, but at least she seems good with everything."

"The sheriff will be fine. Once the wife is on board, the husband will follow."

"Oh, are those your words of wisdom for today?"

"Yeah, you'll see."

Peter was staring at a computer screen when Jack and Lisa walked in.

"Hey, you guys are back already? How'd it go with the McCallisters?"

"It went fine. They're in their rooms and getting settled in."

"Good."

Jack jumped in, "So, what are you two doing tonight?"

Peter replied, "I'm not sure. We had talked about having a quiet dinner in our suite. Lisa, do you have any ideas?"

"A quiet dinner sounds nice. Everything is all set for tomorrow . . . maybe it'll get our minds off everything. But Dad, what will you do?"

"Don't worry about me; I'll be fine. You guys should have some time to yourselves tonight. Get rested up for the wedding tomorrow."

"Then it's settled," answered Peter.

CHAPTER 4

On Saturday morning another beautiful day dawned on the Sea of Cortez. Temperatures were forecast to reach eighty, with a slight breeze from the west. The wedding was set for five, with an outdoor dinner reception at the Marbella following the ceremony. By eight in the morning a crew of more than a dozen were already at work preparing for the big day. Lisa and Peter had decided to go with a simple but elegant wedding, but having it at the Marbella presented a few challenges. The resort remained open, but a portion of the private beach area was roped off for the wedding ceremony and the reception. A private caterer, one who did a lot of business at the Marbella, had been hired to handle the dinner.

The McCallisters were up early; CJ had decided to start his day at five thirty. The good news was that he had slept through the night for the first time. Mia had awakened when he began crying and was startled at first when she realized that the sun was peeking through the drapes. She went quickly to the crib and picked him up.

"Such a good boy!"

Maybe the salt air was to his liking.

With the wedding not slated to start until five, Jack thought he'd spend the morning doing some sailing. He had always done some fishing during his previous visits to Puerto Peñasco, but he wasn't sure his body was ready for that quite yet. He called down to the concierge desk and let them know that he'd like to go out for a couple hours. The concierge, recognizing the room number as belonging to Peter Donnelly's soon-to-be father-in-law, immediately made the necessary arrangements. Jack headed downstairs to grab some coffee and breakfast.

Chuck woke up early as usual, went down to the beach, and watched the sunrise off to the east. Nothing was open quite yet at the Marbella, so once the sun was up he took a two-mile walk on the beach. He hadn't lived near the sea since his college days at UCLA, and walking along the Sea of Cortez made him realize how much he missed the beach. Always an avid hiker, it had been difficult for him to curtail his normal routine following his heart scare. The doctor had told him to take it easy for a week or two, but once that period had passed he was back to doing three to four miles a day at Red Rocks near their Castle Springs home. The stent had done the trick and he really felt better than he had in years. He was seventy-five but felt fifty.

The day passed quickly, with Mick and Chuck doing some fishing and Mia and CJ enjoying the beach. Before they knew it, it was time to get ready for the wedding.

Chuck stared into the mirror on the bathroom wall, fiddling with the tie around his neck. He was trying to make the two ends come out at least somewhat equal in length, but wasn't having much success. He tried to remember back to the last time he wore a suit and tie, but except for the occasional funeral, he hadn't put one on since his days as a NASA scientist, some fifteen years earlier.

"Dad, let me help you."

Chuck looked in the mirror to see his daughter looking at him sweetly.

"Okay, I'm not having much luck. I wore one of these things every-day for thirty-five years, but today it's getting the best of me."

"No worries, Dad."

Mia gently placed her hand on her father's shoulder, turning him to face her. She reached up and tied the tie, getting both the length and the knot perfect.

"Now go get your coat; the wedding starts in fifteen minutes."

Chuck looked at his daughter and welled up with emotion. Ever since his heart attack he had experienced a whole range of emotions, with each feeling greatly enhanced.

The wedding took place on the beach at the Marbella resort, the same beach where Peter and Lisa had talked on the night they first met. And the same beach where things between them had completely unraveled months later when Peter discovered that Lisa was a fugitive from Colorado on the run from the police. And now, a couple of years later, they were waiting to exchange vows on the same beach under a white arch covered in plumeria.

There were eighty guests present; it was a virtual who's who of Puerto Peñasco. Lisa was dressed in a flowing white Bohemian-style dress. She wore her hair down in loose curls. Her bouquet had gardenias, white roses, and baby's breath. Peter was in a gray suit with a pale blue shirt open at the collar. Both were barefoot, something that Lisa had wanted. Their life together would be carefree and fun, and she felt bare feet represented that freedom.

She was in the house, peeking out through the sliding glass doors, waiting for the cue to begin her walk to the arch. Jack was with her, nervously pulling on the sleeves of his suit. He was going to make the trip down the aisle without his walker. It might take him a little more time, but Lisa didn't mind. She was thrilled that her father, a man she had grown up not really knowing, was there for the most important day of her life.

She looked at her dad and said, "I am so happy you're here today. I love you so much."

Jack embraced his daughter and gave her a kiss on the cheek.

"I love you too, sweetie. There's no place I'd rather be. I'm so happy for you."

"Thanks, Dad. Now, if we can just get this show on the road . . . I am so ready!"

"What's our cue?"

Lisa peered back out the glass doors. "When the violinist starts to play. Should be any moment. You ready?"

"I think so, although I have to tell you—I'm kinda nervous!"

"You'll do fine. Just take your time and I'll be on your arm the whole way. Enjoy the moment, Dad."

Just then, the sound of a violin filled the air, with the opening notes of the wedding march.

"Let's go, Dad. It's showtime!"

Lisa took her dad's arm and the two started slowly across the beach toward the arch. White rose petals lined the aisle between the chiavari chairs set out in rows in the sand. Lanterns lined the aisles, each with a candle burning brightly inside. Halfway to the arch, Lisa leaned into her father. "You doing okay?"

"Yep, couldn't be better."

All the guests were now standing, taking in the magical scene. Lisa and Jack nodded and smiled at their friends as they walked toward the arch. Lisa looked up and fixed her eyes on Peter. He locked eyes on her and watched as she and Jack approached. The bride and the groom both had wide smiles on their faces.

Once they were front and center, Jack nodded at Peter as he stepped forward to take Lisa's hand. Jack kissed his daughter on the cheek and whispered something in her ear. She whispered something back and Jack got a bit emotional. He gathered himself, turned to Peter, and offered Lisa's hand to him. Peter gave Jack a hug and he and Lisa took their places under the arch. The minister presiding over the ceremony welcomed everyone and began.

The wedding reception was held on the terrace of the Marbella, just yards from the sand. The guests mingled, enjoying Champagne and myriad delicious hors d'oeuvres, while the newlyweds were busy taking photos on the beach.

"This is quite the spread," Chuck whispered to Mick and Mia, standing on the expansive terrace, taking in the scene.

"I bet just this reception cost more than our wedding and honeymoon combined," answered Mick.

Mia looked at Mick. "Yeah, but I wouldn't trade ours for anything. It was perfect."

Mick took her hand and squeezed it. "I agree, but you have to admit this is really something."

"Yeah, it is. Not a bad place for Lisa to hide out from us a few years back."

"Let it go, Mia. It's ancient history."

"I know, but wow . . . that girl knows how to land on her feet!"

Mick and Chuck both laughed at the comment.

They were interrupted by Pablo, the deejay.

"Ladies and gentlemen, if I can ask for your attention for just a moment, our bride and groom are about to arrive!"

The guests all turned their attention toward the beach to see Peter and Lisa walking hand in hand toward the terrace. The scene was perfect—two gorgeous people looking radiant.

They walked onto the terrace with Billy Joel's "Just the Way You Are" playing as their entrance song.

"Ladies and gentlemen, it is my great pleasure to welcome, for the first time as husband and wife, Peter and Lisa Donnelly!"

Every guest turned to watch as the newlyweds swept across the dance floor in each other's arms. It was like a scene from a movie, a perfect moment.

Once the song ended, the deejay continued, "And now I'd like to introduce the father of the bride, Mr. Jack Keller!"

Jack, who was standing with Mick, Mia, and Chuck, gave a little wave to the guests. He let go of his walker and slowly made his way across the dance floor to Lisa. The two embraced, he gave her a kiss on the cheek, and they danced to Frank Sinatra's "The Way You Look Tonight."

It was an emotional time for Jack and Lisa. Just a few years earlier they had been reunited through the most bizarre of circumstances, and now they were dancing together at Lisa's wedding in Puerto Peñasco, Mexico.

Life was good.

CHAPTER 5

After three months on injury leave, Jack was excited to return to work. His daughter's wedding had gone beautifully, but now it was time to get back to his routine. Jack walked into the Investigations Bureau and shuffled over to his former cubicle. The desk had been completely cleared off; only the phone and a computer remained. He did a quick check of his file cabinets and found them all empty. There was virtually nothing remaining in the place he had spent more than a dozen years. He folded up his walker and placed it in the corner. It was barely seven in the morning and the bureau was deserted. He sat there, wondering where the hell all his stuff was, trying not to get pissed off. Maybe they moved it into storage? He wasn't sure if the sheriff had informed the RCSO employees that he would be returning to work. It had been more than three months since the shooting, and with his injuries Keller had been medically retired. It wasn't his choice, but doctors had told him he'd never be able to keep up with the physical demands of the job. He had argued that as an investigator he didn't need to possess the same physical capabilities as a patrol officer, but Louis Centeno, the CEO of Rocklin County, had decided they couldn't risk keeping Keller onboard as a full-time active duty law enforcement officer. Mick had gone to bat for him, arguing that he could find him a position that bore no risk, but he had been overruled.

However, Mick found a loophole and offered Keller a contract as an independent contractor, eliminating any financial exposure to the county. The county agreed to the arrangement and Jack was back, though his contract limited him to working no more than 999 hours per fiscal year.

Keller sat at his desk and thought about his new position. Having the sheriff go to bat for him was not something he would have ever envisioned. He and McCallister had been constantly at odds; in fact, the sheriff had fired Jack just two years earlier, only to give him his job back when Keller threatened to expose a secret that could bring down the sheriff and allow Scott Lennox, a convicted murderer, to go free. Keller didn't like having to play that card, but felt he had no choice at the time and the move had worked. To say things had been strained between the two was an understatement. McCallister could hardly stand being in the same room as Keller. But all that changed when Keller had taken a bullet—three to be exact—for Mia. He had saved Mia's life and the life of their unborn baby. McCallister would be forever indebted to Jack Keller.

"Hey, stranger. How goes it?"

Keller looked up and saw Mike Laubacher standing at his cubicle.

"Hey, Mike."

"I heard you were coming back on a contract. That's great. We could use the help."

Keller, not one for small talk, responded. "Do you know what they did with all my stuff? Everything's gone."

"They gave your caseload to Bernzott. I'm guessing he has all your shit."

"Well, I'm going to need it back."

"I'm sure you guys'll work it out. Good to see you, Jack."

Laubacher walked away, headed for some coffee in the break room.

With no files, Jack was dead in the water. He tried logging onto the computer on his desk, but the passwords didn't work. It was like he had never fucking worked there, he thought.

"Good morning, Jack."

Keller turned to see who it was and saw Mia standing there.

"None of my passwords work and all my files are missing."

Mia looked at the man who had saved her life. Keller being Keller—Mr. Congeniality.

"I'm sure they'll restore all the passwords, Jack. And I'm sure Mick will talk to you about your caseload."

"What's there to talk about? Laubacher said Bernzott was working my cases. I hope he didn't screw things up."

"I'm sure it'll all get worked out. Mick should be in soon."

Keller didn't respond. Mia decided to change the subject.

"Hey, the wedding was beautiful. We really enjoyed it."

Keller looked at Mia and nodded. "Yeah, it was good. Thanks for coming."

Mia realized that was about as much as she was going to get out of her former partner.

"Okay, I'm going to get to work. It's my first day back, too. I don't even want to think about what's waiting for me in my inbox."

Mia's three month maternity leave was over.

"Yeah, good luck with that."

Before heading to her cubicle, Mia poked her head in Mick's office.

"Just a heads up—Keller's at his desk and wondering where all his files are. He's a bit grumpier than usual."

"Yeah, I gotta talk to him about that."

"Kevin Bernzott took his caseload, right?"

"Yeah, and I'm leaving those cases with him. It was already a hassle moving them to Kevin after Jack retired. Now he's finally got his bearings and is making some good progress on several cases. I don't want to disrupt that flow again."

"Oh, that'll go over well. Let me know when you're going to talk with Keller about that. I think I'll leave the building."

"He'll be okay with it."

"Ummm, no he won't. But you're the sheriff and that's why you get the big bucks."

"Yeah, I keep having to remind myself of that. Speaking of which, I have a re-election committee meeting tonight. Do you want to go?"

Mia hated politics and was less than thrilled about what was ahead for her and Mick. His four-year term was coming to an end and the wheels were in motion for him to run for a second term.

"If it's okay, I think I'd rather stay home tonight and spend time with CJ. Both he and I need to get used to having me back at work. I miss him already."

"No problem. Hopefully it'll be a short meeting. Save dinner for me."

"I will. And good luck with Keller."

Mick thought about what Mia had said about Jack. Might as well get it over with, he thought.

He picked up the phone and dialed his administrative assistant.

"Lucinda, find Jack Keller for me and have him come see me."

"You got it, boss."

Mick contemplated how the conversation with Jack would likely go. He wouldn't be happy, but at least he was back at work, something that Keller had made very clear he wanted.

A few minutes later Keller appeared in the doorway.

"Morning, boss."

"Come on in. Close the door."

Keller looked at him uneasily. The only times a superior had asked him to close the door were times he was being disciplined, or worse. He couldn't be in any trouble yet, so he figured the sheriff was about to deliver news he wouldn't like. Keller maneuvered his walker around and closed the door, then took a seat across from the sheriff.

"Jack, I wanted to talk to you about your new assignment here. After you were injured I didn't think you'd be coming back to work. It was pretty clear that a medical retirement was in your future and so I had no choice but to reassign your cases to another investigator. I'm sure you understand."

"Sure, that makes sense. But now I'm back and I'd like my cases back. It's what you hired me back for, isn't it?"

Mick looked at his best investigator. Mia was right—this wasn't going to be easy.

"Well, yes and no."

"What do you mean, 'yes and no'?"

"I'm going to leave your caseload with Kevin Bernzott. He's up to speed on the various cases and I don't want to disrupt his progress. If I reassign them back to you I think that'll complicate things and could cause problems. You know that, Jack. Cases have a certain momentum and Bernzott has that working right now."

"Then what the fuck am I doing here?"

Mick let the comment go. Keller was upset and that was understandable.

"I want you to work some special projects for me."

"Special projects? What does that mean, exactly?"

"It's a position I've created just for you."

"With all due respect, sheriff—"

"Now, hold on, Jack. You don't even know what the position is about. Let me explain a little about the job."

Keller looked dubious but didn't say anything. He knew Mick was up for re-election and was concerned that his new assignment would be to somehow help him politically. He had no interest in that.

"To start with, I'd like you to do an inventory of the evidence room."

Jack couldn't contain himself. "The evidence room? Are you kidding me?"

"Listen, Jack. Nate Frazier retired a month or so ago I think the evidence room needs a look. An audit of sorts."

"Then have some fucking clerk do it. I'm not the guy for that kind of stuff. I'm a homicide investigator, for God's sake."

"I know that, but, as you know, the chain of evidence is critically important. Things down there have to be run right. If not, we run the risk of a case going south and some asshole walks on a one-eighty-seven."

"I know all that, sheriff. My beef isn't with you wanting a well-run evidence room. We both know that's critical. But get someone else to do it. I'm here to work homicides, not take care of administrative crap."

"I'll make a deal with you. Take on the evidence room and get it all cleaned up. Make sure we're good down there and then I'll start having new cases assigned to you. The next one-eighty-seven is yours."

Keller stared at his boss. He wasn't sure he had much choice but to take the assignment he was being offered. Hopefully someone in Rocklin County would get whacked soon and he'd have a real case to work on, he thought to himself.

"All right. But the next one-eighty-seven is mine, correct?"

"Yes, absolutely."

Keller stood, grabbed his walker, and left the office.

CHAPTER 6

Keller returned to his cubicle and called down to the IT guys. He asked to have his computer and passwords reinstated. Then he walked down to the evidence room and asked to speak to Suzy Gill, the woman generally tasked with retrieving evidence when something was needed by investigators. Suzy had been at the RCSO longer than Keller. The two had good rapport, something Jack knew would be helpful as he did the audit of the evidence room.

"Jack, I had heard a rumor you were coming back!"

"Hey, Suzy. Yeah, it's true."

"What can I do for you?"

Keller looked around. "Is there some place we can talk privately?"

Looking a little surprised, she responded, "Yeah, sure. We can use my office."

Suzy held the door for Jack, and the two moved slowly toward the back of the evidence area.

"So, how are you doing, Jack?" she asked, as the two walked down the hallway.

"I'm okay. Just gotta lose this damn walker. Frickin' doctors."

"You're too stubborn to be using that thing for much longer. I'm sure you'll be back to your old self real soon."

The two entered Suzy's office and took seats facing each other.

"So, what's going on, Jack?"

Jack knew he had to phrase things carefully. He didn't want Suzy to get defensive; he would be needing her help.

"Look, Suzy, I just met with the sheriff and he wants me to do an audit of the evidence room. He said with Frazier's retirement he thought it was a good time for it."

"Yeah, I had heard that that was in the works. I think it's a good idea."

Jack was relieved Suzy was on board.

"Just routine. Gotta keep the chain of evidence above reproach. Hell, you know all that."

"Yes, of course."

Suzy looked like she had more to say. Jack picked up on it.

"You okay with all this, then?"

Suzy stood and went to the door. After closing it, she returned to her chair.

"Jack, we've been friends for a long time. And I feel I can trust you."

"Of course. What's on your mind, Suzy?"

Suzy grew serious and seemed reluctant to continue.

"Talk to me, Suzy. What is it?'

Suzy leaned in toward Jack and lowered her voice.

"Look, before Frazier retired, I went to Commander Espy and expressed concern about how things were being run down here."

"How so?"

"You know, I worked with Frazier for more than twenty years and I have—or I should say—*had* a lot of respect for him. He ran a good shop and the chain of evidence was of the utmost importance, as it should be. I mean, the integrity of the unit was key to the prosecution of hundreds of court cases each year."

"Yeah, go on . . . "

"A year or so ago, I saw a change in Frazier. I think he was having some money problems and he started drinking heavily; sometimes I smelled alcohol on his breath after lunch. He had always been hard working and very proud of the unit. Then it all seemed to take a back seat to his personal problems."

Jack nodded. He certainly understood the alcohol issue, having battled alcoholism for more than four decades. Except for a short setback two years earlier, Keller hadn't had a drink in fourteen years.

"When you say money problems, do you think he did anything stupid like stealing stuff from the evidence room?"

"No, nothing like that. At least I never saw any evidence of that. It was more like he didn't give a shit any more. He'd come in late and leave early. Stuff would pile up on his desk and he'd take forever to get to it. On more than one occasion, I found evidence that he had checked out for someone just sitting on his desk. And then, when the officer or investigator returned it from court, he was a bit lackadaisical about returning it to its proper place. And obviously that was a big no-no."

Keller shook his head. He had seen mistrials declared for less. His mind wandered to the LAPD and the OJ Simpson case and the criticism the department had been subjected to over the handling of evidence from the crime scene.

"No, that's no good. But you don't think anything is missing, do you?"

"No, I've never found anything like that. But because of his sloppiness I'm sure there are things we'd be hard pressed to put our hands on if needed quickly for a criminal trial. But there's something else . . . I noticed Frazier's memory was slipping. Like early-stage dementia or something. I'm no expert, but my uncle went through something similar a few years back."

Keller considered what he was being told. This was not what he had signed on for, but he liked Suzy and was concerned about what she was telling him.

'When was the last time the unit went through any kind of official outside audit?"

"It's been years. Way before McCallister became sheriff."

"Do you remember who did the audit?"

"It's been so long, I can't remember the name of the company. But I could find it."

"Okay, why don't you do that? But in the meantime, don't mention our conversation to anyone. I need to talk to the sheriff first."

"Okay, Jack."

Keller looked at Suzy and could sense her relief. She'd been carrying this burden for a long time and now perhaps she saw a path to making things better.

CHAPTER 7

Chuck loaded CJ into the new stroller he had purchased as a baby gift for his grandson and headed for the door. It was a ritual that he carried out each day—a long walk around the neighborhood. CJ seemed to enjoy it, although he typically fell asleep within a few minutes.

Chuck was feeling good since doctors had put the stent in his heart more than three months earlier. It had taken him a few weeks to get back on his feet and resume his normal activities but he was in full swing now. The walks he and CJ took each day had started out short, just around the block at first, but now they were up to three miles or so. His big plans were to eventually take CJ on hikes up around Red Rocks, but he hadn't told Mia about that. He wasn't sure how she'd feel about it.

As he walked by the neighborhood park he saw a familiar car slowing down as it approached.

"Hey, Dad. How's your walk? CJ sound asleep?"

"Hi Mia. Yep, he's zonked out. How was your first day back to work?"

"Went okay. I sure missed my boy, though."

"I can imagine. I'm almost done here, I should be home in a few minutes. I've got a roast going in the Crock Pot for dinner."

"Sounds great. See you in a few."

Mia could smell the pot roast as soon as she stepped into the house. She took a quick peek in the Crock Pot and saw meat, potatoes, and carrots. Perfect, she thought. She'd put together a salad and they'd be ready to go. She looked at her watch—six thirty-five. She expected Mick home at his usual time, around seven.

A few minutes later Chuck and CJ arrived home and Mia rushed to her son. She unbuckled him from the stroller and held him tightly, kissing his face. The ten hours she'd spent at work was the longest she'd been apart from him. Her heart ached, realizing this would be her schedule now, and the time apart from CJ was more difficult than she had imagined. When's the weekend? she thought, but quickly realized it was only Monday.

Chuck could see how difficult it had been for his daughter to be away all day.

"Mia, he did great today. We did our walk, we watched some TV, he took a couple of good naps, and he ate a ton. He's going to be just fine."

"I know, Dad. But it's just really hard. I'll adjust to it, but it won't be easy."

"You could always stay home with him . . . "

It was a conversation the two had had several times leading up to her return to work. Chuck was a bit old fashioned—he thought it would be best if Mia stayed home and raised her son. It was what he and Mia's mother had done forty years earlier. But times were different now. Different, Chuck thought, but not necessarily better.

"I know, Dad."

"Okay, just thought I'd throw it out there."

"Yeah, for like the thousandth time," Mia replied with a smile.

"Mick should be home soon. Shall we aim for seven for dinner?"

"Yeah, that sounds good. Ah, crap . . . I just remembered he has a re-election meeting tonight."

"How late will that go?"

"Who knows, those people all love to talk."

"Should we eat without him? We can save him a plate."

"Yeah, let's do that. I'm starved."

CHAPTER 8

Keller woke up early and was at the office before seven. As usual, he was the first to arrive. He made a pot of coffee and returned to his nearly empty office. He checked his computer and found that his old passwords worked once again. The IT guys had come through for him. He accessed the RCSO internal network and checked the patrol logs. It had been a quiet night with nothing major going on. He was itching to catch a 187, but for now he'd need to focus on the issues in the evidence room.

He had given considerable thought to what Suzy had told him. It worried him that some case could fall apart because the RCSO couldn't come up with some crucial piece of evidence. God help the evidence technician if it ever happened in one of his cases.

He put together a quick email to the sheriff asking if he could meet with him for a few minutes to discuss the evidence room issues. Then he emailed Kevin Bernzott telling him he was back to work and that he'd be happy to assist on any of his old cases. He knew he was stepping beyond the purview of his duties by offering such assistance to a fellow investigator. If the powers that be didn't like it they could go screw themselves, he thought. They were his damn cases.

He grabbed another cup of coffee and sat in the break room. In his forty-plus year career he'd never had a boring day but with this new "special projects" position he was thinking that might change.

He liked having a caseload—something that he had command of and something where there was always more than enough to do.

A voice startled him.

"Good morning, Jack."

He turned to see the sheriff coming into the room, headed for the coffee.

"Hey, sheriff. I just emailed you requesting a meeting to talk about the evidence room. Do you have time this morning?"

"I've got some time right now, if that works. I need to be at the county admin offices at eight, but I'm free till then. Come on back to my office."

Jack stood, grabbed his walker, and followed the sheriff down the hall to his office. Keller closed the door behind him, despite no one being around at the early hour. It didn't go unnoticed by the sheriff.

"What's up?"

"I met with Suzy Gill yesterday to tell her I would be looking at the operation of the evidence room. She said she was glad because she had some concerns about things down there. She said that before Frazier retired he had been getting a little sloppy. That was the term she used."

"She said that? Frazier was sloppy with evidence?"

"Yeah. She said Frazier was having a lot of personal issues and that he may have been drinking on the job."

"Shit."

"She also said she thought Frazier's memory was fading, like he was in early-stage dementia."

"Yeah, I heard that he was struggling back there. It was clearly time for him to retire."

Keller continued, "I think we need to do an external audit down there. Suzy said we've done that before but it was years ago. Not sure who you call in to do that kind of work, but it's something we need to do ASAP. We need to get a handle on this before a case goes to shit."

"Yeah, I agree. I'll bring it up to the county admin team at my meeting this morning. Tell them it's a necessity. We'll get it done."

"Good. And I'm going to spend some time down there and learn all I can about the whole evidence process. I know how it works peripherally, but I'm no expert. If I'm going to be working on making sure things run properly then I need to know what I'm doing."

"Sounds great. I'll let you know what I learn at my meeting. Speaking of that, I gotta run. Nice job, Jack. It's only been one day and you're already digging in and figuring stuff out down there. Who knows, maybe you've got the makings of being an admin guy."

Mick was smiling as he ribbed Keller.

"Not a chance in hell, boss."

"I know, Jack."

"And remember—I catch the next one-eighty-seven."

"You got it."

Keller shuffled down to evidence to see if Suzy had arrived. He wanted to talk to her more and get a look inside the evidence area. She greeted him as soon as he walked in.

"Good morning, boss."

"I'm not your boss. I'll never be your boss."

"I know, I'm just teasing you."

Jack got right down to business. "I spoke with the sheriff and he's going to get an auditor in here. Did you have a chance to find out who did the last audit?"

"I did. I have the info on my desk."

"Okay, good. Meanwhile, I'd like to take a look at the place. Can you give me a walk through?"

"Of course. Got some time now?"

"Yep, let's do it."

Suzy held up her RCSO ID badge to the security monitor and the door clicked open. They entered the area containing the evidence being stored for more than two thousand cases. Rows and rows of stacked boxes, each containing its own story. From evidence needed in trial to seized and stolen property, it was all there. Jack always felt a little bit in awe every time he was in an evidence room—so many stories, so many lives affected, in so many ways.

"So, how is this organized?"

"Each box or container has a barcode that's tracked through the property system in the computer. We use case numbers. So, for instance, in the case of a homicide, every piece of evidence collected for that case would use the case number assigned to that crime. That way we can track everything by crime. In a one-eighty-seven, as you know, we could have quite a few boxes of evidence. And it it's blood or some other item that needs to be preserved, then those go into the refrigerated area in the back."

"So everything investigators bring in to you gets barcoded, tagged, and logged into the computer?"

"Yep, everything. We have over ten thousand items back here currently. And we need to be able to put our hands on every single item as soon as it's requested. If we can't then that brings up all kinds of problems."

"How often does that happen?"

"In my twenty years down here it's only happened twice. Both cases were dismissed by the judge. He really has no other choice. No evidence, no case."

"I hate to ask, but what kind of cases were they?"

"Not one-eighty-sevens, thank God. One was a burglary and the other was an auto theft, if I remember correctly. The bad guy walked in both cases."

"Shit."

"Obviously, the other thing we need to be very careful of is the chain of evidence. We need to be able to tell the court where each piece of evidence has been every minute it's been in our possession. If an investigator checks out a piece of evidence then that activity is logged into the system. When it gets returned it's logged back in."

"And that's one of the concerns with Frazier. You said yesterday that you'd find stuff on his desk?"

"Yes, on a handful of occasions that happened. An investigator would bring something back and instead of logging it right back in, he'd get distracted and just put it in his office. I think the dementia thing was to blame."

The two walked up and down several rows of evidence. It was like a library, with several aisles of shelving running the length of the building. Each shelf was full of plastic containers, rows and rows of them, each with its own barcode and written case number on the front. The containers were various sizes and could contain virtually anything investigators believed to be important to their cases.

"How do you get to the top rows of evidence? Some of these shelves are eight feet high."

Suzy, who stood no more than five feet tall, pointed out a ladder on wheels in the corner of the room.

"We just wheel that thing over and climb up. Like they do at Home Depot."

Keller smiled at the comment, looking up at the top row of containers. He'd need the ladder to reach them as well, and he was over six feet tall. As he finished his sentence, he stopped and stared at the top row directly in front of where they were standing.

"What's that box up there? I don't see a tag on it."

Suzy looked up but couldn't see what Jack was referencing.

"I can't see up that high."

"Let's check—get the ladder," replied Jack.

Suzy wheeled the ladder over and climbed the steps.

She reached up, grabbed the box, and tipped it toward her.

"It's a UPS box. And you're right, there's no evidence tag or barcode, but there is a name and return address."

"Can you get it down? If it's heavy, I can get it."

Suzy shifted the box, judging the weight.

"No, it's pretty light. I can get it."

Suzy put the box under her arm and carefully climbed down the ladder. She placed the box on the floor and looked at Jack.

"What do you want to do?"

Jack considered the situation. There was no RCSO barcode on the box, just the return address. He knew they couldn't just put the box back on the top shelf and forget about it. They would need to figure out what was inside and then decide what to do about it.

"Let's open it up."

Suzy nodded and motioned for him to follow her to her office. Once there, Suzy grabbed a box cutter from her desk. She carefully cut open the box and peered inside.

"Oh, shit. I hope that's not what I think it is."

She handed the box to Jack and he took a look. He paused, placed the box on her desk, and said, "Lock up your office and don't say anything to anyone. Don't touch the box. I'll be back."

CHAPTER 9

"Is the sheriff in?"

"No, he's across the street at the county meeting with some big-wigs," responded Lucinda.

Jack remembered that the sheriff had told him about the meeting. "What time do you expect him back?"

"Any minute, actually. You need to see him?"

"Yeah."

"He has a pretty full schedule when he gets back, but I'm sure he'll take a few minutes for you."

Jack took a seat and wracked his brain for a scenario that might explain the contents of the box. He couldn't think of one.

As he was deep in thought, he heard Lucinda's voice.

"Sheriff, Jack Keller is here to see you."

Mick looked in the waiting area off his office and saw Keller.

"Twice in one day, Jack? Gotta be a record. Come on back."

For the second time that morning Keller closed the door behind him as they entered the office.

"Geez, Jack. So secretive this morning."

"I need to discuss something with you."

"Sure. Oh, before I forget—I got approval for the audit. We just need to let our budget people know. They'll find the money."

The comments didn't register with Jack.

"I was just down in the evidence room and we have an issue."

"What's the problem?"

"Suzy was showing me around and I noticed a box up on the very top shelf, out of sight. There was no RCSO barcode, just a return address. We got it down and took a look inside."

"And . . . ?" Mick looked a bit concerned.

"There was a human skull inside."

"What?"

"You have human remains in a fucking UPS box in your property room, sheriff."

"That can't be . . . I mean, what the hell?"

"We obviously need to bring in someone to confirm it, but I'll bet a week's pay it's a human skull."

"Jesus, that's unbelievable. I don't understand how—"

"I've been here almost fifteen years and I can't recall any cases involving the recovery of human remains in the evidence room. And if we did recover any, they sure as hell wouldn't be in a goddamn UPS box, brushed aside and forgotten about. This makes no fucking sense."

Mick sat at his desk, bewildered.

Jack looked at him. "We need to call in the coroner to check it out. But like I said, it's human. No doubt about it."

"And this skull's down in evidence right now?"

"Yeah, I had Suzy put it in her office. And I told her not to say anything to anyone."

"Good, let's keep this quiet for now. At least until we get confirmation from the coroner. I'll make that call right now."

CHAPTER 10

Suzy sat in her office with the door closed, staring at the UPS box on her desk. She jumped when she heard a knock at the door.

"Suzy, it's me. It's Jack."

She let him in and closed the door behind him.

"I've let the sheriff know what's going on. He's calling the coroner right now so we can get someone down here to confirm it's human. I suspect they'll be here shortly."

"Human, huh? No way this skull belongs to a cow or a moose or a jackalope?"

Jack laughed.

"Jackalope? That's a good one, Suzy. Good to see you're keeping your sense of humor."

"I gotta tell you, Jack, this is kinda freaking me out. I mean, how long has that been up there?"

"Let's check the package. Gotta be a date on there, but we need to put on gloves. There could be fingerprints on the box, although God knows how many UPS people have handled the box before now. Still, better to be safe."

Suzy grabbed a two sets of latex gloves from the box in her desk. They each slipped on a pair and then looked at the mailing label on the box. It was addressed simply to the RCSO, with the mailing address for the main station. It had been mailed on March ninth.

"Today's May twenty-fifth, so it was mailed about two and a half months ago."

"I swear I never saw that box before today."

Suzy was obviously concerned about the responsibility falling on her shoulders.

"I know, Suzy. Don't worry about that. I barely saw it and I'm a foot or more taller than you. Someone stuck that box up there out of sight on purpose. No idea why, but that's probably what happened."

"It makes no sense why someone would do that."

"How tall is Frazier?"

"Maybe five foot six . . . he's not a big guy."

"So, it's very possible he never saw it up there either."

"Or maybe he did. Could he have stuck the box up on a shelf like that? Maybe the dementia thing."

"Could be. We'll just have to see."

"My uncle started doing all kinds of weird stuff when the dementia hit. I can remember him putting empty milk cartons in the dishwasher and trying to start his car with his cell phone. It was sad to see."

"Did you ever see any evidence that Frazier had reached that point while he was still working?"

"No, nothing like that. Just the stuff I told you about earlier, like putting stuff in his office instead of logging it back in the system, and not always returning things to their proper places in the stacks."

"Have you had any contact with him since he retired?"

"Nope, haven't seen him since his retirement lunch last month."

"Okay, I think I'm going to need to talk with him. Maybe he can explain all this. At least we can hope so."

Suzy's desk phone rang and she saw it was the sheriff calling.

"Hello, sheriff."

"Hi, Suzy. Look, Keller told me about the discovery this morning and I wanted to let you know the coroner's people are en route. Their ETA is probably fifteen minutes. I need to let Keller know. I want him there when they examine the skull."

"He's right here, sheriff. I can let him know."

"That'd be great. And give me a call when they arrive. I need to be there as well."

"Will do, sir."

Suzy turned back to Jack.

"The ETA on the coroner is 15 minutes. I just realized that Tim is here; he came in at nine. He doesn't know anything about this . . . he might be wondering why we're huddled in my office."

Tim Barnes was an evidence tech, and the only other full time employee in the unit.

"I think we can let him know. The coroner walking in here in a few minutes might be a bit of a tip-off," answered Jack with a smile.

"You're sure calm, Jack. I'm sitting here freaking out and you're cracking jokes."

"Just another day at the office for me. But remember, you did nothing wrong, Suzy. And we'll get to the bottom of this."

Suzy sat back in her chair, feeling somewhat relieved by Jack's support.

"I hope so. It's just bizarre. I mean, we've got a lot of crazy stuff in these containers, but human remains? With no identifier? That takes the cake."

There was a knock on the door and Jack reached over and opened it.

"The coroner is here. Asking about 'our box of bones,' whatever that means."

Suzy replied, "Come on in, Tim. I'll explain."

Jack grabbed his walker and struggled a bit to get himself up.

"I'll go meet the coroner."

"Okay, and I'll let the sheriff know. He wanted me to call him when they arrived."

Jack made his way to the front of the evidence room and saw Dr. David Mora and his assistant, Kate McLean, standing in the public area. There was no one else there.

Keller greeted the two.

"I guess they send the big guns when the RCSO discovers human remains in a UPS box in their own evidence room, huh?"

Dr. Mora, who had been the county's coroner for nearly a decade, replied, "Trouble just follows you around, huh, Keller?"

Mora and Keller had an easy rapport and had worked many cases together over the years. Mora was an elected official, but not the typical stuffy, uptight politician.

"You know, just the typical stuff . . . a human skull in a box . . . whatever." Jack shrugged.

Mora chuckled. "Yeah, that's what the sheriff told me. Let's take a look."

Keller led Mora and McLean to Suzy's office.

As they reached the door, Tim Barnes was leaving. All the color had drained from his face. He scooted past the trio without speaking.

Suzy stood as the three came into her office. She shook hands with Mora and McLean and introduced herself.

"So, is this the box?" asked Mora, pointing at the UPS box on her desk.

Suzy nodded and Mora reached into his pocket for some latex gloves.

Just then, Sheriff McCallister poked his head in the door.

"Hey, doc. How're you doing?"

The sheriff and the coroner were well acquainted. As elected officials in Rocklin County, they traveled in the same circles.

"Good morning, sheriff. Good to see you again."

"Sure hope you can shed some light on what we've got here. Maybe tell us this is something other than human."

"Well, let's take a look."

Mora removed the lid and peered inside. He picked up the skull and examined it closely.

"Sorry, sheriff, but what we have here is almost certainly a human skull. I'll have to run some radiographic tests, but I have little doubt."

"Great," mumbled Suzy, still holding onto hope it wasn't human.

Mora continued to study the skull.

"The size and shape tells me this was an adult, probably male. Here, take a look at this."

Keller and Mick leaned over and looked at where Mora was pointing. Jack knew instantly.

Mora continued, "A skull fracture. And a significant one. Likely our cause of death."

Jack nodded, looking at the deep fissure in the skull. Mick, not having ever worked homicide, trusted that the two men knew what they were talking about.

"Baseball bat, maybe?" Jack asked Mora.

"I don't think so, it looks smaller but deeper. More like a golf club, perhaps."

Keller had worked a couple of homicide cases involving golf clubs as murder weapons. The clubs could be lethal, especially irons.

Jack pointed at the wound, "Wait a second, is that a number eight imprinted right there?"

Mora smiled at Keller's attempt at gallows humor.

"Yeah, Jack, the killer chose an eight iron to do his dirty work. He thought he might shank a three iron."

Suzy looked at the two men. Joking about a murder? Her expression caught Jack's attention.

"Sorry, Suzy. Just trying to lighten the mood," Jack replied.

Suzy shook her head.

Mora continued, "I need to take the skull down to my office to take a closer look and run some tests. Jack, you want to come with me?"

"Yeah. Sheriff, you okay with that?'

Mick nodded. "Looks like you caught your one-eighty-seven, Jack."

CHAPTER 11

The Rocklin County Coroner's Office was a nondescript, bunker-like building a half mile from the Justice Center. Unlike the morgues featured on TV crime shows, Dr. Mora's domain had low ceilings and bright fluorescent lighting. Keller parked in the back parking lot in a spot marked *Official Vehicles Only* and made his way to the entrance.

Kate McLean, who along with Dr. Mora had just arrived a few minutes earlier, saw Keller coming through the front doors. She buzzed him in.

"Come on back. We're setting up in room three."

Keller nodded and headed to the examination rooms in the back area of the building. He found Dr. Mora putting on his scrubs.

"Grab some coveralls in there, Jack. You know the routine. Join me when you're ready."

A few minutes later, Keller and Kate McLean joined Dr. Mora at the table.

"Let's take a closer look, shall we?"

Mora carefully removed the skull from the UPS box and placed it on the table.

"As I said at the station, I feel confident that our victim was an adult male based on the shape and size of the skull."

"Any idea on age?" asked Keller.

"On the younger side, I'd say. Maybe between twenty and forty."

"Nationality?"

"Likely African-American."

"How can you tell?"

"The cranial features of various races are generally unique to that race. It's not foolproof but it's fairly consistent."

"Such as?"

"Well, the shape of the eye orbits, viewed from the front. Africans tend to have a more rectangular shape, East Asians more circular, Europeans tend to have an aviator glasses shape."

Dr. Mora continued, "You also have the nasal aperture. Africans tend to have wider nasal apertures, Europeans more narrow. There are other characteristics but those are a couple of examples."

Jack continued, "So, based on all that you believe our victim was African-American?"

"Yes, I'd say almost certainly."

"How about time of death? Any way of determining that?'

"Not really. I could give you maybe a wide range, but it probably wouldn't be of much help."

"Can we get DNA from the skull?"

"Certainly, but we won't get results for several weeks. I can get preliminary results in a day or so, but they won't be a hundred percent. You know how it goes, Jack."

"But it could give us a pretty good idea."

"True."

"So, how do you do the DNA test from bone?"

"I'll cut a small piece from the skull and crush it into powder. It'll look like flour you can bake with. That gets sent to the lab and they'll do their thing."

Jack turned his attention to the wound on the skull.

"The cause of death . . . likely a blow to the head with something sharp like a golf iron?"

"Yes, I'd say so."

"Could it have been something like an axe?" asked Kate.

"No, I really don't think so. That leaves a different kind of mark."

Keller was frustrated—not by Mora, but by how little information they were able to glean from the evidence on the table.

"Okay, I've got work to do. Let me know if you come up with any other theories."

"Will do, Jack. Best of luck."

CHAPTER 12

Keller decided to grab a quick bite to eat at a drive through on his way back to the RCSO. He didn't especially like fast food, but with his hip injury limiting his mobility he found it easier than eating in a restaurant. In the three and a half months since the shooting, he had gained nearly fifteen pounds. He decided to forgo the french fries.

He had only been back to work for two days and had already gotten his wish—a 187 to work. He sat in the McDonald's parking lot, slowly eating his burger, running through various scenarios in his mind. He had worked many challenging cases during his career, but this one seemed particularly daunting. Not having a time of death would be a big obstacle. The TOD was always a good place to start with an investigation. Mora thought a blow to the head was likely the cause of death—a golf club or something similar. They had no ID on the vic, no real clue as to when or where the victim had been killed, and didn't know how the remains came to find a home in the RCSO evidence room.

Should have gotten some fries, he thought to himself.

Jack gathered up the trash from his lunch and drove to the trash can near the parking lot exit. He opened his car window, stuffed the bag into the receptacle, and headed back to work.

"The sheriff wanted you to check in with him when you returned."

Keller looked at Suzy and nodded.

"Did you learn anything about our skull?" she asked.

"Likely an African-American male, twenty to forty years of age."

"Well that narrows it down," Suzy responded, smiling.

"Yeah, no kidding."

"I've got faith in you, Jack."

"Yeah, well, thanks for that."

Jack turned and headed upstairs to see the sheriff.

"You wanted to see me?"

"Yeah, sit down. What did you learn from Dr. Mora?"

Jack ran everything by Mick.

"This is going to be a tough nut to crack," Mick answered, taking in what Jack had reported.

"I need to figure out how that box wound up in our evidence room. That could answer a lot of questions. I need to go talk with Frazier."

"That's a good starting point."

"With Frazier is in the early stages of dementia, it could be a big dead end. He was losing it here near the end."

"Yeah, there's that."

Keller looked at his boss. Yeah, no kidding, he thought. But admin didn't do much about it.

"I'll give him a try. Could yield something."

"Sounds good. You'll be working the case with Mia. I want to put you guys back together as a one-eighty-seven team."

Keller shrugged. He wasn't too surprised. His preference was working alone, but Mia was a capable investigator and she could be of some help to him. And since the shooting they had mended their relationship and were on good terms.

"That'll work. Does she know?"

"Yeah, I filled her in after you left with Dr. Mora. Get with her and let her know where you are with the case and then get out to see Frazier. Keep me posted."

"Yes, sir. Will do."

Keller found Mia in her cubicle catching up on emails.

"Hey, Jack. The sheriff told me about our new case."

"Yeah, let's go out to Nate Frazier's place. I'll fill you in on what I've got so far on the way."

The two stopped by the HR office to get Frazier's address and phone number. He lived on the outskirts of Castle Springs, not far from Mick and Mia's home.

Mia dialed Frazier's phone number but it went to voicemail.

"I guess we'll just drop in. No answer on the phone."

"That'll work," replied Jack.

"So what have we got so far, Jack?"

"Not much, to be honest. I really hope Frazier can shed some light on this thing. We need to find out how that box got into the evidence room. It's job one right now."

Keller filled Mia in on everything else he had on the case.

"Crap, this is going to be a challenge."

"Yeah, but if we get the right break things could fall into place quickly. You never know."

A few minutes later the two pulled up in front of Frazier's house, a modest place in a nice neighborhood. They parked on the street and approached the house.

"Did you know Frazier at all?" asked Jack.

"Yeah, a little bit. Not great buddies, but I did go to his retirement lunch."

"Okay, then you should take the lead. He's more likely to recognize you than me. And being a woman you probably have a better chance of gaining his confidence."

Mia looked at Jack and felt a bit insulted. The comment sounded a little sexist, but she knew he didn't mean anything by it so she let it go.

They rang the doorbell and waited. A minute later a woman came to the door.

"I hope you're not selling anything," she said, as she opened the door.

"No, Mrs. Frazier. We're from the sheriff's department. We worked with Nate."

The woman, who appeared to be in her mid sixties, peered at the two.

"Yes, I remember you," she answered, looking at Mia. "You were at Nate's luncheon."

"That's right, I was. I worked with Nate for almost twenty years. This is Jack Keller, an investigator with the department. We were wondering if we could come in and talk to Nate for a few minutes. Is he home?"

The woman, who looked a bit haggard, replied, "He's home, but I'm not sure how conversant he'll be. He's not well; he has good days and bad days."

"Of course, we understand. But maybe seeing familiar faces might help."

"What did you want to talk with him about?"

Keller jumped in. "We working a case right now and we're hoping he might be able to shed some light on an issue with some evidence."

"Well, I'll be surprised if he'll be much help. Although his memory function can be surprising at times. He'll remember things from the past really well, but he can't remember something you said thirty seconds ago. The doctors say dementia patients have minds like Swiss cheese—their memories have big gaping holes in places."

"Well, maybe this is one of those times he'll remember things," answered Mia.

"I guess there's no harm in it. Come on in. My name's Nancy, by the way."

The three shook hands and Nancy led them to a back room of the house.

Before they entered the room, Nancy said, "Nate's decline has been significant in the past month. Just so you know."

The three walked into a small family room and saw Frazier sitting in a recliner watching television. He was dressed in a bathrobe and was unshaven. A large box of adult diapers sat on the floor near the recliner.

"Nate, you have some visitors. They're from the sheriff's department. You used to work with them."

Frazier looked at Jack and Mia but didn't say anything. It looked like he was searching his memory to make sense of the two people standing in his family room.

Both Mia and Jack were taken aback by the change in Frazier. It was shocking.

Mia stepped forward and offered her hand.

"Hi, Nate. It's Mia. You used to help me a lot down in the evidence room."

Frazier shook her hand, his handshake limp.

"I don't remember you. Are you sure we worked together?"

"Yes, for many years. And this is Jack Keller. He works homicide cases with me. You've met him before, too."

"Sorry, don't recall him either."

"Can we sit down?" asked Mia, pointing to a sofa a few feet away.

"Yeah, I guess so."

The two took a seat.

Jack said, "Nate, we're working on a new case and thought you might be able to help us with it."

"What do you need from me?" Frazier responded, with a shrug.

"I was in the evidence room this morning and discovered a box, a UPS box, up on the top shelf of one of the rows. It was out of sight and impossible to see without a ladder."

Nate peered at Jack for a few moments.

"What were you doing in the evidence room? You shouldn't be in there."

"I was there with Suzy. She was helping me find something and I came across the box."

It wasn't exactly how things went down, but Jack thought it would help the conversation along.

"There's lots of boxes in there."

"That's true, but this one was different. It had no ID on it, and it was up on the top, like it was hidden from sight."

Frazier's expression changed quickly.

"What are you saying? That I did something with evidence from a case?"

Mia stepped in. With a calming voice she reassured him, "No, Nate, not at all. If we couldn't see it up there, then neither could you. We're just trying to find out how it got up there and what case it's connected to. That's all."

Frazier looked at Mia and seemed to calm down. It was clear that he preferred talking to Mia, so she took the lead.

"Did you look in the box?" he asked.

There was no easy way to say it so Mia just came out with it. "We did, and we found a human skull inside."

Frazier sat up in his chair. Mia had his full attention.

"What? That's impossible. There's no damn skull in my evidence room. It's probably a cow. A cow skull—it ain't human."

Jack and Mia's hope that Frazier could shed some light on the case was diminishing quickly.

"We're as puzzled by this as you are. We're just trying to learn whatever we can so we can identify the skull. And hopefully find out what happened."

Frazier's demeanor changed and he folded his arms. It was clear he was done talking.

Mia said, "Okay, Nate. We appreciate your time. If you remember anything give us a call."

Mia handed him her card and looked at Nancy.

"Thanks for seeing us."

She nodded and showed them out.

"That was a dead end," offered Jack, climbing in the car.

Mia looked at her partner. "Pretty much. But we had to do it and now we can cross Frazier off the list. At least for now."

"Unless the skull in the box belonged to a cow."

"Hey, you never know. Moooooooo."

CHAPTER 13

Mick arrived home after seven and found Chuck and Mia talking in the kitchen.

"You hungry, Mick?" asked Chuck. "I've got some lasagna in the oven."

"That sounds great. I didn't have much lunch."

"You want a cocktail now or wine with dinner?"

"A drink now sounds good."

"I'll make it for you, hon," said Mia.

Mia grabbed a bottle from the cupboard, poured her husband a couple fingers of vodka, added some ice from the freezer, and handed it to him.

"Thanks, Mia. Here's to your skull in the box," he said, holding the glass in the air.

Chuck looked at his son-in-law. "Skull in the box?"

"Didn't Mia tell you? Her first week back to work and she's got herself a case already."

"No, she hasn't said anything."

"It's a weird one, that's for sure," Mia answered.

Chuck looked at the two but didn't respond. He didn't want to pry, but was certainly curious about what they were talking about.

"Go ahead, Mia. Tell your dad."

Mia often ran cases by her father. She had found him to be a great sounding board—a retired engineer with a very bright, inquisitive mind. He often raised issues with cases that Mia hadn't considered. And he understood the importance of keeping things confidential, an obvious requirement when she shared things with him.

Chuck listened to his daughter as she told him about the UPS box in the evidence room. He was fascinated; it sounded like something out of a juicy crime novel.

"That's incredible. How did the box end up in the evidence room?"

Mia answered her father. "That's the million-dollar question. We have no idea."

"And the coroner thinks the skull was that of a young male?"

"Mora thinks so. He's running a DNA test to try to get an ID, but that takes time and you never know if it'll get a hit."

Chuck theorized, "It's hard to believe that there wouldn't be a missing person report filed at some point by the victim's family. I mean, someone's dead and the family must be aware their loved one isn't around anymore. You don't just let that go. Unless the family was estranged from the victim."

"Or killed by a family member," Mia replied, considering what her father was saying.

Mick jumped in. "The victim could be from somewhere out of the county and so the family, if they did call it in to law enforcement, called it into the agency where they lived, so we wouldn't have anything on it. We need to broaden out our search ... put it out to all Colorado agencies."

It was a good point and Mia made a mental note to discuss it with Jack in the morning.

Mick continued with his train of thought. "But that still doesn't answer how these bones ended up in a UPS box in our evidence room. And because they were sent to us, that makes me believe the skull belongs to someone from our county. I mean, why else send the damn thing to the RCSO?"

CHAPTER 14

Keller, as usual, arrived early to the station the next morning. He liked the quietness of the place at that hour and was typically there before seven. He checked his phone messages and his emails; there was nothing pressing. He went to the coffee room, made a fresh pot, and poured himself a large cup. He took a seat and stared out the window at the mountains in the distance. He allowed his mind to turn over thoughts about his new case, kind of free wheeling it. The approach had served him well in the past; things he hadn't considered previously would sometimes find their way into his consciousness.

"Good morning, Jack."

Keller jumped at the voice. He looked over and saw Mia standing in the doorway of the break room.

"Hey, Mia. You're here early."

"Learned that from my partner. Didn't mean to startle you. You looked like you were a million miles away."

"Just thinking about our skull."

Mia poured herself some coffee and sat at the table with Jack.

"Any revelations?"

"Not really, just that we need to track down that box today. Where was it mailed from, who sent it . . . UPS should be able to help us with that, and we need to check it out."

"Agreed."

"And at some point the guy's family must have realized he was missing. And what do people do when a friend or family member goes missing?"

"They call the cops."

"So we need to check our missing persons logs. You and I both know that ninety-nine percent of those people reported missing turn up alive at some point. We need to find those people who have been reported missing and haven't turned up."

"Suzy Gill oversees our missing persons unit. Let's check with her this morning and see what she can tell us."

Reginald Gray sat on the edge of his bed trying to clear the sleep from his mind. He looked over his shoulder at Shalon, his girlfriend of six months, and saw she was still sound asleep. He looked at the alarm clock on the nightstand; the red numbers told him it was seven thirty. He climbed from the bed and made his way downstairs. He could smell the freshly brewed coffee as he walked toward the kitchen. Coffee makers with timers were one of the world's best inventions, he thought to himself. He poured a cup and walked outside to get the paper. He was one of those people who still liked holding a newspaper in his hands; he wasn't a fan of online news.

He walked back into the kitchen, spread the paper across the table, and started perusing the headlines. So much depressing news in the world—problems in the Middle East and North Korea, climate change, declining stock prices, and the Rockies in yet another skid.

He turned the pages, looking for any stories about his latest deeds. It had been several weeks and so far there had been nothing. Maybe his guys did it right, he thought. They had assured him there was no chance for discovery, but he had heard that before and knew it wasn't necessarily true. Bodies had a way of turning up.

CHAPTER 15

Jack and Mia pulled into the parking lot of the UPS store on Verdugo Road in Castle Springs. Keller wasn't sure how much they'd be able to tell them, but it was a start. They'd likely need to contact someone at the corporate office to get the info he and Mia needed.

"Good morning. How can I help you?"

The clerk was a middle-aged man who clearly noticed Mia more than Jack when they walked in. Picking up on this, Mia took the lead.

"Hi, how are you doing?" she replied.

"Great, thanks. What can I do for you?" he asked Mia. It was like Jack wasn't even there.

"I was hoping you could help me," Mia responded, lowering her voice and leaning in toward the man.

"Sure, what do you need?"

Mia took the box from under Jack's arm and handed it to the clerk. "I was wondering if you could tell me where this box was mailed from." He took the box and studied the return label.

"Well, normally I'm not supposed to give out that info but let me see what I can do."

"Thanks so much. You're so sweet."

She was laying it on a bit thick, Keller thought, but it was working.

The man, whose name tag read *Billy*, took the box and ran his scanner across the barcode on the label. He looked at the readout on the scanner and said, "It was mailed from the UPS store down in south county."

"Can you tell me which store?"

"The one on MLK Boulevard."

"Does the barcode tell you the name of the person who mailed it?"

Billy looked at Mia. He had already told her too much.

Noticing his reticence, Mia smiled and said, "That's okay, Billy. I don't want you to get in trouble."

Billy shrugged and took another look at the scanner.

"John Taylor."

"And an address?"

Mia was really pushing her luck but she figured there was no harm asking.

"Why do you need all this?"

"Just trying to track down an old friend."

He didn't believe it, but Mia smiled at him and tilted her head to the side.

Billy ran the scanner over the label a second time.

"It's 251 South C Street in Castle Springs."

"Thanks so much, Billy. You've been a great help."

"Sure, no problem. Come back any time."

Jack grabbed the box from the counter and the two left the store.

"I should've waited in the car. I didn't say a damn thing in there."

"Maybe if you smiled more, Jack," ribbed Mia.

"I don't think that has anything to do with it."

Mia didn't waste any time once they were back in the car. She googled the address Billy had given them.

"No such address. Shocking."

"John Taylor sure as hell is a dummy name. I wouldn't even bother googling it, there's probably a million of them."

"Any benefit to visiting the UPS store down there? Could we get anything more from them?"

"No harm in it. Let's give it a try," Jack answered.

Twenty minutes later they were walking into the UPS store on MLK Boulevard. There was a totally different vibe to this store. The clerk, a man named Vince, hardly acknowledged them when they entered.

Jack took the lead. "Good morning. We were wondering if you could help us with something."

The clerk noticed the box under Jack's arm.

"You need to mail that?"

"No, actually this is a package we received recently and we're not sure who it's from. Wondering if you could tell us by looking at the barcode."

They already had that information from Billy, but sometimes good detective work meant shaking the trees a bit. You never knew what might fall in your lap.

"No, you'd have to check with corporate for that."

Vince played by the rules. Mia didn't have the same influence over this guy, Jack thought.

"Yeah, I'd hate to go through the hassle of all that. How about when the package was mailed? Can you tell me that?"

"No, man, check with corporate."

They were at a crossroads. They could badge the guy and that might work, or it could cause him to totally shut down. Given that he wasn't getting anywhere, Jack felt he had nothing to lose. He took out his badge and showed it to Vince.

"We're here on official police business. I just need a little bit of cooperation. Can you help us out here?"

Vince looked at the two.

"You speak English, don't you? Corporate, man."

Mia pointed at the corner of the store, up by the ceiling.

"You've got security cameras. Your rudeness is on video. We'll be sure to mention that to corporate security when we contact them."

"Do what you gotta do, lady."

Mia and Jack turned and left the store.

"Asshole," Mia muttered as they walked back to the car.

"What happened, Mia? Your charm didn't work on good ol' Vince."

"He's obviously gay."

Keller laughed. "Yeah, that must be it."

They reached the car, stopped, and looked at each other.

The word *PIGS*, written in large letters, was traced in the dirt on the windshield.

"You see Jack, this is why I keep my car nice and washed."

Jack shrugged, "Let's get outta this dump."

As they headed north on I-25, Mia googled the 800 number for UPS security. She got the number and placed the call.

"Good morning, this is Mia Serrano with the Rocklin County Sheriff's Department in Colorado and I was wondering if I could get some assistance."

"Sure, what do you need?"

"I'm working a homicide here in our county and was wondering if I could get some help reading a barcode on a package that was sent from one of your stores."

"Can you read me the number?"

"Sure, hold on a sec."

Mia grabbed the package and read off the barcode number.

"The package was mailed from one of our franchised stores in Castle Springs, Colorado."

Mia didn't want to burn Billy so she played dumb. "Which store?"

"The address is 10851 Martin Luther King Boulevard."

"And can you tell me the name and address of the sender?" Mia asked, wanting to confirm what Billy had told her. No reason to believe he wasn't being truthful but thought she'd check just the same.

"The customer's name is John Taylor. The address is 251 South C Street in Castle Springs."

"Perfect. You've been so helpful. I appreciate it."

"Will there be anything else?"

"Oh, yeah, one more thing. I noticed that the MLK store has video cameras."

"It's required of all franchisees."

"Do you know how long they keep the tapes?"

"It's all digital, so they should have a record going back at least ninety days."

"So when Mr. Taylor came in the store on March ninth to mail the package, that would be captured on the surveillance cameras, correct?"

"Yep, unless for some reason they were inoperable. But that would be in violation of the franchise agreement. They're required to keep them in good working order."

"Is there a way to tell what time the customer came into the store to mail the package?" Mia asked, trying to narrow down the time frame so they wouldn't spend all day staring at video.

"Sure, it looks like the package was mailed at 11:09 am."

"Wow, that's fantastic. So, how do I go about getting the video for the time the package was mailed?"

"I can do that. I can pull it from here and email you the video. I'll pull video covering ten minutes before and ten minutes after the 11:09 timestamp just to be safe."

"Wow, that's awesome. I gotta tell you, I talk to a lot of corporate security people and you're the best."

"Thanks, I appreciate that."

"Let me give you my email address. How long will it take?"

"Give me an hour and I'll send it to you."

"Perfect."

Jack looked at his partner. "Damn, woman—you are on fire today."

CHAPTER 16

As promised, the video arrived in Mia's inbox less than an hour later. She called Jack and he came to her cubicle.

"Let's see what we've got."

Mia clicked on the email and the two waited a half minute while the video downloaded.

They both peered closely at the screen as the video started to play. The image was surprisingly clear, not like the typical grainy images usually recorded by inferior equipment. They timestamp in the corner of the video read 11:00 am. They could clearly see the people in line at the counter, a half dozen in total.

"Let's see who's got our package," Jack said.

"The third guy in line. He's holding a box. No one else has a box that size. It matches."

"See if you can zoom in."

Mia tried manipulating the screen but to no avail.

"Nothing. Let's hope we get a better view of the guys face as he moves up in line."

The customer with the box reached the counter at 11:04 am.

"It's not him; he's too early. Our guy mailed the package at 11:09. Unless they don't actually process it until a few minutes later, after he's left. Let's watch what they do with the package."

Jack and Mia stared at the screen. The clerk took the package and scanned it while the customer was getting the money from his wallet.

"Shit. Not him."

"Okay, let's see what happens next."

The timestamp read 11:06 as a new customer walked in carrying a box that looked like the one containing the skull. By then the line had thinned out and there was only one customer ahead of him. The new customer reached the clerk at 11:08. A minute later the package was scanned.

"That's our guy."

The two watched in silence as the video played on.

"There. He turned toward the camera," said Jack.

Mia hit the pause button. The picture was slightly blurred from freezing the image, but you could make out the face. It was sufficient to put it on a news release and ask for the public's help in identifying the person.

"Mark Archer can put this out for us," Mia added.

"How do we get the photo off the video?"

Mia looked at Jack. Technology wasn't his strong suit.

"I can print it off the screen or we can send the video to IT and have them pull the photo. Given the picture is a bit blurred I'd suggest our IT people do it. They might be able to clean it up a bit."

"Let's do it."

Mia emailed the video to IT with a quick explanation of what they needed. The best image of the person was at the nine minute, forty second mark, so she included that information in her email.

"Okay, done. Let's go see Mark Archer and let him know what's going on so he can do his thing."

It was a short walk to Archer's office in the administrative section of the building. His office was next to the sheriff's.

Archer was on the phone when Jack and Mia arrived, but he waved them in. They took seats and waited for him to finish the call. A minute later he hung up the phone and turned his attention to the detectives.

"What's up, guys?"

Keller took the lead and filled him in.

"Can you get this guy's photo out to the media?"

"You said it's off a video feed?"

"Yes, from the UPS store down in south county."

"I'd rather put out a short video rather than just a freeze frame of the guy's image. The media will give it more play if it's a video clip. They'll eat it up."

Mia looked at Archer. He knew his stuff, that was for sure.

"Then let's do the video clip. I've got our IT guys working on it. I'll make sure they send you a clip, not just a single image."

"Perfect."

"It's only a few seconds; the rest of the video just shows people waiting in line."

"Okay, I can make that work."

Archer looked at his watch and saw that it was nearly eleven.

"We'll miss the noontime newscasts but we can hit it hard at five, six, and ten."

"Let's do it."

CHAPTER 17

Mark Archer downloaded the video from IT and looked at the footage. He edited it down to a manageable length; fifteen seconds or so worked best for television newscasts. Anything longer and people lost interest. The attention span of the average American had shrunk in Mark's opinion, a result of a society that wanted everything fast and at their fingertips. He himself wouldn't watch any videos posted on Facebook longer than a half minute. It was a disposable world. People had more time than ever but they were always in a damned hurry. He put together the video and saved it to his computer. He turned his attention to writing the accompanying press release that would explain the video. He was careful not to share anything about the skull in the evidence room, just that the person in the video was a "person of interest." It was a term that the police used often to mean they didn't have enough evidence to put out an arrest warrant on someone but they were pretty sure the person was involved in a crime.

If he included the salacious details about a skull being mailed to the cops it would garner a lot more attention, but he was confident that the video he was sending out was sufficient. The media loved video; the story would air at or near the top of the newscasts throughout the Denver area. He had checked the various news sites and saw it was a slow news day, which was perfect to get his news spread far and wide.

Once he finished with the press release he attached the video and hit *send*. Ten minutes later his phone started ringing.

CHAPTER 18

Jed Nixon was as high as a kite, sitting on the deck outside his double-wide trailer, staring intently at the stars above. Every once in awhile he'd see a shooting star and would just about lose his shit. He'd jump out of his chair and whoop it up, doing a little dance. The meth he had injected thirty minutes earlier was doing its thing and the show in the sky was spectacular . . . at least to him and his imagination.

His trailer was situated in a run-down park just outside Aurora, far enough from the city lights to get a good view of the night sky. He paid just three hundred bucks a month for the spot, and his income from peddling meth covered that and some very basic living expenses. He should have more disposable income, but a lot of what he made he put right back into meth. He was hopelessly addicted and knew it was just a matter of time before he messed up yet again and found himself back in prison.

But prison wasn't so bad and he would free himself of the meth demon while in custody. It was kind of his routine. He'd been in prison four times in the last decade, each time for drug use or distribution, and each time he'd gotten clean and sworn he'd never use again. But he knew he was weak and that he'd fall back into the same rut soon after his release. Which is exactly what happened, each and every time.

But this time he had more to worry about than just peddling the shit. He had graduated up and paid his dues to the shot caller of his meth network. The word had come from the top—he needed to kill someone who had fucked up big time. He didn't want to do it but he knew if he didn't, then he'd find himself on the big man's hit list. He had a pretty easy gig as a middleman in the network and didn't want to upset the proverbial applecart. So he carried out his duty like a good soldier, killing the guy who had snitched. It was an easy hit; he knew the guy and the poor sucker never saw it coming. A crowbar to the head had turned out the guy's lights, and Nixon disposed of the body using a wood chipper. He loved the movie *Fargo*, and it had been a lifelong dream to put someone through a chipper.

Turns out it was easy to get one at the local rental business in Aurora. The hard part was cleaning the chipper afterward. The entire unit was covered in blood and he had to go back and rent a power washer from the same place. Took him two hours to get all the blood out of the thing but he had managed to get it done. Of course he knew that if the cops ever checked it for blood they would find some traces and they'd know something was up. He had seen as much on *Forensic Files*. Those dudes were smart! But he'd rented it under a phony name and address and he had paid cash. He should be in the clear, he thought.

He had been high on meth when he killed the guy. He wasn't sure what possessed him to keep the guy's head; maybe it was some kind of sick trophy. He knew killers and rapists often did that; he had met a fair number during his prison stints. They loved bragging about what they had done and telling him their trophies let them relive their deeds. Those puppies were sick! So he kept the head, but no such thrill had happened for him.

And it was no easy task beheading the guy; it took several big whacks with an axe that he kept at his place. The spinal cord, it turned out, was a mother. Thick and tough to hack through, but he had managed it. He had wrapped the head in a trash bag and kept it in the closet of the guest room in his trailer. But after a few days the thing began to stink, and he got a bad whiff of it every time he walked into the trailer. He didn't have many guests to his place (none, really) but what if someone did come over? The landlord or one of those damn Jehovah's Witnesses, or maybe the cable guy?

He became concerned and decided he needed to do something with it. He hated the cops and, once again, while in a drug-induced state, he decided that he would mail it to them. Kind of egg them on . . . rub their noses in his murder. He cleaned up the skull really well and sent it off. Later he thought better of it, but it was too late—it was already on its way to the Rocklin County Sheriff's Department courtesy of UPS. But that was two and a half months ago and no one had come knocking at his door, so he was pretty sure he was in the clear.

Another shooting star crossed the sky and Jed jumped up and did another little jig on his deck. At a little before ten he stumbled into his trailer and hit the power button on his cable remote. He wanted to catch another couple episodes of *Breaking Bad*. He loved that show, kind of humanizing what he did for a living. Glorifying and legitimizing those in the meth business. The guy was a chemistry teacher, after all.

He stared at the television screen; that good-looking anchorwoman on the Channel 8 ten o'clock news had caught his attention before he could change the station.

"We have breaking news tonight from Castle Springs. The Rocklin County Sheriff is asking for the public's help as they try to identify a 'person of interest' in a possible homicide case they are investigating. Mark Archer, spokesman for the RCSO, wouldn't offer many details on the case, just that they are looking to question this individual. The person's image was caught on video mailing a package at the UPS store on MLK Boulevard in Castle Springs on March ninth of this year. Here, take a look at the video."

Nixon lowered himself slowly onto his sofa, staring at the screen and watching the video of himself mailing the package at UPS. The picture quality wasn't great but he was definitely recognizable.

"Shit. I'm a dead man."

Nixon knew he had no time to waste; enough people knew him around town that he'd be dimed off by somebody. Hell, he thought, the phone to the sheriff's department was probably already ringing. There was certainly no shortage of people who wanted to see him behind bars, or, better yet, dead.

He jumped to his feet and looked around his trailer, trying to think about what to take. He'd need to pack up his dope and the cash he had stashed in the freezer, a stack of hundreds, fifties, and twenties shoved in a Popsicle box, nearly five grand in all. He had used the box for quite awhile, and despite having his place ransacked twice, no one had found the cash.

He ran into the bedroom and grabbed the Tupperware box under his bed that contained the meth. Somehow he wasn't as careful with the dope as he was with his hard-earned cash. He grabbed a duffle bag from the closet, tossed it onto his bed, and started shoving clothing inside. He added the Tupperware container to the bag and headed for the kitchen. He grabbed the Popsicle box and placed it on the top of the duffle bag. He took one more quick look around and couldn't think of anything else of importance to take with him. He left the trailer and headed for his car.

A neighbor standing in his bathrobe and watering the small patch of grass outside his trailer saw Jed as he hustled quickly to his '95 Chevy truck.

"Man, you look like a bat straight outta hell. Everything okay, Jed?"

"Oh yeah, just going to visit my sister for a couple days. Be back on Thursday. Keep an eye on my place, will you?"

"I didn't know you had a sister. Where's she live?"

"Billings."

Nixon didn't have a sister and he wasn't sure what made him say Billings. He had never been there.

"Beautiful country up there in Montana."

"Yep, sure is. Hey, I gotta run. See you Thursday."

CHAPTER 19

Mark Archer had decided to stay late at the office, wanting to see if the news coverage about their person of interest generated any calls. Ever since he and Angela Bell had broken off their relationship three months earlier, he had been spending more and more evenings at work. He lived alone and an empty house wasn't really his thing. He missed Angela, but the truth was he also thought quite a bit about Rachel Gillespie, the soon to be divorcée he had begun seeing around the same time he broke up with Angela.

It was a good decision, because within five minutes of the story airing, the 911 center received three calls from people identifying the man in the UPS video.

Mark recognized the dispatch center phone number from his caller ID. "Archer."

"Hey, lieutenant, this is Annie down in dispatch. I've got some info for you on the guy we're looking for in connection with the one-eighty-seven."

"Whatcha got, Annie?"

"Putting out the video worked because we got three calls, all identifying your suspect as Jed Nixon. I ran him in the system; his real name is Adolph Nixon, age twenty-eight, with priors for drug peddling. He's a white male, six feet, and one hundred forty-five pounds. Lives in a trailer park up in Aurora. Looking at his booking photo and sure enough, it looks like your boy."

"That's great, Annie. Email me everything you've got."

"Are you still here?'

"Yeah, just getting caught up on some paperwork. And I wanted to see if the news story tonight triggered any memories on our suspect."

"Well, it did the trick. Nice work, lieutenant!"

"Thanks. Get me the info and I'll see if we can get some deputies up to Aurora tonight."

"Will do, sir."

Archer hung up and dialed Jack Keller's cell. He was confident he'd answer; the guy was a notorious workaholic. Jack picked up on the second ring.

"Keller, our video aired at the top of the ten o'clock news tonight and resulted in three calls from people all identifying your one-eighty-seven perp."

"Outstanding. What can you tell me?"

Archer ran things down to Keller and offered to have deputies travel the twenty miles or so up to Aurora.

"No, that's okay, lieutenant. I'll run up there myself."

"Take some backup, Jack. The guy is a one-eighty-seven suspect, after all."

"Yeah, I'll put a call into the CO's office. I'm sure they can spring a couple of guys loose for an hour or two."

"Keep me posted, Jack."

"Sure, lieutenant."

Keller hung up and grabbed his coat. He didn't plan on calling for any backup, he would just pay a little surprise visit to Mr. Nixon. No harm, no foul . . . it was the way he rolled.

Archer sat in his office and reflected on the conversation he'd just had with Keller. He felt uneasy, thinking that Keller might not follow his suggestion to ask for backup in Aurora. It wouldn't be the first time Keller went rogue; he had a reputation for playing things a bit loose. He picked up the phone and dialed down to the watch commander's desk.

"CO's desk, Bob Elder speaking."

"Hey, Bob, this is Archer. Has Jack Keller called the CO's desk tonight asking about getting some backup for a run up to Aurora?"

"No, haven't heard from him. What's he need backup for?"

"We need to talk with a person of interest in a one-eighty-seven case. He said he'd call and get a couple of deputies to go with him. My concern is that he'll just go up there alone."

"Wouldn't be the first time."

"No, and given his physical limitations right now, I don't think he should go up there unaccompanied."

"Want me to go ahead and send a couple units? We're slow tonight; I can spare them."

"Not yet. Let's see if he calls asking for them. He just learned about the guy in Aurora not ten minutes ago. Maybe he'll call shortly."

"I'll call you as soon as he calls me. If he calls in, that is."

"If he doesn't call in the next fifteen minutes, then send the deputies. I'll forward you the guy's location info in Aurora."

"You got it."

CHAPTER 20

Keller accelerated once he entered the northbound I-25. Aurora was a quick twenty minutes with no traffic from Castle Springs and at that late hour he knew it would be clear sailing. He assembled his thoughts while on the drive, trying to determine the best way to approach Mr. Nixon. Keller had learned through experience that it was usually best to downplay the interview to the interviewee. Take a Columbo-style approach, soft peddle the questions like he was just there to tie up some loose ends. Build rapport with the guy and make him feel comfortable, basically leading him down the yellow brick road until he was waist deep in his own shit.

The video from the UPS store was fairly good quality and if three different viewers saw the footage and all identified the guy as Nixon, there was a very high likelihood that he was their guy. Of course, it was said that everyone had a doppelgänger, but what were the odds the guy had a virtual look-a-like twin living in the greater Denver area? Not very likely, Keller reasoned. No, this was the guy. But what was he doing mailing a package to the RCSO with a human skull?

It was possible the guy didn't know what was in the package, that he was mailing it for a friend or something. Of course, when push came to shove, Keller knew that's exactly what the guy would claim. "Wait, there was a skull in that box? My buddy told me it was See's candy! I had no frickin' idea!"

Keller chuckled at the thought. It was even funnier to him if the guy really had no idea what was in the box. Holy crap, the guy would think . . . a human skull?

But his intuition told him otherwise, especially after reading the guy's rap sheet. He was no choir boy. The guy peddled dope, and Keller had no patience or tolerance for dope dealers. It was bad enough that guys like Nixon sold dope to anyone with a buck, kids included. But Keller knew that the dope trade was a mean, dirty business and that a homicide wasn't unusual if it cleared the decks as far as competition was concerned. The gangs in Los Angeles, Miami, and other major cities all knew that it was kill or be killed when it came to the drug trade. Denver had its share of problems as well, and sometimes those problems spilled onto the streets of nearby communities. Rocklin County wasn't immune to them; in fact there had been a significant increase in drug-related issues during Keller's fifteen years at the RCSO. It wasn't approaching the level of problems he'd seen in St. Louis during his career there, but it was disconcerting nevertheless.

He followed the directions he was being fed by the Waze app on his phone. Mia had turned him on to it a few months earlier. Keller wasn't particularly tech savvy but he found the app easy to use and highly accurate. Within a few minutes of exiting the freeway in Aurora he was at the entrance of the Wagon Wheel Trailer Park.

He pulled in, looking for a map or directory of the park. He had Nixon's address, space number eighty-three, but didn't want to have to meander through the park looking for the right trailer. He pulled in a hundred yards or so and saw a clubhouse of sorts. He stopped in front and saw a large display of the park. Bingo, he thought.

He gazed through the window of his car and found space eighty-three. There were no street names, just lanes of roadway with numbers marked indicating the trailer spaces. Committing the location to memory, he made a few turns and was soon approaching the trailer. He parked in a red zone marked as a fire lane and approached the trailer on foot. He left his walker in the car.

The lights were out, not unusual given that it was nearly eleven. He gave some thought to requesting backup but he really didn't want to wait. If the guy had gotten word that his photo being shown on the news, then he could easily be in the wind already. Or he could be oblivious to it and blissfully sound asleep in the rickety old trailer. He walked up to the door, pounded heavily, and waited.

Nothing.

He pounded again and waited, his hand on the gun in his side holster. Still nothing.

Keller noticed that a light in the trailer next door had come on. He turned his attention to the light, realizing that he had probably disturbed the people inside with his loud knocking.

The door in the neighboring trailer popped open and a middle-aged man came out.

"Can I help you? It's pretty late to be paying someone a visit, don't you think?"

"I'm sorry to have bothered you. I'm looking for Jed Nixon but he's not answering."

"Yeah, I can kinda tell you're looking for him. Damn, you woke me up from a sound sleep."

"Again, I apologize. Have you seen Mr. Nixon?"

"I saw him earlier tonight. But he ain't home now. Went to see his sister."

"He told you that?"

"Yep, said he'd be back in a few days."

"When did you talk with him?'

"Who are you, and what do you want with Jed?"

Keller would rather not give himself up to a nosy neighbor, but saw no other choice.

"I'm Investigator Keller with the Rocklin County Sheriff's Office. I'm here on official police business."

Keller said it with authority, stepping toward the neighbor, hoping to intimidate him. His hip hurt but he ignored the pain to put up a good front.

"At this hour? Must be important."

"Like I said, I need to speak to Mr. Nixon."

"Is he in some sort of trouble?'

"No, I just need to talk with him about a police matter," Keller lied.

"Well, that ain't gonna happen, at least not tonight. 'Cuz like I said, he's gone to Montana to see his sister."

"Do you have a cell number for Mr. Nixon?"

"Why would I have his number?"

Keller was growing impatient.

"What's your name, sir?"

"Why? Am I in trouble now?"

"No, sir, I'm just trying to find Mr. Nixon."

"Can't help you there. Now, if you don't mind, I'm going back to bed."

Jack tried not to let a heavy dose of sarcasm punctuate his words, but was unsuccessful.

"You have yourself a good evening, sir."

"Yeah, you too." As the neighbor turned to go back inside, Jack heard him mutter *asshole* under his breath.

One of Aurora's finest residents, he thought to himself.

Keller turned his attention back to Nixon's trailer. He noticed a window on the side where the curtain was open, so he walked around to take a look. Peering in he couldn't see much, given the dark conditions. He had a flashlight in his car so he turned to get it. As he walked the short distance to his car he glanced over at the neighbor's trailer. He could see the man peering out at him. Get a life, Jack thought. He opened the car door and grabbed the flashlight from under the seat. He walked back and shone the light through the window.

He moved the light to shine around the trailer, but there wasn't much to see. Off to one side there was a ragged old sofa and a small table with just one chair. Seemed that Mr. Nixon lived alone. He moved the flashlight to peer at the other side of the trailer and noticed a flickering light. He stared at the source and saw a small television set. It was angled away from him but as he looked closely he could see Jimmy Fallon on the screen. Keller wasn't a huge fan of late night TV but he knew enough to know he was watching Denver's Channel 8. And he knew that late-night television followed the late evening news-casts. Maybe Nixon had gone to visit his sister in Montana but the guy had left his TV on. That told Keller that he very likely left in a hurry, forgetting to turn off the set. More evidence that Nixon had indeed seen himself on the news and fled the scene. There might or might not be a sister in Montana, but he was clearly on the run.

"Stop right there! Hands up where we can see them!"

"What the hell?" Keller thought as he raised his hands and very slowly turned toward where the shouting was coming from.

Standing not thirty feet away were two Aurora PD officers, guns drawn, focused on Keller.

The nosy neighbor must have called the cops on him, Keller surmised.

"I'm law enforcement, Rocklin County Sheriff's Department, here on an investigation."

The two officers kept their guns aimed at Keller's chest.

"Got some ID?"

"Yes, and I'm armed."

"Okay, slowly put your weapon on the ground."

Keller obliged, bending over the best he could, to place his Baretta on the ground at his feet.

The two Aurora cops saw how gingerly Keller was moving.

"You say you're from the RCSO?"

"Yes, here on a one-eighty-seven investigation."

"Funny, we didn't hear anything about another agency coming into our jurisdiction to conduct a murder investigation."

"This is unfolding very quickly, I didn't have time. My apologies."

The two Aurora officers stared at Keller for a few more seconds.

"Let's see your ID."

"It's in my coat pocket. I'll reach in slowly and get it."

The Aurora cops watched as Keller produced the ID.

"Where's your badge?"

"I don't have one. I retired medically a few months ago and the department brought me back to do one-eighty-sevens. All I have is the ID," replied Keller, handing over his ID.

One of the cops took the ID and looked it over.

"Wait a minute . . . Jack Keller. You're the guy that got shot in Denver at that press conference."

"Guilty as charged."

"Damn, you saved that female deputy's life. She was pregnant, wasn't she?"

"Yes."

"And you took out that dirtbag. Damn, you're a hero to me, man."

Keller didn't say anything but gave the officer a little nod.

Both Aurora cops holstered their weapons.

"Sorry for this. We didn't know."

"Of course, no worries. And I'm sorry I didn't let you guys know, but like I said, this thing just started really rolling an hour ago."

"So, what's the case?'

Keller offered a cursory summary, leaving out the part about the skull in the UPS box.

As the officers were listening, they noticed the neighbor coming out of his trailer.

"Would it be possible for people around here to get some sleep?"

The officers looked at the man, then at Keller.

"Adam Henry," he said in a lowered voice. Adam Henry was unofficial police code for asshole.

"Gotcha."

"Sir, we're sorry. We'll keep our voices down. Now go back inside your home."

The neighbor looked like he was going to respond with something nasty but thought better of it. He turned and went inside his trailer, but gave Keller a little wave first.

"So, is there anything we can help you with here, Keller?"

"Not really. Looks like our subject is gone. Must have gotten wind that we were looking for him."

"Okay, send us the four-one-one on the guy and we'll make sure it's put out as a BOLO to all our patrol officers."

"Appreciate that. I think I'll make my way back to Rocklin County."

"Okay, have a good rest of the evening. And Investigator Keller—it was a pleasure to meet you."

Both officers shook Keller's hand. Jack was a little embarrassed by the attention. He definitely preferred flying under the radar.

Just as the officers were climbing back in their patrol car, two RCSO patrol cars pulled up to the trailer.

"Aw, shit," Jack muttered under his breath.

CHAPTER 21

Mark Archer woke to his alarm, set as usual for 5:00 a.m. He grabbed his phone from the nightstand and quickly scrolled through his emails and text messages. He was pleased to see nothing of significance. He opened the RCSO watch commander report covering all evening shift activities and read the entry from Commander Elder about Keller and his visit to Aurora.

Damn Keller, going rogue as usual, he thought. But more disappointing was that Nixon was gone. A statewide BOLO had been put out on him but so far, nothing. Elder's entry was very lengthy and detailed, and outlined the possibility that Nixon was on his way to Montana. That BOLO needed to be extended to the western US, Archer thought, not just Colorado.

He climbed out of bed, took a quick shower, and headed to the office.

Jed Nixon was sure the cops would have figured out it was him in the video; plenty of people knew him and the video was pretty clear. The tip line had probably lit up like a Christmas tree as soon as the video aired. He imagined the cops had probably already hit his trailer in Aurora and he considered what they might have found there when they searched it.

He had packed in a huge hurry, taking the important stuff—the dope and the cash. Everything else was replaceable. There wasn't anything in the trailer that would tip them off to where he might be headed. If the cops talked to his neighbor and he told them about his "visit to Montana," that might send them off on a wild goose chase and buy him some time.

With this in mind, he headed south on the I-25, and by early morning he was in Las Cruces, New Mexico. He checked into a fleabag motel for $34 for the night, paid cash, and decided he'd get some sleep before heading out again. He had a cousin in Tucson and thought he could crash at his place for a day or two, at least until he figured out what his next steps would be. His cousin, Pauley, had a bit of a checkered past himself and would understand his situation. Where he went from there was anybody's guess. He just knew he would never return to Colorado; that life was over. He grabbed his phone and sent a quick text to his girlfriend, Marina, telling her he'd be out of town for a few days. He'd think of something else to tell her down the road. Marina had her own share of problems, so she'd understand if he disappeared for a while. Their relationship had started when they were busted together at a party in Aurora. Both were high and the arrest had resulted in both of them doing a few days in county lockup.

Keller, despite a restless night, was back in his office before seven. He made himself a very strong cup of coffee in the empty breakroom and took a seat in his cubicle. He queried his computer, checking for any updates on Jed Nixon's whereabouts. By now, he had been on the run for more than eight hours. He could be anywhere, even out of the country if he had gotten on an airplane.

Something told Jack that Nixon wouldn't have done that—he was most likely in a vehicle. After returning from Aurora the night before

Jack had checked the DMV database and found a car registered to Nixon, a 1995 Chevy truck. He had immediately put out an ATL, or attempt to locate, on the vehicle, but now, eight hours later, Nixon was still on the loose.

Jack read the CO entries in the department log outlining his actions the night before. He knew he had overstepped his bounds and that he should not have gone to Aurora without backup. He'd hear about it, no doubt. Whatever, he thought. He'd been called on the carpet countless times in his nearly forty-year career.

Keller entered the info on Nixon into the national police database. The APB would go everywhere, but Jack knew it was no guarantee they would nab him anytime soon. Nixon would be run in the national database only if he encountered some kind of police contact. That would yield a hit but if Nixon was smart he'd behave himself. A taillight out or going ten over the speed limit could land Nixon in prison. But small stuff like that had put countless criminals in jail, so Jack knew putting Nixon into the system was worth doing.

CHAPTER 22

Jed Nixon didn't sleep well. The bed in the motel was lumpy and soft. Restful sleep eluding him, he tossed and turned most of the night, not able to free his mind from his current situation. He'd been in trouble before, but never for murder. Probably shouldn't have hacked the guy up, he thought. But the asshole was a snitch and he had no patience for people like that. The drug trade had certain rules and turning in one of your own simply wasn't tolerated. The guy had to pay for his deeds and Nixon had made sure he did. Jed closed his eyes and pictured the last moments of the guy's life. Sheer terror on his face—no doubt he knew what was coming. The crowbar had done the trick; there was really no need to behead the guy And the chipper, that was just to make sure there was no body left behind to find. The only mistake he had made was to send the guy's skull to the sheriff's department. That was a dumb mistake, but when you're strung out on meth you do stuff you can't really explain.

Nixon picked up his phone to check how far he was from his cousin's place in Tucson. Looked like an easy drive, about six and a half hours. He'd be there by late afternoon. He thought about calling and letting Pauley know he was coming for a visit, but thought better of it. Better to just drop in so his cousin couldn't turn him away. His history with Pauley had been difficult; the two hadn't always been on the best of terms. But he hadn't seen him for a couple years so a drop-in visit should be okay, especially when he explained that he was in a jam. He gathered up his stuff and was back in his truck and on the road a few minutes later.

Pauley Nixon was sleeping off a drunken binge when his doorbell rang. Screw it, he thought. He didn't want any Girl Scout cookies. The damn girls had been canvassing his neighborhood for days. But when the bell kept ringing, he decided he'd better check. Looking through the peephole he saw it wasn't a Girl Scout. He opened the door.

"What the hell, Jed?"

"Hey, Pauley. How you doin'?"

"This can't be good. Come on in."

Jed slipped in and Pauley closed the door behind him.

"Long time no see," Jed offered, trying to keep the mood friendly.

Pauley surveyed his cousin, standing in his living room.

"What's wrong Jed? You in some kind of trouble?"

"Why do you assume that? Can't a guy just visit his cousin?"

"Haven't seen you in a couple years and you show up unannounced in the middle of the day. Last time I heard from you you were living in Colorado somewhere. Tucson is a long way from Colorado, Jed. What's going on?"

"How've you been, Pauley?"

"Just great, Jed. Now tell me what's happening here."

"I need a little help, that's all."

"What did you do now? You in trouble again?"

"Yeah, okay. I'm in a little jam."

"Figures. Come on in, tell me about it."

The two walked over to the sofa and sat down.

"I need a place to land for a little bit, that's all."

"I ain't no hotel, Jed."

"I know that, I just need a little time. I won't be no bother. You'll hardly even know I'm here."

Pauley looked at his cousin. The guy was trouble, and who knew what he was up to now. He'd have to hear the whole story before he agreed to anything.

"What did you do, Jed?"

"It ain't no big deal, Pauley. It'll blow over."

"What'll blow over?"

Jed realized he wasn't getting anywhere with his cousin. He'd need to come clean.

Pauley pushed the issue. "You need to tell me exactly what's going on before I let you stay here. I need to know."

Jed looked around the room, unsure if he should tell the truth or make up a story.

Pauley could sense Jed's apprehension. He decided to put an end to the conversation.

"You know what, get the hell out. I don't need this right now."

"I'm family, Pauley. You gotta help me."

"I don't have to do anything, Jed. I owe you nothing."

"Pauley, I screwed up. Real bad. I need to stay hidden, at least for awhile."

"Great, so you want me to harbor a fugitive?"

"You say it that way and it sounds bad."

"You have ten seconds to tell me what you did or you can walk out the door and never come back."

"All right, all right—'"

"Spill it, Jed."

Jed folded his arms.

"I killed a guy. He was a snitch and he had it coming. I had to do it, man."

Pauley closed his eyes, slowly shaking his head.

Jed continued. "You don't do that, man. You don't snitch on people.

The guy was a dirtbag and I did what anybody else would do."

Pauley opened his eyes. "So the cops know it was you?"

"Yeah, I guess."

"Why do you 'guess'?"

"My picture was on the news."

"Aw, shit, Jed. You gotta be kidding me."

"I wish I was. It was on last night."

"So that's why you're in Arizona. What kind of news were you on? Just local? Like in Colorado?"

"I don't know, man. I assume so. Who cares about a Colorado case except people in Colorado?"

"Let's hope it stayed in Colorado. Did they use your name in the story?"

"No, just my photo. Asking people to call the cops if they recognized me."

"Shit."

"But I should be okay here, right? No one in Arizona is looking for me. If I just hang out here for a little while, just till the cops lose interest—"

"The cops aren't going to lose interest in a murder case, you dumbass."

"They will if they can't find me. Some other case will come along and they'll forget about it."

"If they don't find you in Colorado, they'll put it out to other states, including Arizona. And the cops will have you in their computers, nationwide. You need to disappear, man."

"That's why I'm here. I need your help."

"You've put me in a bad position, Jed. I've got problems of my own, you know? I don't need yours, too."

"I'm sorry, I just didn't have anywhere else to go. Come on, we're family."

Pauley looked at his cousin. He had an idea.

"Look, I was heading out in a couple of days. Maybe we can work something out."

"Really, Pauley? That would be great."

"Ever do any fishing?"

"Fishing? Yeah, I guess so, when I was a kid. Why?"

"I've got a job working on a fishing boat. It's hard work but it pays pretty well."

"What are you thinking? That I could do that with you?"

"Yeah, it'll get you outta here for a few months, too."

"A few months? What kind of fishing?"

"A charter business. I'm in pretty good with the guy. He's always looking for good help."

"I don't know, Pauley. Sounds like a lot of work."

"You don't got much of a choice, Jed. You need to get out of here."

"Where's the job?"

"Mexico."

"Mexico? I don't want to go to Mexico."

"Well, you're going to be living there for a few months so get used to the idea."

"And when's this happening?"

"I was going to go a few days from now but now we'll move it up. We'll leave in the morning."

Jed sat and contemplated his situation. Yesterday he was living in Colorado, peddling a little meth, living pretty well. Now, just two days later he was on his way to work on some fishing boat in Mexico.

"The only issue is getting you across the border."

"Getting over the border? Shit, that doesn't sound good."

"It's possible the guards at the crossing will have your name in their computer. If the Colorado cops have put it out nationally, they'll catch you red-handed as soon as you try to cross."

"So then how exactly are we going to do this?"

"I cross the border all the time. The guards know me. They usually just wave me in. They know I work the fishing boats down there."

"And if they don't just wave you in? What then?"

"Then we got problems. Got any money with you, Jed?"

He looked at his cousin, and replied, "A little."

"How much?"

"About five grand."

"More than enough. For a grand, they'll look the other way. At least that's my understanding from folks that have had to get someone across."

"A thousand bucks?"

"Hey, you got yourself into this mess. A grand is pretty damn cheap if it gets you out of the country for awhile."

"So, we try to get into Mexico, but if we get caught then I'll have to cough up a grand. Is that the plan?"

"Yeah, pretty much."

"And how are you going to smuggle me in?"

"In the trunk of my car."

"Jesus."

"They've never searched my trunk. I'm sure it'll be fine. And like I said, if for some reason they want to check the trunk then the bribe will get you in. But I don't think that'll be necessary."

"Damn, this makes me nervous."

"Yeah, well, it should. Now go get some rest. We leave first thing tomorrow."

CHAPTER 23

Sheriff McCallister sat on the edge of his bed perusing the watch
commander's log from the night before. It was how he started each
day, checking on the activities of his department while he'd been sleeping. If something major had happened—homicides, officer-involved
shootings, etc.—he would get a phone call in the middle of the night,
but the more mundane stuff would be listed in the report. A good start
to his day was when he opened the log and saw the words "Nothing
significant to report." He loved those days!

But today was not one of those days. He read the entry about Keller's
trip to Aurora. He tried to control his anger as he reread the entry.
Maybe it was a mistake to bring him back on contract. He couldn't be
doing this stuff, especially with his physical limitations.

"What's wrong, Mick? You look pissed."

He looked up at Mia. "Your partner running amok, that's what."

"Keller? What'd he do this time?" Mia asked, her hand on her hip.

"The video clip Archer put out last night got several hits. It came
back to a guy in Aurora. So instead of waiting and getting some deputies out there, Keller headed up there alone."

"He what?"

"You heard me."

"My God, I'm his partner on this one-eighty-seven and he didn't
even call me?"

"Nope. Keller being Keller."

"So, what happened?"

"He went up there but the guy was in the wind."

"He could've called the Aurora PD and they could have sat on the guy's place until we get our people in place. Keller's an idiot."

"Let's both meet with him first thing this morning. Tell him he's gotta knock this shit off or I'll cancel his contract."

"I'll say more than that. Damnit, he pisses me off!"

Chookie Thompson sat on her living room sofa sipping her morning coffee. She had endured yet another sleepless night worrying about her stepson, Tracey. She hadn't seen or heard from him in weeks. He had disappeared before, but never for this long. Her birthday, which was more than a week ago, had come and gone and she hadn't received anything from him. No phone call, no card, nothing. He had never missed her birthday, and she knew in her heart that something terrible had happened to him. Tracey wasn't a perfect son by any stretch of the imagination. He'd had his troubles and run ins with the police, but he had a good heart and Chookie knew her stepson would eventually outgrow all the foolishness and get his life together.

CHAPTER 24

Reginald Gray didn't grow up with the goal of becoming a drug kingpin in Rocklin County. He was born into the middle class; his father was a plumber and his mother a secretary. They didn't have a lot of money growing up in Atlanta, but he always had a roof over his head and enough to eat. Most of the people he'd come to know during his rise through the ranks of the drug trade came from less; they were typically poor with screwed up family lives. It was a cliché, but true—absentee father, mom working two or three jobs—he could see why people blamed their circumstances for their criminal ways. But the bottom line was that each was free to choose his or her own path, including him. Geez, he would often think—I sound like a damn Republican.

His plan, after graduating high school with a sparkling 2.3 GPA, was to attend Piedmont College in Athens, Georgia. Piedmont certainly wasn't the only college in Athens. Athens was also home to the prestigious University of Georgia Bulldogs, which was why he accepted a full-ride scholarship to Piedmont—to get noticed by U of G basketball coaches and scouts.

He had been a star basketball player in high school, averaging more than twenty points and fifteen rebounds per game. At six foot, five inches he was big for high school basketball, but at the college level players that size with his skill set were a dime a dozen. Despite that he was determined to play division one basketball. He had received a few college scholarship offers upon graduation but it was all small school stuff. He was determined to play in the NBA one day and going off to some obscure college wasn't the way he envisioned reaching his goal. Plus, Piedmont was sixty miles from home in Atlanta and he was ready to spread his wings outside the influence of his parents.

He found success at Piedmont, at least in the basketball world. He quickly became a dominant player and led the Lions to a state championship. A couple U of G basketball scouts did take notice, but no offer came to transfer to the big-time Bulldogs. He was too small to play center at the division one level and he wasn't quick enough or a good enough shooter to play forward or guard. He was pigeonholed as a center and couldn't escape it. After his sophomore year he began to realize his NBA dream wasn't going to happen and he became bitter and frustrated.

At an off-campus party one day a friend offered him a joint and for the first time in his life he accepted. It had been no easy thing avoiding the influence of drugs in high school and college, but with random drug testing required for all athletes at Piedmont he never wanted to take the chance. His basketball future was simply too important to him to risk using weed or any other drug. But after two years at Piedmont, his dream of playing in the NBA was quickly turning to dust, and he gave weed a chance. The high gave him a relaxed, calm feeling—something he hadn't felt with the constant pressures of school and basketball.

It was the off season and basketball wouldn't begin again for several months. There was no drug testing during the break so Reggie felt free to experiment with weed and then eventually ecstasy and cocaine. Within a few months his drug use was becoming a daily routine. His grades slipped and basketball seemed like a distant memory. His basketball scholarship at Piedmont was dependent on him playing, obviously. As the time approached for his junior season he realized that he'd need to stop using or risk failing a drug test. If he failed, his basketball career would be over and his scholarship would end.

That scholarship had allowed him to attend Piedmont without the need for a job. But with the added expense of his growing drug habit he found himself short on funds. The freebees that he been offered by Frankie Solis, his local dealer, were over and he needed money. So when Frankie suggested that he could do a little side gig peddling weed, it was easy to say yes. No big deal, he thought—just provide a little dope to his close buddies on campus. Filling a need, essentially. He'd be an entrepreneur, just like the ones he saw on *Shark Tank*. Only his business wasn't legal or legitimate.

At first Reggie peddled the dope to just his circle of friends, but eventually Frankie gave him more latitude. He was netting a few hundred dollars a week and suddenly the scholarship from Piedmont didn't seem that important. He was living in the dorm and he knew he was good until the end of the year. Basketball wouldn't start up again till Christmas, and he wasn't about to tell anyone he wouldn't be playing anymore. He was done. His dreams of playing for the U of G or any other division one school were dashed. At the age of twenty-one he was too old. His time had passed.

But Frankie saw something in Reggie, namely a very large circle of friends and a willingness to work hard and take chances. Calculated risks, not stupid stuff like many of those in his army of dope peddlers would take. Reggie was smart and he seemed to want to expand his efforts. There was some real money to be made, and Frankie needed someone like Reggie to be his sergeant, so to speak.

Within a few months Reggie was overseeing half a dozen sellers. He took a piece of the action and with the sale of meth, weed, and ecstasy he was pulling down more than a grand a week. Life was good, the work was easy, and the world of basketball faded to black. But the most important decision he made was to cut back his personal use of the drugs. Frankie had warned him about those underlings who had done well at first, only to fall victim to their own addictions. Their earnings went right back into the purchase of drugs, which was good for Frankie, expanding his profit margin. But it was hard for him to keep good people under him. Reggie, it seemed, wasn't falling into this trap. Frankie had high hopes for his new sergeant. He needed someone to climb the ranks of his growing distribution network. Good people were hard to find!

CHAPTER 25

Rachel Gillespie arrived ten minutes late for her coffee date with Mark Archer. It had been three months since their affair had started and she needed to play things just right with him. Keep him waiting a bit. She checked her makeup in the car mirror and spritzed some fresh perfume. Her sweater was just tight enough and showed a bit of cleavage. A quick application of lip gloss and she was ready to go.

Mark sat inside Bean Crazy nursing a black coffee. He glanced at his watch, noting Rachel was late. Not unusual; she tended to run a few minutes behind. He thought about his situation, wondering how exactly he had arrived at this point in his life. He and Angela had had a great thing going, but that had ended three months earlier. He had caught her in a lie; not a white lie, but one that was felony stupid. Literally.

Arranging for a bomb to be thrown through the window of Channel 8 just to raise TV ratings was a major screw up. It still shocked him that she would do such a thing. They had been together for nearly three years and in that time he had never seen anything indicating she was capable of such a stunt. They hadn't spoken in three months, since the shooting involving Mia, Jack, and the sheriff.

He had spoken to the sheriff only once about it, right after he had discovered what she had done. Mick, too, was shocked. He knew Angela, both professionally and personally, and would never have guessed she would do such a thing. The sheriff was conflicted about what, if anything, to do about it. On one hand, she shouldn't get away with it, but on the other hand Angela had done him a huge favor a couple of years earlier. That favor, essentially covering up the truth about the most sensational case in Rocklin County history, had helped send a murderer to prison. If the truth ever got out it would certainly result in the killer being released from prison. The judge could order a new trial, or given the misdeeds of the sheriff's department, the judge could simply release Scott Lennox and he would be a free man.

Mark shuddered at the thought. Scott Lennox was absolutely guilty, he had admitted as much, and if the sheriff had to cover up something to make sure he went to prison, then so be it.

"Hello, Mark."

Absorbed in his thoughts, he was startled by the voice. He stood quickly, knocking over his chair. He reached down and righted the chair.

"I'm sorry I surprised you. You look like your thoughts had you a million miles away."

"No worries. I was just thinking about an old case."

"Must have been a tough one."

"Yeah, it was. But it was a long time ago. So, how are you doing?" Mark asked, pulling out a chair for Rachel.

"Good, thanks."

"Glad to hear it. You look great."

"Aren't you sweet."

"So, what have you been up to these days?"

"Just busy with everything. I filed the divorce papers last week."

She didn't waste any time getting down to things, Mark thought.

"That's gotta be tough. Sorry you're having to deal with all that."

"It had to happen. It was a long time coming. I should have done it years ago."

"Yeah, but there was Kendra and you wanted to keep things together for her sake."

"True, but in retrospect I don't think I did her any favors by waiting."

"How so?"

"My marriage wasn't exactly the example I hoped to convey to my daughter. It was loveless and kids certainly pick up on that."

"That's true. But she's young and can figure things out on her own. She's a smart young lady. You did your best, Rachel."

"Yeah, I know all that. But with what happened to her on that campus, I don't know—it's just been a really rough year, I guess."

Mark reflected on the incident at Wilson High School. Kendra had been taken hostage by a disturbed young man who had held a gun to her head. Mia had taken him out, saving Kendra's life. But the shooting had received a lot of attention and the fallout from the incident was ongoing. Mia had just returned to work after a three-month maternity leave.

"You'll get past it, Rachel. The future is bright for you and Kendra. She'll go off to Colorado State soon and start her life."

"Yeah, that's another thing. I'm worried about her going so far away. I can't get the image of her held captive by that kid out of my mind. I know it's irrational, but what if something like that happens again and I'm seventy-five miles away?"

"It won't happen again. It was a bizarre situation and she'll be fine in Fort Collins. It's a great school and has a great reputation for being a very safe campus."

"I know all that, Mark. But my head can't quite process it."

"Sounds like you've got a little PTSD going on. It's not unusual. Victims feel it all the time."

"PTSD?"

"Post-traumatic stress disorder. Traditionally, soldiers were the ones diagnosed with it. But in recent years the scope of PTSD has been broadened and psychologists now know that victims of crime can experience strong effects of PTSD as well."

"I've heard of it. I didn't know victims of crime could have it."

"Yeah, it's very common."

"That's good to know, I guess. At least it explains a little of what I've been feeling. I mean, I have crazy, vivid dreams about what happened that day at the school. Thank God I wake up and realize it was only a dream and that the horror is over and Kendra is safe."

"Perfectly normal. Have you thought about seeing someone about it?"

"No, not really. I feel like I should be able to get past this on my own. I mean, Kendra seems fine. She's back to a normal life, and here I am, still struggling."

"Everybody's different. Don't beat yourself up over it. If it's how you feel, it's how you feel. No shame in talking to a therapist about it."

"Do you know anyone I can talk to?"

"Actually, I do. The RCSO uses a local therapist here in Castle Springs. Her name is Dr. Analee Lusetti. By all accounts, she's very good."

"Maybe I'll check her out. Couldn't hurt."

"You should do that. No reason to battle your feelings alone."

Mark hesitated, then continued.

"About twenty years ago, when I was new to the spokesman role, I handled a particularly difficult triple homicide. A dad, going through a divorce, murdered all three of his kids. Suffocated them in bed. All under the age of six. To this day, it's the worst thing I've ever seen."

"Oh my God, that's unbelievable."

"He did it to spite his estranged wife. He actually called her after he had killed the children, telling her she could come over and pick up the kids. It was a joint custody kind of thing, his weekend with the kids. Anyway, she came over and instantly knew something awful had happened. She said she could see it in his face. She ran in to check on the kids and discovered what had happened. She comes out screaming and and finds him standing in the living room, smiling. He puts a gun to his head and pulls the trigger."

"That's pure evil. And you had to respond to the scene?"

"Yeah, I got there maybe thirty minutes after it happened. Anyway, I had nightmares after that case. In fact, I slept with the light on in my bedroom for several days afterwards. I knew it was over, the perp was dead, so it didn't make any sense that I felt that way. But the point is I did feel that way. But I never asked for any help. It was back in the day when cops tried to maintain a certain machismo. You were weak if you admitted something got to you. So, I just lived with it. Over time I got over it, but in retrospect I should clearly have gotten some help."

Rachel thought of her own situation, going through a divorce. Maybe it was a good thing Kendra was away at school. Tim was a lousy husband, but he would never do anything to their only child. He loved Kendra, she was sure of that.

Mark sensed where she was with her thoughts.

"Rachel, I didn't mean to upset you with that story. My point was that there's nothing wrong with seeking a little help when you struggle with your feelings. I don't know Tim very well, but from what I've seen, that isn't in his makeup."

"Oh, I know. He'd never harm her. But my God, what an awful thing."

"Let's talk about something else."

CHAPTER 26

Mick couldn't believe how fast the three years had passed since his election as sheriff of Rocklin County, The term was four years and he knew he needed to start planning for his reelection run. He and Mia had discussed whether or not he should run, but at forty-eight years old he was simply too young to retire. And besides, he loved the job. The administrative and political part of the position weren't high on his list, but the leadership he had brought to the RCSO had resulted in happy deputies and a falling crime rate. In fact, crime was down more than twenty-three percent since he had taken office, something he credited to community policing and some very good work by his deputies and detectives. He didn't see anyone in the horizon angling to run against him, but his philosophy was to always run like you were in the fight of your life. His strategy was to keep three particular groups happy and content, at least to the best of his ability.

First, there was the rank and file. He had meetings with the deputies' union every month, listening to their concerns and grievances, and trying to be fair with them. Some of their requests were a bit on the outrageous side, like the time they had asked for a twenty percent annual raise, but he listened just the same. He had always maintained an open-door policy and had made a point to attend the wedding every time one of his deputies got married. With more than a thousand deputies, he and Mia had been to more than fifty weddings during his three years in office. The deputies recognized his efforts and appreciated that they had his ear. He had little doubt that the deputies' union would support him in his reelection efforts.

Second, there was the community. He spent a great deal of time interacting with the public. Not just glad-handing at events, but real connection. Mark Archer hosted a weekly TV show for the RCSO that shared information with Rocklin County residents. The show was live and allowed Archer to take phone calls from viewers. That could get a bit dicey at times, but for the most part it served the department well. Mick would often sit in on the show and answer questions as well. He had personally attended more than a hundred community meetings each year. Listening to residents' concerns and just being there went a long way in gaining support for the department. The RCSO had been the first department to do webcasts and still continued them a decade later because they also contributed to an open line of communication between the sheriff and the community.

Third, there was the media. *Open* and *transparent* were the buzzwords everyone used, and they sounded good, but it wasn't always easy. Colorado, like every state, had very strict privacy laws protecting deputies, especially following controversial cases such as officer-involved shootings. The media wanted all the details all the time, but that just wasn't always possible. But when there was a question about what could be released, Mick erred on the side of publishing the information. It had served him well, and kept most reporters happy. Although he had had a handful of tough moments with reporters and editors, especially Angela Bell and Denise Elliott. Both were very aggressive and had some issues with the RCSO. The department's relationship with Angela had soured since Mia's officer-involved shooting and Angela's subsequent breakup with Mark Archer. Denise Elliott was very pushy and one of those reporters who wasn't happy unless you gave her every detail about whatever was going on.

He checked the calendar on his phone and saw he had two community meetings that day. He was scheduled to be the lunch speaker at the Noon-Timer Lions Club and had an evening meeting with the Cabrillo Neighborhood Council in north Castle Springs. He texted Mia to let her know that he'd be late getting home that evening and to eat dinner without him; he'd grab a sandwich somewhere.

Mia was sitting at her desk going over her notes in the skull case when her cell went off. She checked the caller ID and saw it was Rose Cochran calling. Cochran was her attorney from Los Angeles, whom Mia had hired to sue attorney Leland Simpson after he had made defamatory comments about her involvement in the shooting death of Alex Washington. Mia, who had saved Kendra Gillespie's life when she took out the young man holding Kendra hostage with a gun to her head three months earlier, had made the decision to sue. She was asking for ten million dollars, an outrageous sum, but one that she knew would get a lot of attention from the media. She knew, as Rose Cochran had warned her, that she was unlikely to collect anything from the legendary attorney, but she certainly had his attention. The shooting had caused a monumental shift in Mia, and she was determined to strike a victory for all those officers crucified in the press and the community following a shooting. The ignorance some people showed following these incidents was astounding, and Mia was determined to do something about it. Her lawsuit against Simpson was an important first step.

Mia answered the call.

"Good morning, Rose. How are you doing?"

"I couldn't be better, Mia. How are things going in Colorado?"

"I'm doing okay. Things are slowly getting back to normal. I'm back at work now."

"That's fabulous. It's got to feel good to get back in your routine. How's CJ doing?"

"He's great. Three months old and already thirteen pounds. He's always smiling and looking around. My dad is watching him for us during the day. I miss him so much but my dad is really great with him."

"I'll bet Chuck loves being a grandpa! I can totally see him in that role. Does he have CJ going with him on his hikes yet?"

"Just on walks around the neighborhood so far. He's out pushing that stroller up and down all the streets in Castle Springs. The doctor doesn't want him out on anything super strenuous right now. So Red Rocks isn't quite on his routine yet, but I'm sure it will be soon."

"That's great to hear. Glad he's doing well."

"Thanks. So, what's new with the case?"

"Not too much. As you know, it's going to take a while to wind through the system. But I will do everything in my power to keep it fresh in the eyes of the public."

Mia smiled at the thought. Rose Cochran made quite a career for herself taking on controversial cases that allowed her to get in front of the cameras and talk about the outrageous behavior of whomever it was she was targeting. The public largely knew she was a grandstander, but they ate it up. People loved all the drama and with social media it wasn't hard to get a few million people to follow her every step. Although Cochran was in her seventies, she and her staff had mastered Twitter, Facebook, Instagram, and Snapchat. They could make all these avenues come alive promoting whatever she was doing. She'd make the rounds of all the gossipy shows—*The View, Access Hollywood, TMZ*—always wearing her traditional baby blue attire.

"I'm sure you will, Rose. So we just hold tight for now, then?"

"Yeah, it'll be a couple more months before we have any court appearances. And of course, when that happens we'll get it on the front page. Gotta keep Simpson's toes to the fire."

"That sounds great," replied Mia, wondering a bit about the purpose of Cochran's call.

"So, listen. I'm going to be out in Denver next week. I've got another client out there I need to meet with. I'll only be in town for a short visit but I'd love to get together with you and Mick and meet CJ."

"Sure, that sounds good. We should be around. Just let us know when you're in town and we can make that happen."

"Perfect. Oh, and I'd love to see Chuck, too."

Mia smiled to herself. She remembered Rose and her father getting very flirty with each other on her previous visit. It was strange for her to see her dad carrying on like that with a woman, but he was a widower and Rose was divorced, so why not she thought.

"Of course. We'll have you over to the house for dinner. That way you can see everyone."

"Perfect, Mia. I'll be in touch. Have a great day."

CHAPTER 27

Angela Bell sat in a production meeting, daydreaming as the others talked about the various stories listed on the whiteboard in the Channel 8 conference room. She hated these meetings, much preferring to be out reporting or sitting at the anchor desk reading the news from the teleprompter. She knew the meetings were a necessary step in the process; they got everybody working on the same page. But as a twenty-year news veteran having worked in a half dozen media markets, she was pretty much over it. Either bring me the news to read or send me out on a juicy story.

The daily shooting and stabbing stories were the same every day. Throw in a couple of stories about the Denver City Council or the Colorado Legislature, and you had half the newscast filled up. Add sports, weather with the pretty, young weather girl, an animal story if you were lucky, and maybe a couple of touching human interest stories, and the hour-long newscast was complete.

Smile at the camera, connect with the audience, pretend you're talking to each viewer personally . . . it was all formulaic, but it worked. While ratings were down (everywhere, not just at Denver's Channel 8), the news division still made money. This profit center had benefited from cutbacks in staff and paying much lower salaries than in the past. The days of big money were gone; reporters really didn't make all that much. Unless, of course, you were in a top-ten media market. Be an anchor in New York or LA and you were rewarded with huge salaries, often a million or more dollars per year, just for reading the news. But as a reporter or even an anchor in a smaller market, you'd be lucky to earn much above a living wage. Fifty grand a year was not unusual. And the videographers, producers, and editors typically earned less.

Angela, with her longevity, experience, and excellent on-camera presence, earned $140,000 per year. But Denver was a pretty good-sized market. It wasn't LA or New York, but for a woman coming from rural North Dakota, she had done well for herself.

As her assignment editor droned on about some community center opening in Longmont, her mind drifted to Mark Archer. Their big blowup had occurred three months earlier and the two had hardly said a word to each other since. Mark had sent a few cryptic text messages, and her responses had matched his tone. They needed to be at least cordial to each other due to their jobs—he was the spokesman for a major police agency in Channel 8's viewing audience.

But the truth was she missed him. They had three years invested in a relationship that was, for the most part, wonderful. Mark was certainly the best man she had ever been involved with. She was nearly forty and had never been married. She had truly thought Mark was the one she'd be with for the rest of her life. They were very compatible and shared the same media world experiences. He totally got what she did and appreciated her for doing it well.

But when he essentially accused her of arranging for that bomb to go through a Channel 8 window during a live broadcast, that was something she couldn't overlook. Trust was obviously a huge factor in any relationship and if he didn't trust her, then that was going to be a big issue. The problem was it was the truth. She had arranged for the bomb, albeit a small one, to be thrown through the window that night. But she had the guy throw it through the front window where no one was working at that hour. It seemed like a small prank to her back then, but in retrospect it was a truly stupid thing to do. Ratings were one thing, but jeopardizing her relationship with the man she truly loved was just stupid. She wished she could somehow undo it all. No one was injured and there was little damage, but, obviously, she couldn't go back in time.

She had thought Mark would eventually come around and they could mend the break. But three months had passed and there had been no real attempt by either to get their relationship back on track. In another troubling development, she had heard that Mark was already seeing someone else. Men move on so damn quickly, she thought. She wasn't ready to date anyone else—she didn't want anyone else. Maybe she should reach out to him again and see if she could get a feeling about where he was with things.

Her mind went to the Scott Lennox trial two years earlier. Lennox had murdered his business partner and was tried and convicted for that crime. He was currently in a Colorado prison serving twenty-five years to life. The then-married Lennox had been assisted in the homicide by his girlfriend, Lisa Sullivan. Sullivan had agreed to testify for the prosecution in exchange for her freedom. It was a controversial move by the district attorney, and one that didn't sit well with the Rocklin County Sheriff's Department. Mick McCallister, who at the time was running for the office of sheriff, was particularly incensed by the DA's decision. But it was out of his hands and the deal was made. A few days after Lennox's conviction, McCallister was elected sheriff.

Just prior to the jury's deliberation in the case, Angela had learned the shocking truth that Lisa Sullivan was Jack Keller's daughter. It was a bombshell that she knew could destroy the case against Lennox. If word somehow got out that Jack Keller, the lead investigator in the case, was Sullivan's father, then the judge would certainly declare a mistrial. And Mick McCallister would have a major problem on the eve of the election.

When she learned of the situation, Angela knew she had a major decision to make. Sit on the story and not say anything? Scott Lennox was clearly guilty of murder; there was never any doubt about that. If she went public with what she knew then a murderer would almost certainly go free. The story would be huge, though—it would go national at least. And that national attention could lead to something for her in a larger media market. It was all very tempting, but in the end she decided to sit on the story. So Scott Lennox was convicted, McCallister won the election, and her relationship with Mark Archer was stronger than ever. Mark knew that she knew the truth about Keller and Sullivan so he was grateful for her keeping quiet. A greater good had come from her decision to stay quiet, Mark had told her. It wasn't ideal and it didn't always feel right to her; it was essentially a coverup, but it was something she could live with. Going public with what she knew and allowing Lennox to walk on the murder was simply too high a price. The truth would have to take a back seat.

But now her relationship with Mark was over. She pondered that and allowed her mind to consider what would happen if she came forward with the truth. The likely fallout would be that Lennox would be freed from prison and probably be given a new trial. McCallister would face a huge backlash and might well be unsuccessful in his upcoming re-election efforts. Mark would be furious with her and any hope of reconciling with him would be dashed. Clearly, no good could come from it.

But what would Mark do if he *thought* she might tell her story? Would it cause him to rethink their relationship? It wasn't the way she wanted to get him back, but it could open a dialogue with him and that could lead to something good.

But how could she broach the subject?

CHAPTER 28

Mia texted Rose Cochran to invite her to dinner at the house. It seemed like a good plan, as Rose would only be in town for the one night. She was scheduled to leave on the first flight back to LA in the morning.

She arrived by limousine a few minutes after six, greeting everyone in the McCallister family with a quick hug.

"Where's that beautiful baby?"

"He's in his crib, taking a nap. Let me see if he's awake," Mia replied.

"No, no, don't wake him up for me."

"He's due up around now. I'll go take a peek."

Mia left the room and Rose turned to Mick and Chuck.

"So, how are things going, sheriff?'

"Going well, thanks. I've got a reelection campaign to put together so I've been busy with that."

"Good for you. That's great that you'll have another four years at the helm of the RCSO. So, have things calmed down with respect to the OIS?"

"Yeah, I haven't heard anything about it for a while. Although I do wonder what Leland Simpson will have up his sleeve next."

"Maybe nothing—he got reamed pretty good with his ridiculous comments after the OIS about Mia being pregnant. I did everything I could to put him in his place, so he may be still licking his wounds.

But wait till the next step in the lawsuit comes around. He'll wish he'd never taken the case."

"Sounds good to me."

Rose turned her attention to Chuck.

"And you, young man, how are you doing?"

"Just great, Rose. I'm back to my old self, better than ever."

"That's great to hear, Chuck. Remember you owe me a hike in Red Rocks. You promised."

"Oh, I haven't forgotten. Too bad you don't have more time. It's supposed to be beautiful here tomorrow but Mia tells me you have an early flight back to Los Angeles."

"Yeah, I have to get back. I have a very busy rest of the week, or I'd take you up on your offer."

"Rain check, then."

"Absolutely. I'm going to hold you to that, Chuck."

Mia came into the room, holding a slightly groggy CJ.

"Oh, my, let me get a look at that beautiful boy."

Mia smiled and handed CJ to Rose.

She cuddled him and gently stroked his cheek.

"He's perfect. I love babies at this age. My grandchildren are all older now and I miss this."

"How many grandchildren do you have?" asked Mick.

"I have six, but the youngest is almost ten so it's been awhile since I held a little one like this. So precious."

Chuck watched Rose cooing at CJ. She didn't look like a woman with six grandkids, he thought. She seemed much too young for that. Too bad she had to leave so early the next morning; a hike with this woman would be nice.

Mia glanced at her father and saw a look on his face she hadn't seen before. She remembered how he and Rose had carried on a bit at the hospital before his heart procedure. It was very odd to see her dad flirting with someone. Her mom had been gone for more than ten years, so there wasn't anything wrong with him showing interest in another woman, but still, it was weird.

"I better give him back to you Mia or I just might take him with me back to LA."

Mia smiled and took CJ.

"Let's move to the living room where we can be more comfortable. Dinner will be ready in about thirty minutes. Can I offer you a drink, Rose?" Mick asked.

"That would be great. White wine, if you have it."

"I can do that. Chuck, your usual?"

"That would be great, Mick. Here, let me show you to the living room, Rose."

Chuck took Rose by the arm and led her out of the room.

Once they were out of earshot, Mia turned to Mick.

"Geez, they'll be moving in together by the end of the week."

Mick laughed. "I think it's great, Mia. Chuck does seem a bit taken with her."

"And vice versa, I'd say."

"No harm in that. And remember she lives a thousand miles away. If anything happens it'll have to be a long-distance relationship."

"Oh, God, I'm not ready for that."

"Well, let's not get ahead of ourselves. It's just a little banter between the two."

"Yeah, I know. But it's definitely weird to see."

"He could do worse. At least she's not twenty-five," Mick replied, nudging Mia in the ribs as they walked to the kitchen.

"Don't get any ideas, big boy."

"Me? I'm the most happily married man I know."

"Even with your post-pregnant wife? I still need to lose a few pounds."

"Those pounds? They're all in your boobs! And personally, I'm good with that."

"Oh my God, listen to you. Such a sick mind, Mr. Sheriff."

"Just saying. You're more beautiful to me now than before CJ."

"Good to hear. But you're still a pervert."

"Thanks, honey. I'll take that as a compliment."

"I'm sure you will."

Mick poured a glass of chardonnay for Rose and vodka on the rocks for both him and Chuck. He took the drinks into the living room where he found Rose and his father-in-law sitting close together on the sofa. They were giggling about something and she had her hand on his arm.

Looked like Mia was right, he thought.

CHAPTER 29

LaNiece Jackson was still reeling from her son's death. It had been a long three months since Jaquon was shot to death by the RCSO and she was having a very difficult time coming to grips with what had happened.

Her son had been trouble since junior high and had really gone south after his cousin Alex Washington had been killed. Jaquon had a deep hatred toward the police and when a deputy took his cousin's life, something inside Jaquon just snapped. He was filled with hatred and rage and was determined to do something to get justice for Alex. The only justice he knew was street justice and that ultimately brought about his own death.

LaNiece wasn't shocked by what happened. In fact, she had shared her concerns about Jaquon with her Uncle Floyd a few days before Jaquon died. Floyd was concerned as well and had gone to Jaquon's apartment the day before his death. He tried talking to him about things but it was no use. After the visit, Jaquon and his live-in girlfriend, Alondra, got into it and Jaquon took off. Twenty-fours hour later he was dead at the hands of RCSO investigator Jack Keller. What happened during Jaquon's last twenty-four hours was unknown; no one knew what Jaquon was doing after fleeing following the argument with Alondra.

But one thing was clear—Jaquon had gone to a Denver hotel with the intention of killing the woman who had shot and killed Alex. The woman, who happened to be married to the sheriff of Rocklin County and seven months pregnant, was there with her attorney spouting off about the shooting. Jaquon opened fire but was shot and killed by Keller before he could hurt the female deputy. But he did seriously injure Keller in an exchange of gunfire, and the wounds Keller inflicted on Jaquon proved fatal. Mia went into premature labor soon after the shooting and delivered a four and-a-half-pound baby boy.

LaNiece buried Jaquon five days later in a small church service with just family present. The media didn't care about his death; not a single reporter attended the funeral. The police took him out and no one cared. Of course, the fact that he had gone to the hotel that day to kill a deputy didn't generate much sympathy from the public or the media. But Jaquon was her son and he didn't deserve to die that way, she thought. He had a good heart; he was just struggling with the difficulties of life. Just as his life was about to get back on track—she was sure of it! But the cops took him out like a dog, just like they took out Alex.

When Alex was killed, his mother, Danesha, who was LaNiece's first cousin, was contacted by an attorney who offered to sue the RCSO on behalf of the family. She wouldn't have to pay a dime, they told her. That lawsuit was proceeding and the family was sure to get rich—she just knew it. But no attorneys knocked on her door after Jaquon died; clearly no one cared. But what the cops did to him wasn't right. Couldn't they have shot him in the knee or just shot the gun out of his hand? Why not use a taser or a baton? It was what people called "excessive force." Why weren't people outraged? Why weren't there protests in the street like there were for Alex?

Just because attorneys weren't contacting her didn't mean she had no case. She decided to take things in her own hands. If the attorneys weren't coming to her, she'd go to them. She grabbed her iPhone and searched for attorneys. Dozens appeared on the screen, all bragging about the cases they had won for their clients. This shouldn't be hard, she thought. There were plenty to choose from. But which one? She scrolled down, doing a quick read about each one.

Almost all said they wouldn't charge anything, just take a percentage of the winnings. That was fair, she thought. No money out of her pocket—that was important because she was broke. If she had to share the winnings, she was okay with that, as long as she got to keep most of the money.

After reading more than two dozen entries, a name popped up and she instantly got a good feeling. Aquarius Morales, attorney at law. You don't pay unless we win your case. Personal injury is our specialty, we win 98% of our cases!

Her first name was Aquarius? LaNiece knew this was the right person. After all, LaNiece's birthday was February second and she was an Aquarius! It was like a sign from God. She hit the contact button and was quickly talking to a real person. No answering machine, no phone tree hell—she liked that. Good customer service, not some impersonal law firm with a thousand employees.

"Can I help you?" the voice said.

"Yes, my name is LaNiece Jackson and I need to hire an attorney."

"Well, you've called the right place. Tell me about your case."

LaNiece proceeded to explain her situation, trying not to get emotional. But halfway through she lost it and began to cry. She apologized to the nice woman on the phone.

"That's okay, I understand why you're upset. Your Jaquon was taken from you. Any mother would be devastated by this."

"So, can you help me?'

"Well, normally we take personal injury cases. This is really a wrongful death case."

"But my Jaquon was injured, worse than injured—he was murdered!"

"Yes, that's true. But typically personal injury cases involve traffic accidents, trips and falls, things like that."

"But my case is worse than that, they took my Jaquon from me!"

The woman paused for a few seconds before responding. She was trying to calculate what the case could mean financially. Maybe a quick settlement with the county, just to make the case go away. They wouldn't want the hassle or the publicity. On the other hand, maybe they would welcome the publicity—show their residents they were tough and weren't going to pay off on what was essentially an extortion case. Either way, it was worth the risk.

"Okay, I think we can help you."

"Oh, thank you! When can I talk to Aquarius?"

"You're talking to her, LaNiece. Think of me as a one-woman band."

LaNiece didn't have GPS in her 1997 Honda Civic, but the Waze app on her iPhone worked great. She plugged in the address for Aquarius Morales's office and was on her way. The office was located in the Montebello neighborhood close to downtown Denver. LaNiece was familiar with the area as she had a former junior high school classmate living there. She had visited her a few times in recent years but as often happens she had fallen out of touch with the woman.

She followed the verbal commands coming from her phone. She chuckled each time Mr. T's voice told her where to turn. The Waze app allowed for different voices to give the necessary directions and warnings. She had tried them all before settling on her favorite, the 1980s TV star Mr. T.

"Look out sucka, hazard ahead!"

LaNiece looked around and sure enough there was a ladder in the street being dodged by the cars in the lane next to her. She navigated safely around it.

After a few more turns Mr. T advised, "You've arrived at your destination. The location is on your right."

LaNiece glanced over and saw a dilapidated two-story brick building with the address on the front. One of the numbers was dangling at an angle but the address was still readable. Hmmm, she thought . . . not what she pictured when she thought of an attorney's office. She found a parking spot half a block from the building and pulled her Civic in nose first. Parking was free, something rarely found in an area so close to downtown.

She walked quickly to the building as she sensed the neighborhood wasn't a particularly safe one. Graffiti was prevalent and there were weeds growing up through cracks in the sidewalk. Several buildings had broken windows. She walked into Morales's building and located a directory on one of the walls in the lobby.

Aquarius Morales, Attorney-at-Law - Room 232

She looked around and saw an elevator. She walked over, pressed the button, and could hear the lift come to life, squeaking and grumbling. Not feeling good about the elevator she looked around again to see if there were stairs. Not seeing any she stayed put and waited half a minute until the doors opened. The ride up was slow and noisy but once on the second floor she quickly found room 232.

She opened the door and realized that it was just one room. No reception area, just a woman in her fifties with her hair in a bun. She was Hispanic and wore no makeup. She was dressed in some kind of Aztec-looking dress, very colorful and flowing. The woman was attractive, but definitely a free spirit, LaNiece thought.

"I'm looking for Aquarius Morales."

"Well, you've found her. And you must be LaNiece?"

"I am," she answered, extending her hand.

"Nice to meet you, LaNiece. Please, have a seat."

LaNiece looked around at the tiny office. The place was smaller than the bedroom in her apartment in Castle Springs. There was only one chair; there wasn't really room for any more than that. She pulled the chair up to the front of Aquarius's desk and sat down.

"Would you like some coffee? I have a Keurig if you're interested," she said, pointing over her shoulder.

"No, thanks. I'm fine."

"You look a little surprised at my office setup here."

"A little bit; it's just not what I pictured."

"No worries, I like to travel light, you know? Most attorneys carry a huge overhead—all those fancy downtown offices, large staffs, mahogany desks, expensive lunches. I think differently—my clients come first and I keep my overhead low so I can charge them a very competitive rate. Guess what my hourly rate is."

"Oh, I have no idea," LaNiece answered, a bit concerned as she had gone in thinking she wouldn't be paying anything.

Aquarius picked up on the concern.

"Now remember, I'm taking your case on what they call a contingency basis. You won't be paying me anything until your case settles."

"Okay, that was my understanding on the phone. That's good."

"No worries. Okay, with that settled, guess my hourly rate."

"I've really no idea. Maybe fifty dollars per hour?"

"Oh, LaNiece! You kidder, you!"

LaNiece wasn't sure what to say. The most she had ever made in her life was $9.50 an hour. That was at the Castle Springs 99 Cent Store when she made floor supervisor.

"Too low?"

"Let me put things in perspective. A Denver attorney with all the trappings I mentioned a minute ago would charge clients a minimum of three hundred dollars per hour and some get as much as four hundred."

"Oh my God. I had no idea."

"Because of my arrangements here, I charge only a hundred and fifty an hour. You see my strategy?"

"Yes, I see what you're doing."

"And still, I win ninety-eight percent of my cases. All that superfluous bullshit doesn't matter. It's results in the courtroom that really count."

"That's true."

The reality was that Aquarius Morales rarely, if ever, actually went into a courtroom. Her strategy was to cut and run—get a quick nuisance settlement offer from the big bad insurance company or government agency and keep forty percent.

"So, are you ready to get down to business?"

"Yes, I think so. I want justice for my Jaquon."

"Then, it's justice we'll get. That and a bucket full of money. Jaquon would be proud of what you're doing. You aren't going to go away quietly. The RCSO must pay for their sins."

"Amen. It ain't right what they did to my boy. They need to pay."

"And pay they will. Before we get started I just need you to sign this contract. It outlines everything we talked about on the phone."

Aquarius slid the document across the desk and handed LaNiece a pen.

LaNiece looked at the pen and remarked, "Hey, that's a Ninety-nine Cent Store pen. Aisle five."

CHAPTER 30

I t took Pauley some time to rouse Jed. "Time to go. Get your ass outta bed."
Jed opened his eyes a bit and saw his cousin standing over him. The reality of his situation came rushing back. He was heading to Mexico.

"All right, all right. Give me a minute."

"We leave in ten. Pack your shit."

Pauley left the room and Jed gave himself a minute to get his mind focused, contemplating his life. It was a mess, that was for sure, and now he was going to be working on a fishing boat hundreds of miles from Colorado. At least the cops would never find him down there. But he hoped the move was temporary and he'd be able to return to the States. Maybe things would cool down and the cops would lose interest in finding him at some point. Doubtful, but he could entertain the thought . . . it gave him some hope.

He checked the clock on the nightstand—6:30 am.

He grabbed his cell and sent a quick text to his girlfriend, Marina.

"Let's go, Jed. Move it!" came a shout from the hallway.

"Yeah, yeah, I'll be ready in a minute."

"We need to get a move on," replied Pauley, coming into the bed-room to see if Jed was up and about.

"What the hell are you doing?"

"Sending a text. Chill bro."

"You fucking idiot! Cell phones can be tracked by the cops!"

Jed's eyes got wide.

Pauley grabbed the phone and quickly removed the battery. "We gotta destroy this phone. I can't believe you're that stupid!"

"Shit!"

"Have you been sending texts to her before this morning?"

"Yeah, I sent her one yesterday from New Mexico."

"Great, Jed. Why don't you just send the cops your trip itinerary?"

"I'm sorry, man. I didn't even think about it."

"Please tell me this is a burner phone."

"No, it's mine."

"God, you are major-league stupid!"

Pauley dropped the phone on the hardwood floor and stomped on it with his heavy boot. A few sharp blows and the phone was destroyed. One piece flew under the bed.

"We'll get you a burner phone today. Don't give that number out to anyone except me. Got it?"

"Yeah, okay."

"Now move it."

Jed climbed from the bed and threw on a pair of shorts and a tank top. He brushed his teeth and within a few minutes he was sitting in Pauley's Toyota sedan. Jed hoped that he'd be able to cross the border sitting in the front seat, not squirreled away in the trunk. He was a little claustrophobic and the idea of being hidden away in a dark, cramped space was discomforting.

"It's a two-hour drive to the border. We should be in San Martin by ten. That'll give us enough time to introduce you to Jeremiah. He's the guy that runs the charter I work."

"What if he doesn't want to hire me? I've got no experience."

"I'm pretty tight with him. He'll hire you. I'm not worried. Besides, they're always looking for people to work the charters. People are always coming and going. The timing worked out perfectly. You need to get out of the country and this gig is exactly what you need."

CHAPTER 31

Chookie Thompson spent yet another sleepless night worrying about her son. He had disappeared into thin air. Her concern had shifted from wondering what he had done to a serious concern for his well-being. Her maternal instincts were on overdrive and she just knew something was seriously wrong.

She had developed a distrust of the police after being lied to by a detective a few months earlier. The guy—what was his name? Jack something—had posed as a salesman to try to get information about her stepson. He had flat-out lied to her and her son had been arrested, largely as a result of her confiding in Keller about her stepson's whereabouts.

The look he had given her after the arrest, a slight nod to her outside Chookie's Pub, where Tracey had been arrested, really pissed her off. But now her son had been missing for weeks and she saw no other option but to call the sheriff's department. Given his checkered past she wondered how much attention they would give a missing person report on Tracey, but she couldn't worry about that now. She picked up her cell and dialed 911.

"Sheriff's department, what is your emergency?"

"It's not really an emergency but my stepson has been missing for a pretty long time and I think something may have happened to him."

"How long has he been missing?"

"About two and a half months."

Normally the dispatcher would refer someone calling in about a missing person to the detective bureau, but this call caught the dispatcher's attention. She thought about the person of interest flyer issued the night before and remembered it was connected to an unidentified body.

"Hold on, I'll transfer you."

At least she was getting somewhere, thought Chookie.

"Mark Archer."

"Hi, lieutenant, this is Stella down in dispatch. I've got a nine-one-one call from a woman reporting that her stepson is missing. Says he disappeared about two and a half months ago. I think that matches up with your unidentified body and thought I'd keep her on the line. You want to talk with her?"

"Absolutely. Thanks for the heads up, Stella."

"No problem. I'll put her through to you."

"This is Lieutenant Archer. May I help you?"

"I want to report a missing person. Can you help me with that?"

"Certainly. Who is it that's missing?"

"My stepson. I haven't heard from him since March."

"Has he done this before? Gone missing for any period of time?"

"Not like this. I know something is wrong. I can just feel it."

"Okay, tell me about your stepson."

"His name is Tracey Thompson. He's twenty-four years old and—"

The woman began to break down.

"That's okay, take your time. I know this is hard."

"He's a good boy. He hasn't always made the best decisions but he's a good boy at heart. You know what I mean?"

Archer had heard it all a thousand times before. All moms loved their children and believed they were, deep down, good people. And maybe it was true, but Archer had seen plenty of examples where people weren't always good deep down. He'd seen lots of plain old-fashioned evil.

"Of course. Can you describe your son for me?"

Archer wanted to see if the description fit their subject. If not, he would pass the woman on to the missing persons detective and things would take their normal course.

"He's a good boy, really."

"I'm sure he is. Can you give me a physical description?"

"He's twenty-four, about six feet tall, with a thin build. Brown hair and brown eyes. What else do you need to know?"

"How about race? Tattoos, other distinctive features?"

Archer didn't care about tattoos, it was race that he was most interested in. But he knew to couch the question carefully.

"He's black and has a lot of tattoos. I can't think of anything really distinctive. He has a great smile," she added between sniffles.

"I'm sure he does."

Archer felt hopeful with the description the woman had offered. It was enough to hand to Keller so he could run with it.

"So can you help me?"

"Yes, but I'm not the one who does these investigations. But I will personally speak to the detective and have him call you when he comes in. Can you give me a number where you can be reached?"

"Sure, my number is 303-555-1976."

"And your name?"

"Chookie, that's what everyone calls me."

"Okay, you should be hearing from a detective shortly."

Archer called Keller's cell number to let him know about the lead. It was still pretty early, but he knew Jack was an early riser like him. Jack picked up on the first ring.

"Keller."

"Jack, it's Mark Archer. I just got a call from a woman who says her son is missing. She hasn't heard from him since March, and he fits the age and race of your victim. Sounds like it could be your skull in a box. Told her she'd be hearing from a detective shortly."

"Text me her contact info and I'll give her a call."

"Will do."

A minute later Jack's phone pinged. He opened the text and read: Caller's name is "Chookie" and her number is 303-555-1977.

Jack stared at the screen, shaking his head. But it made sense.

It would be an interesting phone call, Jack thought, contemplating what he might say to Chookie. He thought back to meeting her some four months earlier, posing as an out-of-town salesman named Danny, dropping into Chookie's Pub for a quick drink. The ruse worked and a conversation with her produced information on the whereabouts of her stepson. She had learned of Jack's true identity later that day when her stepson was arrested outside the bar.

And now, given this new development, he knew that the skull could well be her stepson's. Ratting out a fellow gang member often brought swift street justice.

He contemplated how he'd handle the call. Should he tell Chookie up front who he was and risk her shutting down the call? It had been more than four months. Would she recognize his voice? His conversation with her at the bar that day had been fairly lengthy, so it was possible she would recognize the voice and figure out who he was. Probably best to have Mike Laubacher make the call. He had no history with the woman.

Mia looked at her cell and saw Keller listed on the caller ID.

"Good morning, Jack."

"Good morning. What's your ETA this morning?"

"I'm about to leave for the office so probably fifteen minutes or so. What's up?"

"We just got a call from a woman reporting that her stepson has been missing for two and a half months. The description matches our skull in the box. Archer talked to the woman and now we need to do a follow up call."

"That's great news. So, you just wanted me to know?"

"You're always telling me to include you, so there you have it."

Mia considered what Jack was saying. It didn't make a lot of sense—she'd be seeing him in minutes when she arrived at the office, so why the call?

"Okay, I do appreciate that. Anything else you want to tell me about this lead?"

"Yeah, I know the caller. I think it's best if we have Laubacher make the contact."

"How do you know her?"

Mia grew concerned about another Keller entanglement. The hidden relationship between Jack and his daughter, Lisa, had been a nightmare. Now what, she wondered.

"You remember the arrest of the knuckleheads who bombed your place?"

"Of course."

"I got one to rat out the other after leaning on him pretty good."

"Yeah, I remember. So how does this caller tie in with all that?"

"The caller is the stepmother of the one who rolled over. I was a little less than straightforward with her when we spoke back then. It was the only way I could get my hands on the assholes that did that to you and your dad."

"And now this woman is reporting her stepson has been missing for months?"

"Yep. The timeline matches up nicely."

"It sure does. So you want Laubacher to call her and keep you and me out of it. Is that it?"

"Yeah, I think that would be best."

"Okay, Laubacher it is. See you in a few."

CHAPTER 32

Laubacher made the call and got all the pertinent information from Chookie. There was no mention of Jack during the conversation, nor was there any outward hostility toward the RCSO for arresting her stepson. Chookie was a very worried mom and both Mia and Jack believed she had reason to be concerned. There was a good chance the skull belonged to Tracey Thompson aka Iceman. Fortunately they had Iceman's DNA on file; getting that sample was a requirement of the plea deal he had struck with the DA.

After getting the rundown from Laubacher, Mia said to Jack ,"We need to get the DNA checked. I'll call and let Dr. Mora know about Iceman. He should be able to check for a preliminary match."

Keller replied, "Yeah, that's job one right now. Once we have a positive ID then we can move forward. Retrace his steps, check his contacts, phone records, all that."

"Agreed."

Mia placed the call to Mora's office and let them know. By lunchtime they had the news they were hoping for. The preliminary search confirmed, with more than 99% certainty, that the skull in the box did indeed belong to Tracey Thompson.

"We need to let Chookie know," Mia said to Jack.

"Let's hold off for now. I don't want to spook Iceman's friends. Better if we fly under the radar for a bit."

"That's not right, Jack. We have a mom who's worried to death about her stepson. She should be told."

"We'll tell her, just not at this particular moment. We need to do some digging first."

"Tomorrow, then. It's not right to keep this from her."

"I'm not so sure. I mean, we only have a preliminary DNA match. We should wait until it's confirmed one hundred percent."

"The prelim match gave it a ninety-nine percent chance it's him. Come on Jack, we can't stall. We owe this mom the truth."

"We'll tell her once we have the truth, one hundred percent."

Mia looked at Jack. He wasn't going to budge so she let it go.

"So, where do we go from here?"

"Let's pull his phone records. The arrest report should have them. We can get a record of his calls on and just before March ninth, the day the package was delivered to UPS."

"That's a good starting point, but just because the package was sent on March ninth doesn't mean he was killed that day. In fact, given that the skull had virtually no skin or other biological material he was probably killed earlier than that."

Mia had a good point and Jack nodded his agreement.

"We'll check his phone records from the day he was arrested to the day the package was mailed. I'm guessing his phone blew up after he ratted out Shorty. Let's see if there are repeat phone calls from any given number."

"I'll get busy with that."

"Okay, and I'll pull up everyone associated with the 120th Street gang that had any past contact with Iceman."

"Let's talk in a couple hours and compare notes."

"That works."

CHAPTER 33

The border between the United States and Mexico is more than 1,900 miles long with over one hundred crossing points. Going from San Diego into Tijuana, where tens of thousands of people cross each day, can take hours with the significant security measures in place. At the border crossing from Lukeville, Arizona into Sonoyta, Mexico, the security measures, by comparison, are minimal.

It was just before nine when Pauley, with his cousin Jed in tow, entered the town of Lukeville, about forty miles north of the border crossing. They pulled into the parking lot of a Denny's restaurant to have breakfast before they entered Mexico.

Jed turned to Pauley, still concerned about the plan for crossing the border. "And you don't think they're going to check the trunk?"

"They never have before, so we'll be fine. Just relax and eat your breakfast."

Jed poked at the eggs on his plate. His appetite was gone, his stomach churning with the idea of what he was about to do. Life in a Mexican jail terrified him more than facing murder charges in Colorado. He had heard horror stories about what happened in those jails. He wanted no part of that, and considered telling Pauley that he'd rather take his chances on the run in the States. Have breakfast and then hightail it out of there.

Pauley could see the angst on his cousin's face.

"Stop worrying, bro. It'll be fine. And besides, we have a backup plan if the trunk thing doesn't pan out."

Jed thought about the money. A thousand bucks was no chump change but if it got him into Mexico then it would be worth every penny.

The two finished their breakfasts in silence.

Mia was able to access Iceman's cell phone records fairly quickly. What used to take days now took minutes, due largely to improved technology and court decisions allowing police to access phone records. She went back to the date of Iceman's arrest and looked at the incoming and outgoing calls from that date to when the skull was mailed. During that period there were more than 1,300 calls listed. Most were incoming and very brief, under a minute. Just enough time for someone to say his piece and be done with it. Mia had no doubt that Iceman faced a torrent of backlash when he ratted out Shorty. Gang members and drug dealers didn't look kindly on snitches. Turning on his friend had very likely cost Iceman his life. It was all part of the gang existence. *La vida loca* was the common mantra—*the crazy life.*

Mia looked at the printout of calls, listed by time received or time called. Several numbers jumped out because they appeared dozens of times. She jotted them down so she could run them in the system. Given that they were dealing with people involved in illegal activities, she knew the chance that these numbers were attached to burner phones was high. The disposable phones were purchased for cash, used for a brief period, and then discarded by the owner, making them untraceable. But she needed to do her due diligence—maybe she'd get lucky.

She was really hoping that one of the numbers might match up to Jed Nixon. She and Keller were confident that he had done the job on Iceman, but it would solidify their case if they found a series of calls between the two. But Mia knew it was also entirely possible that Nixon and Iceman didn't know each other, with the order to kill Iceman coming from the top. Jed Nixon could just be the guy who was ordered to carry out the hit.

She looked at the dozen or so numbers that popped up the most on the list and entered them into the database. Nothing came back. No hits, meaning they belonged to burner phones.

Not surprising, but disappointing just the same, she thought.

"I'm going to pull over and pop the trunk. Don't waste any time climbing in. We don't need anybody seeing what we're up to."

They were ten miles from the border on an open, deserted stretch of highway. Pauley peered out the windshield, looking for any aircraft above. He knew the border security people often patrolled the area from the sky. He didn't see any planes, nor were there any cars in sight. He quickly braked, pulled off to the shoulder, and popped the trunk.

"Go—get back there!"

Jed opened the door, ran to the back, quickly climbed into the trunk, and closed the door on himself. Pauley accelerated and within seconds was back at highway speed. The border was just ten minutes away. He thought about Jed in the trunk and wondered if there would be enough air for him. The thought hadn't occurred to him previously, but now that his cousin was back there he was concerned. He should be fine, he thought. There should be enough oxygen in there for him to get him over the border.

CHAPTER 34

Keller was very familiar with the 120th Street gang. Nearly half of the homicides he had investigated while at the RCSO had some affiliation with the drug activities of Rocklin County's most notorious gang. Idiots, he thought, living a lifestyle that would likely get them killed. He had no patience for it.

He was often asked about the gang by Rocklin County residents concerned that somehow the gang violence might spill over into their lives. He had a standard response for these people—"Don't be a gang member or drug dealer, don't argue with strangers, and don't get involved in love triangles. If you follow these simple rules there's a high likelihood you'll be vertical at the end of the day."

The response was trite, but it was true. Gang violence was largely committed between the gang members themselves and did not involve innocent bystanders. In Rocklin County the odds of dying in a traffic collision were much higher than dying in a gang-involved shooting. But no one stayed awake at night concerned about driving down the roadway while many worried about gang violence.

He pulled up FIRs in the computer and searched Iceman's information. FIRs were field interview reports, documentation made by a deputy when he or she found something suspicious but the activity didn't rise to the level of being illegal. Gang members hanging out together, people acting suspiciously, and other such situations could all be documented in a FIR. The deputy would complete the form and it would be entered in the system. Investigators could enter someone's name and quickly find any FIRs that mentioned the person. Who they were with and what they were doing would all be listed on the screen. It was an invaluable tool for law enforcement and could provide a starting point for detectives. FIRs had led to the clearance of countless crimes.

Under Iceman's file Keller saw that he had been FI'd more than a dozen times in the past year. Largely random stuff—drinking in public, loitering, and associating with known criminals.

Keller looked for names of associates who popped up more than once. Keller knew that Iceman's killer might not have been one of his regular buddies, but it was a good place to start.

Two names jumped out; one, not surprisingly was Shorty, and the other was a Charles Kaufman. Shorty was in county lockup, and therefore had an alibi, so Keller queried the computer for more information on Kaufman and a whole laundry list appeared on the screen.

Kaufman had been FI'd more than thirty times in the past year; it was clear that deputies had their eyes on him. His rap sheet was extensive; he had more than a dozen arrests under his belt going back three years. The arrests were mostly drug related, with a couple for battery. Keller shook his head when he thought about Kaufman being out on the street, but drug-related crimes were rarely prosecuted to the fullest extent of the law. There had been a material shift in the philosophy of what constituted a serious crime; the public largely looked the other way if the crimes were "victimless," like drugs and prostitution. Keller knew better than to think of these crimes as victimless. He had seen the problems that occurred in society when these crimes were left unchecked. Colorado was a national leader in the legalization of marijuana and Keller knew that in due time the people of his state would start to pay the price for that.

Keller looked further into Kaufman's history and learned that he was, in fact, currently in jail. He looked at the intake information;

Kaufman had been in lockup for more than six months. It couldn't have been him, Keller thought to himself. A dead end. The case for Jed Nixon being Iceman's killer was growing stronger by the minute.

CHAPTER 35

As Pauley approached the Mexican border he peered toward the gate. There were no other cars and he considered pulling over and waiting for some other travelers to cross. He thought that falling in behind other vehicles might increase the changes they would just wave him through, but it was mid-morning and there just wasn't much in the way of traffic. He took a deep breath and approached the gate. The guard motioned for him to roll down the window.

"*Buenos dias,*" said the guard.

Pauley didn't recognize him.

"*Buenos dias,*" he replied.

"Where you headed, sir?"

"San Martin. Doing some fishing charters down there. I come through here a lot."

The guard looked at Pauley but didn't reply. Pauley thought maybe he had said too much, trying to be a bit too friendly. The way people can be when they are trying to hide something. Nervous chatter.

"Can I see your ID?"

"Sure."

Pauley pulled his wallet from his back pocket and produced his Arizona driver's license.

"How long will you be in Mexico?" the guard asked, looking at the license.

"A few months. Then I'll be headed back home to Arizona. Gotta make a buck, you know?"

Damn it! Shut the hell up, he thought.

"Where's your gear?"

"It's all on the boat. I'm just a working stiff."

"I can relate," replied the guard, handing Pauley back his ID. "Okay, have a good day. Hope you catch your limit."

Pauley gave the guard a little wave and slowly accelerated away from the gate. They had pulled it off. Now he just needed to find somewhere to pull over and let Jed out of the trunk. He hoped he hadn't suffocated back there.

The resort town of Puerto Peñasco, Mexico, was a shining jewel on the Sea of Cortez. Located just an hour or so from the US border, it was a popular spot for the wealthy from Arizona to visit. Twenty years earlier it had been nothing more than a dot on a map, a tiny village known primarily for its fishing. But Peter Donnelly had a vision and through his efforts the town was now a major tourist destination, visited by nearly a half million people a year. Even celebrities had found the place to be a nice escape; the beaches of Cabo and Cancún were crowded so when you really wanted some peace and quiet, Puerto Peñasco was the place.

Donnelly had built the Marbella Resort, a five-star hotel, to cater to the wealthy. Fishing charters were a big part of the operation. People wanted a chance at catching the prized marlin. There were several charters a day, with visitors paying exorbitant amounts for the experience.

San Martin was a smaller, less conspicuous fishing village. The only reason anyone would go to San Martin was to fish. It was located twenty miles north of Puerto Peñasco and had a niche market catering to clients who couldn't afford the extravagance of the thousand-dollar-a-night rooms at the Marbella.

Jeremiah Kubilos was the captain of one of the half-dozen charters that launched from San Martin. His boat, the *Dolorosa,* had been part of the San Martin fleet for more than a dozen years, and was now doing more than two hundred fishing excursions a year. Pauley had worked his way up and was the lead crew member on the *Dolorosa.* As such he had some say as to the makeup of the rest of the crew, something he was counting on to get his cousin on his boat. If that didn't work, he was confident he could get him on one of the other charters, but his preference was to have Jed on the *Dolorosa.* He needed to keep an eye on him and make sure he didn't do or say something stupid.

Jed had survived the thirty minutes in the trunk, but when Pauley had finally found a safe place to pull over and let him out, he was shaking and drenched in sweat. It took him the rest of the drive to San Martin to calm down.

"Okay, so here's the plan. When we get there we'll check into the employee quarters and I'll introduce you to my boss. Like I said before, he's always looking for new crew members. I'll tell him you're my cousin and I want you on my boat. Shouldn't be a problem."

"And if he says no?"

"Then we go to plan B—get you on one of the other charters. It's not ideal, since you've never worked on a boat before, but you'll be fine."

"If I end up on another boat, won't they expect me to know what I'm doing?"

"If that happens, I'll talk to the captain. Don't worry about it."

CHAPTER 36

Reginald Gray had watched the evening news two nights earlier and had seen Jed Nixon highlighted as a person of interest in a Castle Springs-area homicide. The whole thing was a mess, and he knew he would need to take care of it. Good people were hard to find, he thought. You give someone a job to do and they always seem to muck it up. Very frustrating.

Three months earlier, he had ordered the hit on Iceman, really having no choice in the matter. Iceman had committed a mortal sin—snitching on a fellow gang member. Reginald had no choice but to send a clear message to everyone in his network—go against the gang and there would be a steep price to pay. Jed Nixon was someone he hardly knew, just a cog in his wheel, delivering meth to the places it needed to go. But with Nixon's photo being shown on the news he knew he'd have to take care of things. If Nixon was picked up by police, as he invariably would be, then there was a good likelihood he would spill his guts. Giving the cops a higher-up in the drug network would earn Nixon some serious points and likely keep him from getting the gas in Colorado. Life in prison was something a guy like Nixon could handle. So Reginald knew it was important that he find Nixon before the cops did. He grabbed his cell phone and made a call.

Jed and Pauley were quickly approaching San Martin.

"You need to come up with another name. Jed Nixon isn't going to work anymore."

"Even down here? I thought I'd be safe in Mexico."

"You can't take any chances. The Mexican authorities aren't overly cooperative with the US but you never know. So come up with something before I introduce you to the captain."

Jed considered what his cousin was saying.

"Butch Coolidge."

"Wow, that was quick."

"You asked me for a new name, there you have it."

"And where exactly did you come up with that?"

"*Pulp Fiction*. Bruce Willis's character. Love that movie."

Pauley thought about it, considering whether his cousin should take a name that people could be familiar with. Then he considered the types of people who took charters out of San Martin. Average, middle-class folks, mostly. The kind of people who might well remember a violent cult classic from the 1990s. He didn't want Jed taking any unnecessary chances.

"Change the last name to Coleman and that should work."

"What's wrong with Coolidge? It sounds cool."

"Yeah, well, if someone remembers the movie they might start looking sideways at you. You really want to risk it? For a 'cool' name?"

Jed considered what his cousin was saying.

"Alright. Butch Coleman."

"Good. Now we'll need to get you an ID with that name. It'll run you some cash."

"How much?" asked Jed, thinking about his shrinking supply of money.

"Five hundred for a decent fake. It'll be worth the investment."

"Jesus."

"You wanna go to prison, dumbass? Sometimes you gotta spend a little dough and this is one of those times. Besides, we saved a grand getting you across the border in the trunk. The way I look at it is you're ahead of the game."

"Yeah, all right."

"I know a guy in San Martin that can do the job. We'll stop there before we get to the boat."

CHAPTER 37

Aquarius Morales wasted no time filing a wrongful death law-suit against the Rocklin County Sheriff's Department. For good measure, she also named Mick McCallister, Jack Keller, and Mia Serrano-McCallister in the suit. Once she filed it, she wrote a press release and sent it to every media outlet in Colorado. If she was going to get a nice, quick settlement check she needed to rattle as many cages as possible. Getting the lawsuit in the news was key to her strategy. Cities and counties didn't like bad publicity so there was a good chance Rocklin County would reach out to her and offer some quick cash to keep her from getting too much attention. It happened more than people realized—stub your toe on a crack in the sidewalk and the county would pay a quick ten grand to make it go away. Defending frivolous lawsuits was expensive and it made financial sense for the county to just pay it off. Of course, there were those who thought the county shouldn't cave so easily. All the ambulance-chasing attorneys knew about the county's practice of making quick payouts and many made a decent living filing such lawsuits.

Aquarius Morales was one of those attorneys.

Angela Bell read the press release from the Law Offices of Aquarius Morales. She shook her head. Just another attorney out to make a quick buck. But it was news and she knew Channel 8 would likely cover it. This lawsuit was in response to a highly-publicized shooting and it couldn't be ignored. She had never heard of Aquarius Morales and a quick Google search didn't really offer much besides a rather amateurish website offering legal services. Angela couldn't find anything else about her, no list of successful cases and nothing much in the county court system. Who was this woman? And how did the mother of Jaquon Jackson, the man killed by Jack Keller at the Mia Serrano-McCallister press conference three months earlier, come to hire some no-name attorney?

She walked into the office of the Channel 8 assignment editor, Diane Hafen.

"Diane, did you see the release from the attorney hired by Jaquon Jackson's family?"

"Yeah, I was just reading it. I'm surprised it took her a whole three months to sue."

"Yeah, usually it's three days. But I've never heard of this attorney. A Google search turned up basically nothing. She's a nobody."

"She's in it for the publicity or a quick settlement score. Take her forty percent and then chase the next ambulance."

"So, do we cover it?" Angela already knew the answer, but felt compelled to ask.

Hafen looked at Angela, "Of course we cover it. It's news and it's sensational. It'll get the case back on the front page and we could use the boost in our ratings. Pull the tape of our studio getting firebombed and include that in your story. That should be good for a few ratings points."

Angela felt her stomach churn. She had put all that behind her and was hoping not to revisit it—too many bad memories.

And Mark Archer's handsome face popped into her mind.

Mark Archer sat at his desk reading the press release from Aquarius Morales. Denise Elliott at Channel 2 news had tipped him off, texting him about it and then emailing him the release.

He picked up the phone and dialed the sheriff's cell.

"Good morning, Mark."

"Hey, boss. I just got a forwarded email from Channel Two. It's a press release from a Denver attorney who's been retained by Jaquon Jackson's family. Looks like mom is filing a wrongful death claim against the county."

"I've been wondering about that. No real surprise we're getting sued—happens in every shooting. I wonder what took her so long?"

"No idea, but the attorney, Aquarius Morales—have you ever heard of her?"

"No, can't say that I have. I'm surprised that Leland Simpson isn't all over this. He's the go-to guy when it comes to suing police agencies."

"Yeah, I had the same thought. But maybe Simpson has his hands full with the lawsuit for Alex Washington's family. And representing another member of the same family might be a conflict of interest for him."

"Since when has that ever stopped an attorney like Simpson?"

"Yeah, point taken. But for whatever reason, we have a new attorney to deal with. Another possibility is that Simpson didn't want the case. Alex Washington's family has a decent shot at getting a substantial sum from the county. Jaquon came to that Denver hotel intent on killing Mia. If it wasn't for Keller . . . "

Mick's voice trailed off as he relived that horrible day.

"Yeah, this case has got to be a stinker for Morales. A jury isn't likely to show much sympathy for Jaquon, not that it would ever get that far."

"No chance of that. She's just looking for a quick cash settlement."

"I googled Morales and there's really nothing on her. She's a real low-level player in Denver. Makes no sense that Jackson's mom would hire her."

"Maybe she's a friend of the family?"

"Could be. I guess we'll see soon enough."

Angela mustered up her courage, her stomach churning with anxiety. She dialed the number she knew by heart.

Mark was in the middle of answering an email on his laptop in his office when his office phone rang. He glanced over and saw the number on caller ID. Whoa, he thought.

"Hey, Angela," he said in his best professional voice.

"Good morning, Mark. How're you doing?'

"Good, thanks."

He's not real chatty, she thought.

"I assume you've seen the press release from Jaquon Jackson's family's attorney?"

"Yeah, I saw it."

Short, trite answers. Not rude, but not very personal. Maybe this call was a mistake.

"Have you ever heard of the attorney? Aquarius Morales . . . sounds like a song from the 60s."

Maybe a little humor would loosen him up.

Mark chuckled. "Maybe a member of The Fifth Dimension."

A bit of the old Mark. Angela returned the laugh.

"Can you officially comment about the lawsuit?"

Mark paused, knowing Angela knew the answer to that question. He never commented about pending litigation. It was the policy of virtually every police agency in the country.

"Nope. Just the standard 'I can't comment at this time,' etc. You know the routine."

"Yeah, I know, but I have to ask."

"Of course."

Back to short, business-like responses. The call was ending.

"Hey, I've been meaning to ask you—how's Mia doing? How are she and the sheriff adapting to parental life?"

God, back to sounding like a reporter. *Parental life?* She had never used that term before. What the hell?

"They're both doing fine. Mia's dad is taking care of CJ now that Mia is back to work. I think she's really missing the baby, though."

"Yeah, that's got to be tough."

A long pause. The moment of truth had arrived. Angela continued.

"Hey, listen, I'm going to be in Castle Springs tomorrow night. Are you interested in maybe getting a drink?"

Mark was a bit taken aback by the invitation. He hadn't seen Angela in more than three months and was involved with Rachel now. But he felt a little pull and before he could overthink it, he replied.

"Sure. When and where?"

CHAPTER 38

Jed Nixon, now Butch Coleman, wasn't pleased about the five hundred dollars he had to lay out for the fake passport with his new name. His money stash was dwindling but at least he knew he'd be making a little money on the fishing charters. He just had to get used to what his life had become. He was on the run and a dwindling pile of cash was the least of his worries. Fortunately, Jeremiah Kubilos had agreed to having him on the charter. So Butch would be with his cousin, learning the ropes. Kubilos did pause a bit when shaking Butch's hands, commenting about how soft they were. But Pauley had assured him that his cousin was up to the task. The charter would start the next day so Butch had twenty-four hours to get accustomed to his new surroundings.

After the conversation with Mark Archer and with marching orders from Diane Hafen, Angela wrote the lawsuit story for the noontime newscast. She wanted to downplay the firebombing at Channel 8, but knew she really couldn't bury it. Hafen had specifically mentioned using file footage of the bombing, so she put it in the story. It was a slow news day and the story made its way to the top of the cast.

She pushed the negative thoughts about the bombing from her head and focused on the date she had made with Mark. She needed to finalize her strategy for getting Mark back in her life.

CHAPTER 39

The Forest Inn was a Castle Springs institution, a downtown bar that had been in existence for nearly one hundred years. It catered mostly to upscale visitors and business people visiting the Denver area. Angela arrived ten minutes after eight, confident that the always-on-time Mark Archer would already be there. She didn't want to appear overanxious. She spotted him sitting at a table in the corner, already nursing a scotch and soda.

Mark stood as Angela approached the table.

"Hey there," he said, giving her a little hug and kiss on the cheek. Angela took that as a good sign.

"Hope you weren't waiting long. Traffic was heavy coming out of Denver."

"No problem. What would you like to drink?"

"A chardonnay would be great."

Mark gave the waitress a little wave and she came over.

"Chardonnay for the lady."

Angela settled into her chair.

"Thanks for meeting me. You look well."

"No complaints, just busy as always."

No compliment back, Angela thought. Maybe this was a mistake. She carried on.

"Yeah, me too. It never slows down."

"I saw your coverage of the Jaquon Jackson lawsuit. Very balanced, I thought."

"Yeah, well, I try. I mean, the lawsuit is a joke. No jury would ever award her a dime."

"I noticed you included the Channel Eight firebombing in the story."

Angela wasn't sure where Mark was going with this. She hadn't been there even a minute and he was bringing up this sore subject.

"My assignment editor's idea. She insisted."

"It was a big part of the story. I can understand why she'd want it included."

"About that, Mark . . . "

Mark looked at Angela. Was she about to come clean about things? He gave her a little nod.

"Look, we said some difficult things to each other back then. And I didn't like the way we left things. I was out of line."

Mark looked at Angela and could see this wasn't easy for her. Was an apology coming?

"It was a tough situation," offered Mark.

"It was, but there's no excuse for what I did. I let my job get in the way and I did a really stupid thing."

Was Angela finally admitting that she had arranged for the bomb at Channel 8? He needed to hear her say exactly that, no tiptoeing around things. He asked her straight out.

"Did you arrange for the bomb through the window?"

Angela looked at Mark then lowered her eyes, staring at her glass of wine.

"Yes, I did," she said softly.

"I appreciate you being honest with me about it, Angela. I know that wasn't easy for you."

"What I did—I mean . . . it wasn't my best moment."

"No, it wasn't."

Angela looked back at Mark.

151

"Is the department still looking into it?"

"No, not really. It's been four months and has been largely forgotten, except by me."

Angela felt a wave of relief that the department wasn't focusing on it. But Mark was another story.

"Can you forgive me?"

Mark thought back to two years earlier when Angela had the opportunity to spill the beans after learning of the relationship between Jack Keller and his daughter Lisa Sullivan. Angela could have gone public with what she knew, but if she had, a killer would likely have gone free. She had buried the story and so Mark felt he owed her this one. It could also serve as an insurance policy of sorts—keeping Angela from ever telling what she knew about Keller and his daughter. If she ever did feel the desire to go public with it, then he'd have the firebombing story to tell. If word ever got out about what she had done, it would certainly end her television career in Denver.

"Yes, I forgive you."

"Thank you. I've been carrying this around for months. I can't tell you how good it feels to get that off my chest."

"Let's just move on. Put it in the past."

"Deal."

Cresencio Valenzuela had his marching orders. Reginald Gray had made it clear—find Jed Nixon and take him out before the police got to him. Gray couldn't afford to have Nixon turning state's evidence against him. The whole thing had been botched and now Gray had to clean up the mess. Sometimes Reggie wondered if there were any competent people left.

Mark and Angela finished their drinks and, with a quick hug and kiss on the cheek, departed the Forest Inn. Mark got the sense that if he had suggested the evening continue at his place, she would have agreed to it. But he was seeing Rachel now and he needed to be true to that relationship. While they hadn't made a commitment to anything exclusive, he really liked Rachel and didn't want to mess things up with her. Starting up again with Angela would just complicate things. It was better to sit tight, but he couldn't deny the chemistry between them. Once the apology was made, the two had fallen into easy conversation.

It was like they had never split up.

CHAPTER 40

"**H**e's not home."

Cresencio Valenzuela looked over at the man peering out of the window of a rickety trailer in a mobile home park in Aurora. Valenzuela was standing at the door of Jed Nixon's home and was pretty certain Nixon wasn't home. From a distance, he had surveilled the trailer for more than two hours and there had been no evidence of anyone around. No car, no signs of life in or around the trailer. The man in the neighboring trailer looked harmless enough; maybe a conversation with him could shed some light on Nixon's whereabouts. Valenzuela moved from the door of Nixon's trailer over toward the window from where the man was speaking. He wanted the neighbor to get a good look at his six-foot, seven-inch, three-hundred-and-fifty-pound frame. His size was something Valenzuela knew how to use. Intimidation without saying a word. Once he reached the neighbor's window he was actually looking down on him despite the trailer being on a raised foundation. It didn't go unnoticed.

"Any idea where he is?"

"He left a couple of days ago. Said he was going to visit his sister."

"Any idea when he might be back?"

"No, he didn't tell me any of that."

"Do you know if the sister is local?"

"Montana, at least that's what he said."

"Did he happen to tell you her name?"

"No, we're not that close. Just said he was headed up there for a visit."

Valenzuela looked at the man and didn't see any outward signs he wasn't being straight with him. He reached into his jeans pocket, pulled out a business card, and handed it to the neighbor through the open window.

"If you see him, could you give me a call? I'm a private investigator with a Denver law firm. Mr. Nixon is the beneficiary of a life insurance policy held by a relative and it's imperative we speak to him right away."

"Sounds like he's coming into some money. Good for him—maybe he can move out of this place."

"Well, we need to speak to him to make that happen. Thanks for your time."

Once Valenzuela was out of sight, the neighbor looked at the card.

Robert Gonzales the card read, with a phone number listed below. The neighbor tucked the card into his shirt pocket and closed the window.

Valenzuela drove back to Rocklin County, contemplating what the neighbor had told him. Nixon had left a couple days earlier, which lined up with the time his photo was shown on the news. Montana could be a good place to run to and hide out with a sister for awhile. But his gut told him Nixon wasn't in Montana, that it was just a bullshit story he told his nosy neighbor. So the question was—where the hell was Jed Nixon?

Angela felt a great sense of relief after her meeting with Mark. She had come clean. It felt good to get it off her chest and he seemed to accept her apology. Once that conversation was out of the way they had talked for more than an hour, getting caught up on each other's lives. She really had missed him. Now she just needed to figure out a way to get his mind and attention away from Rachel Gillespie.

CHAPTER 41

Jack and Mia were at a standstill in the Tracey Thompson murder investigation. The focus at this point was to find Jed Nixon. His photo was out there but no one else had called in a location on him. The story was a few days old and the public had largely forgotten Nixon. They needed to get the story out there again, to a wider geographic audience—nationwide if possible.

"Mark, what can we do to get Nixon's photo back on the news?"

Jack and Mia were in Archer's office, updating him on the investigation. Jack let Mia do the talking.

Mark replied, "Are you ready to share the fact that we're in possession of just the victim's skull? If so, I can get this story on the national news, no problem. But are you okay with sharing that much information?"

Neither Mia or Jack wanted to put out that information on the case, but they were starting to realize it might be necessary.

"Can we put out a limited amount of new info, just enough to get the media interested again?" asked Mia.

"Sure, but to get the national attention it needs to be a bit sensational. That and we need to catch a slow news day."

"How much do we need to say?"

"That we have only part of a dismembered body."

"What about the fact that it was discovered in our property room? We can't say that," replied Mia.

Mark said, "No, we leave that part out. But by leaving some holes in the story we'll actually peak their interest even more. So that all works."

"Do we need to say it was a skull?" asked Jack.

"Yeah, I think so. It's sensational and that's what'll get the media attention you want."

Jack shook his head. He didn't like putting out anything to the media, but he knew that the case needed a boost and Archer knew how to do it.

Mia continued, "So how do we say this, exactly? Aren't they going to want details?"

"Of course, they always want details, but I don't have to give them any. We control the message and that gives us the power."

"I think we need to do this. Jack, your thoughts?"

"I don't like it, but yeah, we need to get this thing moving again."

Mark responded, "Okay, give me a half hour or so and I'll draft a press release. I'll email it to you both to make sure you're good with it. Once you give me the go ahead I'll put it out. Keep your fingers crossed that no big story breaks in the meantime."

"Sounds good. We really need to talk to our victim's mother. We need to do the right thing and tell her that her son is dead. If we're going public with this we have to."

Jack nodded in agreement. It was time. "We'll have Laubacher do it."

Mark wasted no time putting together the press release. It was simple and direct.

For Immediate Release:

The RCSO is again asking for the public's help in finding a person of interest in a Rocklin County homicide case. The victim has now been identified as Tracey Thompson, 24 years old, of Castle Springs. Mr. Thompson's body was dismembered and only his skull has been recovered at this time. His identity was determined using DNA testing.

The RCSO will release no further details of the killing except to say that we are continuing to look for Jed Nixon, age 28, of Aurora, Colorado. His photo is available via electronic means at the bottom of this release. While Mr. Nixon is not considered a suspect at this time, it is imperative that investigators speak with him.

Lt. Mark Archer, RCSO (303) 555-1527

Once he had approval from Mia and Jack, he sent it electronically to every media organization in the nation. His phone started ringing three minutes later.

Mike Laubacher had delivered death notifications on a handful of occasions. It was never easy and not something a person ever grew accustomed to doing. It was just one of those difficult but necessary tasks that generally fell to detectives.

He knocked on Chookie's door and waited patiently. After half a minute, the door opened a crack and he could see a sliver of a woman's face in the shadows.

"Who is it?"

"I'm Investigator Mike Laubacher from the Rocklin County Sheriff's Department. I need to speak to the mother of Tracey Thompson."

Chookie slowly opened the door and peered at Laubacher. Looking at his face, she instantly knew her stepson was dead. A deep, guttural sound emerged from her, followed by a haunting wailing that could only come from a mother. Laubacher had seen it before.

He quickly stepped into the foyer of the modest home and placed his arm around Chookie's shoulders. There were no words; he just tried his best to comfort the devastated mother.

CHAPTER 42

"I want to handle this story personally."

Diane Hafen looked at Angela Bell, who was standing in her office doorway holding the cryptic release from Mark Archer.

"Go for it. You were a major part of it the first go 'round. See if you can get more than what's in the damn press release. The RCSO is being real secretive with this case."

Angela quickly left the station and headed for the RCSO headquarters in Castle Springs. The thirty-minute drive gave her time to put her thoughts together—not only about the murder investigation, but about Mark Archer.

Archer expected a big response to his press release and he wasn't disappointed. Within thirty minutes he had more than a dozen calls from as far away as Florida. Given the number of reporters asking for on-camera interviews, he knew he'd have a very busy afternoon. He gave some thought to just doing a press conference, essentially taking care of all the reporters at once. But reporters liked the feeling of getting an exclusive—a one-on-one interview with the person in the know was ideal. Except for an RCSO staff meeting scheduled that day, his calendar was clear. The interviews would allow him to skip the staff meeting—an added bonus to handling the reporters individually.

He felt his cell vibrating in his coat pocket. He reached in and saw it was Angela calling.

"Hey, how you doing, Angela?"

"Hi, Mark. I'm on my way to the RCSO right now. Can I get you on camera about your dismembered body case?"

"Sure, I'll be here all day. There's been a lot of interest in the case."

"Well, no surprise there. You put 'dismembered body' in the release and everyone takes notice. I'm sure that wasn't unintentional."

"Ummm, no. We need to get the word spread far and wide on this thing."

"Okay, I'm about ten minutes out. Can we do the interview right away so I can get it on the noontime newscast?"

"You're first on the list."

"Sweet—thanks!"

"See you in a few."

Mark spent nearly the entire day doing on-camera interviews, fourteen in total, and by five in the afternoon he was finished. He turned on the television in his office to see what the coverage was like and was happy to see that all four Denver stations had the story at the top of their newscasts. Most importantly, two of the national networks had picked it up. The strategy had worked.

CHAPTER 43

Rachel Gillespie was busy putting together a salad for dinner. She had the television on in the living room adjacent to the kitchen and had it tuned to Channel 8 news. She had a weird curiosity about Angela Bell, given her past relationship with Mark. The two were no longer seeing each other but nevertheless she felt the need to keep an eye on her. Channel 8 news had become a regular viewing habit.

"We have breaking news from the Rocklin County Sheriff's Department tonight. Here's Angela Bell with the story."

Rachel walked quickly into the living room and stood in front of the big-screen TV.

"The Rocklin County Sheriff's Department released some morbid details today about a recent homicide case. As you may remember, a few days ago the department asked for the public's help finding a person of interest in the case. That person, Jed Nixon, twenty-eight, of Aurora, is still being sought for questioning. The department hasn't said he's a suspect but they are very interested in finding him. I had a chance to talk with Mark Archer, the RCSO spokesman, about the case. Here's what he had to say."

Rachel stared at the screen as Angela and Mark appeared together. She felt a little twinge of jealousy as the interview began. Don't be stupid, she thought. It's a news interview, not a date.

"Lieutenant Archer, there's new information about the investigation into a recent murder the RCSO is investigating. What can you tell us about that?"

"Detectives have determined that the victim in this homicide case is Tracey Thompson, twenty-four years old, of Castle Springs. His identity was determined using DNA."

"And it's my understanding that only the victim's skull has been recovered?"

"Yes, that's true. And the DNA testing done on those remains allowed us to make the ID on Mr. Thompson."

"Can you tell us more about how the victim's skull was found?"

"At this time we won't be releasing anything further about that part of the investigation. We're looking for a person of interest in the case—a twenty-eight-year-old man from Aurora identified as Jed Nixon. We're actively seeking Mr. Nixon for questioning in this case."

"Is he your primary suspect at this time?"

"No, he's just a person of interest right now. Anyone who knows of his whereabouts is urged to call the RCSO."

"There you have it. If you know the whereabouts of Mr. Nixon, be sure and give the RCSO a call. This is Angela Bell reporting."

Rachel watched as the interview wound down. Before cutting away, the camera stayed an extra second or so on a wide shot of Mark and Angela. The twinge of jealousy Rachel had felt just a minute before quickly returned when she saw Angela put her hand on Mark's arm.

"Damn it," she muttered to herself. "Not good."

Rachel waited a day before sending Mark a text inviting him to lunch. She was concerned about what she had seen at the conclusion of the news interview. Angela touching Mark's arm, she feared, was a sign that she was still interested in him. She needed to reconnect with Mark—they hadn't seen each other in over a week. There had been a couple of friendly, innocuous texts, but nothing beyond that. She knew he was interested in her and there had been a connection between them. Not just physically, but emotionally as well. They clicked and the conversation between them was always easy and fun.

Free for lunch today? I'm buying :)

Mark was in a staff meeting when he received the text. He typed out a response.

Sure, let's go somewhere expensive :)

You got it, I'm thinking Big Macs :)

That'll work if I can get fries with it

How about Larsen's on 5th street in CS?

Noon?

Perfect

Mark thought about the situation. He was involved with Rachel but now Angela had reemerged on the scene. Nothing had really happened when they had drinks a few nights earlier, but the spark that had been there in the past was back. That much was clear.

CHAPTER 44

The latest news story about the search for Jed Nixon didn't yield any promising new leads. As Mark had predicted, the story had received excellent coverage; within twelve hours every news agency in Colorado had run with the story, as well as CNN and Fox. The dismembered body angle had done the trick. But so far, the only calls the RSCO had received were dead ends.

It seemed Jed Nixon was in the wind.

"So, what's next, Jack?"

Mia had come to Jack's cubicle, her head poking over the wall.

"We need to check Nixon's social media accounts. Maybe there's something there that could give us an idea as to his whereabouts."

Mia nodded. She knew that most people posted way too much personal information on the Internet, especially if they were young. Nixon was in his late twenties so it was likely that he had some kind of social media presence.

"Maybe Facebook?" asked Jack.

"We can check, but it tends to be for older people now. People Nixon's age are more likely on Instagram, Twitter, and Snapchat. Those are the ones we need to run down."

"I know about Twitter; haven't heard of the other two."

"Come on, I'll show you."

Mia came around the desk so she could see the screen of his computer. She took his seat and started searching.

"Let's run down Facebook first. I doubt anything will be there but we can at least eliminate it."

Jack squinted at the screen, then grabbed his reading glasses from his coat pocket and put them on.

Mia went to her Facebook account and typed *Jed Nixon* in the search line. "It's a bit of an unusual name, so maybe there won't be too many Jed Nixons."

She and Jack watched the screen as the search turned up a total of three hits. They peered at the pictures to see if any of them matched. Two of the matches were easy nos—the Nixons displayed were much older than their suspect. The third one had no photo. Mia clicked on it.

It was a dead end; the person lived in Australia.

"Okay, as I expected, our boy isn't on Facebook. Let's try Instagram."

"Do you have an account?" asked Jack.

"I do. I don't really use it much, but I can use it to search for Nixon."

Mia clicked out of Facebook and accessed her other accounts, but her searches yielded nothing useful.

CHAPTER 45

Peter and Lisa were settled into a nice routine at the Marbella. Married now for just over a month, Peter was busy running his various businesses and Lisa had resumed her volunteer work with the children of Puerto Peñasco. Prior to her abrupt departure from Mexico three years earlier she had become involved at the mission school, teaching English to some very poor kids. The work was the most rewarding thing she had ever done and she was very happy to be back at the school. Peter loved that she was busy with it. He knew the need was great and the fact that she chose to work with the kids instead of living a life of leisure lying on the beach all day spoke volumes about his bride.

"Hey, how was your day?" she asked.

Peter looked at his beautiful wife and felt a sense of calm come over him. It was always wonderful to come home and see his bride, no matter how busy or crazy his day had been.

"Long. Very long. Staff meetings, budget meetings, meeting after meeting. Sometimes I feel like that's all I do."

Lisa looked at her husband. These types of comments were becoming more and more commonplace. The fun of building the business was gone; now he was left with running the business and it wasn't what he excelled at. He was a creative person and liked imagining things, building things; he was a visionary. It was in his blood.

"Maybe you need to rethink things a little bit. You could turn over the day-to-day management to someone else. That would give you the freedom to do what you do best, Peter."

It was a conversation they had had before. The issue was who to turn things over to? He didn't have a strong second-in-command and had been a bit neglectful in building a succession plan.

"In theory that would be a good thing, but to who? That's the issue."

"I know, but have you really tried? I mean, there are people out there who are very capable. Is there anyone in the States that you know with resort management experience? You must have contact with these types of people."

"Not very much anymore. I did earlier in my career, when I was busy building this place. But it's been years since I've networked with people capable of running a place like the Marbella."

"Maybe so, but there are people out there. You just need to find somebody. One is all you need. Maybe do a slow transition—bring someone on board and take six months or a year to make it happen. You could work hand in hand with the person until you feel confident they're ready to take the reins. And if they have questions or struggles, you're still right there. Just a phone call or cup of coffee away."

"Yeah, I know you're right. Maybe the time has come. I'll put out some feelers and see what I can find."

Lisa walked to her husband and wrapped her arms around his neck. She kissed him gently on the cheek and he sighed a little bit.

"Come on, let's celebrate this decision. I'm proud of you, Peter Donnelly. And now I'm going to show just how proud I am."

Peter and Lisa moved quickly to the bedroom and undressed each other. Peter wrapped his arms around his wife and pulled her close, his lips lightly touching the inside of her earlobe.

"I love you. I want you," he whispered.

She responded by arching her neck; a breathless moan started from deep inside her.

"Oh, God—"

His lips and tongue moved down her neck.

After a short, vigorous session of lovemaking, Lisa and Peter lay in each others arms, catching their breath.

"Remind me why don't we do this every time I come home in the evening?"

Lisa teased Peter, nibbling on his ear. "Because I don't want to spoil you, big boy."

"You should spoil me more often. That was wonderful."

"Yeah, it seems like you needed that. I'm happy to help out."

CHAPTER 46

Mark walked into Larsen's a few minutes before noon. Offered his choice of tables, he picked one toward the back. Given he was in Castle Springs he knew he would likely be recognized and since he was meeting Rachel he'd rather not have the distractions. Generally, he didn't mind people approaching him in public places; it was part of the job. He had been the face and voice of the RCSO for nearly two decades and people in town certainly knew him. Between the weekly RCSO TV show and all the news interviews he had done he was a Castle Springs staple. Occasionally someone would get in his face, not liking something he had said publicly or perhaps angry with the actions of the RCSO. This was especially true following controversial police shootings; there were always those quick to criticize. On some occasions people would shout at him or make obscene gestures. He just gave those people a quick wave and went about his business. It came with the territory.

Rachel walked into the restaurant but didn't see Mark. His car was in the parking lot, so she asked the hostess.

"He's in the back. Come with me."

Rachel followed the young woman as she wound through the maze of tables. Near the back she saw Mark sitting at a table for two. He stood as he saw them approach and gave Rachel a kiss on the cheek.

"Hey, Rachel."

"Are you being antisocial today?" she responded with a smile.

"No, it's just nice to be in a quiet place sometimes. It gets crowded here at lunch and generally they seat me back here if I ask."

"I understand."

"So, how's your day going?'

"Good, just busy running errands and given that I'd be in town today I thought I'd reach out about lunch."

"Glad you did."

So far, so good, thought Rachel, though she was still concerned about what she had seen during the news interview two nights earlier.

"And how's your week going?'

"Fairly hectic. We're actively looking for someone connected to a homicide committed a few months back, but so far no luck. The guy has proven elusive."

"Yes, I saw some news coverage on that case. Channel Eight, I think."

Rachel was fishing, but Mark didn't bite.

"We got some great coverage on it. We publicized the fact that the victim had been dismembered and it received the coverage I'd hoped for. Sensational and salacious—just what the media feeds on."

"That speaks volumes about society today, I guess. Sad, really."

"Yes, but it's human nature. When you pass a car accident on the highway, do you look?"

"Yeah, I guess I do."

"There you go."

"I saw you talking about it on the news. You did great, as always."

"Thanks, Rachel. I appreciate that."

Still, no bite.

The waitress came over and handed them menus.

"No hurry, just wave me over when you're ready to order."

"We will, thanks."

"Ummm, miss—can I get a glass of chardonnay?" Rachel asked.

"Sure, no problem," replied the waitress.

"I wish I could join you, but I'm on duty," Mark said, looking at Rachel. "Of course, I hope you don't mind I ordered something."

"Not at all," Mark responded, thinking about the last time Rachel had ordered a glass of wine with lunch. They had ended up at a hotel and he'd left with a swollen bitten lip.

CHAPTER 47

K eller walked to Mia's cubicle.

"Looks like Jed Nixon has a cousin in Arizona."

"Oh yeah? How did you find that out?"

"A LexisNexis search. Pauley Nixon is the guy's name. Lives in Tucson."

"Tucson, huh? That's far enough away from Colorado to give Jed a little breathing room."

"It's also an hour or two from the Mexico border. Wouldn't surprise me at all if Jed was hightailing it out of the US."

"Wouldn't be the first time."

"I've got a buddy with the Tucson PD. He worked with me years ago in St. Louis. I can give him a call and run things down to him."

"Sounds good. Keep me posted."

Keller placed the call to the Tucson Police Department and was able to speak to his friend Daniel Cordell. Cordell, now a commander with the TPD, ran Pauley Nixon on his computer. A laundry list of contacts and arrests popped up.

"Your boy is here. Looks like he's got a half dozen arrests and a bunch of other miscellaneous contacts with us. Drugs mostly, and a couple of battery charges that didn't stick."

"What's the address?"

"Twenty-eighty Redbeam Avenue. It's in South Tucson."

"Any chance you could spare someone for a little bit? Maybe sit on the house and watch for our boy Jed?"

"Yeah, that's doable. The guy is wanted for a one-eighty-seven— we're happy to help."

"I'll send you what I've got on him. How soon can you set up on the house?'

"I can have someone out there this afternoon. Just get me the info."

"I'll email it to you as soon as I hang up, Dan. I really appreciate the assist."

"No problem, Jack. Great hearing from you."

CHAPTER 48

Mick knew it was never good news when Louis Centeno, the Rocklin County Chief Executive Officer, called for a meeting. He was a bean-counter type and Mick found their conversations stifling and largely useless. Theirs was an unusual relationship given Centeno wasn't technically Mick's boss. As the sheriff, Mick answered only to the voters—he had no real boss. But as the CEO for Rocklin County, Centeno had tremendous power—he, along with the County Board of Commissioners, controlled the sheriff's budget. And given the financial needs of the sheriff's department, with an annual budget of more than a hundred million dollars, Mick needed to at least keep the peace with Centeno.

"Have a seat, sheriff."

Mick sat across from Centeno in a chair that was strategically placed directly in front of Centeno's desk. It was a power move by Centeno, intended to remind the people he called to his office that they were inferior to the CEO.

"What's up, Louis?"

Centeno didn't like being referred to by his first name. He felt it too casual and not respectful of his position, which was exactly why Mick always referred to him that way.

"We're getting sued. Well, let me rephrase that—the sheriff's department is getting sued."

Mick wasn't really surprised by this. Law enforcement agencies got sued every day.

"By whom?"

"Jaquon Jackson's mother. He's the young man who was shot and killed by your investigator, Jack Keller."

Mick looked at the little bean counter sitting at his oversized desk. He paused before responding.

"Oh, yeah, the mother of the man who tried to murder my wife and who nearly killed Jack Keller. That Jaquon Jackson?"

"Yes, that Jaquon Jackson," replied Centeno, irritated by Mick's question.

"And she's suing because we killed her son—"

"Yep, asking twenty-five million."

"That's it? Why not twenty-five billion?" Mick asked sarcastically.

"You can kid all you want, sheriff, but we now have to spend valuable time and resources defending this suit."

"The suit is total bullshit—you know it, I know it, everyone knows it. It's just a money grab, plain and simple. Tell them to shove it."

"I'm glad you can be cavalier about this, sheriff, but if we do that I'll have to bring in an outside attorney and we're talking tens of thousands of dollars at least. If it drags out we could be looking at well into six figures to defend this."

Mick could see where this was heading.

"It's bullshit, Louis. Don't give in and offer to settle. We need to stand up and show people we have some balls."

"Look, in theory I agree with you. But if we offer maybe fifty grand this thing goes away and it never gets any media attention."

"Maybe we want to get some media attention on this. Show our residents that we aren't pushovers. The vast majority of Rocklin County taxpayers will think we are doing the right thing by fighting it. For God's sake, Louis, the piece of shit nearly killed Jack Keller. He's still dealing with his injuries. Let's see how a jury feels about awarding even a dollar to this woman after seeing Keller limp into the courtroom."

"We can't take that chance, sheriff. You know how juries can be—it's a crapshoot. And if we somehow get some people on there who are sympathetic at all to this grieving mother, then we could be paying out a much larger amount than the fifty grand. Ultimately, it's just a financial decision. You know that."

"Don't do this, Louis."

"I need to speak with the commissioners but my recommendation will be to offer fifty thousand to settle."

Mick knew it was useless to try to argue with Louis once he had made up his mind. He shook his head, stood up, and walked out of the office.

CHAPTER 49

The Tucson PD sat on Pauley Nixon's house for more than ten hours. A white paneled van with bold advertisements on the sides boasting $79 to unclog any sink or toilet was parked on Redbeam Avenue, two doors down from the modest home. Inside sat two very bored detectives. They were in radio contact with Dan Cordell, reporting in every so often that there had been no activity at the house. They were about to clear the scene when they saw someone approach the house.

"Is that our boy?"

"No, the photo doesn't match. But let's see what this guy is doing."

Both detectives watched intently as the man, short and middle-aged, walked to the front door. The man took out a set of keys and fiddled for the right one. He opened the door, walked in, and closed the door behind him.

"What do you want to do?"

"Let's see how long he's in there. Maybe he lives with our subject."

"That could take all night. We've been here ten hours. I say we pay the guy a visit and have a chat."

"So, we go in and fix his toilet?"

"Yeah, let's get changed."

The two men grabbed coveralls from the back of the van.

"You wanna be Floyd or Ernie?"

"I wanna be Ernie."

The two detectives slipped the coveralls over their khakis and golf shirts. They grabbed a tool box and headed for the house.

"I'll take the lead," said Floyd.

The man answered the door quickly and looked surprised by the sight of two plumbers standing before him.

"Can I help you?"

"Yeah, you called about a stopped-up toilet."

The man stared at the two men in coveralls.

"No, I didn't call. I think you have the wrong place."

"Is this twenty-eighty Redbeam?"

"Yeah, but I didn't call for a plumber. This isn't even my house."

"It's not your house?"

"No, I'm just a neighbor watching the place for my friend."

"Any chance your friend called for a plumber?"

"I doubt it, he's in Mexico."

"Huh, well I guess we got the address wrong."

"Yeah, no worries."

As the two detectives turned to go, one stopped, looked back over his shoulder, and said, "I've got a place down in Mexico. It's great this time of year. Where'd your buddy go?"

"He's working down there, so it's not really a vacation for him."

The detective chuckled. "Well, that's a switch—someone from the US going down to Mexico for work."

The neighbor smiled. "He goes down there to work on a fishing boat. Pays the bills, I guess."

"I do a lot of fishing when I'm down at my place. Caught a marlin last year."

"Yeah, he says the fishing is great."

"So where did you say he goes?"

"San Martin. Maybe an hour south of the border, I think."

"Oh yeah, I've heard a lot of good things about the fishing down there. Hey, sorry to bother you."

"Yeah, no problem."

"Good news, bad news for you, Jack."

"Whatcha got?"

Cordell ran down the information about Jed Nixon being in Mexico working a fishing charter. Keller knew about the small fishing village of San Martin—it was just thirty minutes from Puerto Peñasco, home of Lisa and Peter.

Jack headed up to the sheriff's office.

"I've got a pretty good lead on our boy Jed Nixon."

"Yeah? Whatcha got, Jack?"

"Tucson PD tells me he's in Mexico working on a fishing charter. He's there with his cousin."

"Where in Mexico?"

"That's the interesting part. He's in San Martin—about thirty minutes from where my daughter lives."

"How reliable is this information?"

"The undercover team they put on his cousin's place talked with a neighbor. The guy had some pretty specific information as to where the cousin was, but technically we don't know for sure that Nixon is with him."

"So there's a chance this is a wild goose chase?"

"Yeah, it's possible, I guess. But everything up to this point has Nixon being with his cousin. And now his cousin is off to Mexico. That scenario plays perfectly for Nixon—he can get out of the country and get lost down there."

"So, what do you want to do, Jack?" Mick already knew what Jack would be suggesting, but thought he'd at least ask.

"I want to go down there and check it out. It won't cost the county a dime. I can stay with my daughter and Peter can send his plane to get me. It's a no-brainer, boss."

"And what about your partner, Jack?"

Jack looked at the sheriff. He hadn't considered Mia in his plans. He shifted uneasily in his chair, realizing that he hadn't even briefed her on this latest development.

"All this just happened, sheriff. Like fifteen minutes ago. Mia is welcome to come along. They have plenty of room at the Marbella."

"So, you haven't told her any of this?"

"No, like I said—it all just happened."

Mick give Keller a look. He wanted him to get the message about keeping his partner in the loop. It was one of Keller's biggest downfalls. He was a lone ranger and it didn't sit well with Mick.

"How many times have we talked about this, Jack? You run off on new investigative leads and leave your partner in the dust. And I'm not just saying this because it's Mia. You have a long history of this crap."

"My bad, sheriff. I'll talk to Mia and let her know what's happening."

"Yeah, you do that."

"No problem. So I have your approval to go down and find Nixon?"

"Yes, with two caveats. One, you bring Mia with you. I don't want you down there going rogue on me."

"Okay, what's the second thing?"

"I'm giving you forty eight hours. That's it. If you can't find him within that timeframe then it's not going to happen. I don't want this dragging out. It's not a vacation, Jack."

It was a cheap shot, but Mick wanted to send a message. He knew Keller wouldn't take advantage of the time in Mexico. He was a bulldog on every 187 case. If Nixon was down there Jack would probably have him in custody in hours.

"Of course, sheriff. I won't need forty eight-hours. Hell, I may be back here the same day."

"Let's use *we*, not *I*, Jack. Team player."

"Of course, I didn't mean—"

"If you and Mia do snag him we'll need to figure out how to transport him back to the US."

"I say we just put him on Peter's jet and bring him home. It won't be an issue."

Mick considered what Jack was saying. Typically subjects arrest-eded far outside the jurisdiction of the RCSO were transported back via public transportation—namely commercial airliner. Getting Nixon transported on a private jet, while certainly not routine, shouldn't present any problems. In fact, it would be much simpler.

"Okay, that'll work. Now you just need to make that happen. When do you want to leave?"

"ASAP. I'll go and brief Mia and we can leave as soon as she can get organized. I'll call Peter and see how quickly he can get the jet up here."

Mick thought about the logistics of Mia being gone for a couple days. With CJ in their lives now things were a bit more complicated. But Chuck would step up as usual and it was all doable.

"Okay, make it happen."

"Will do, boss."

CHAPTER 50

Jack and Mia were on Peter's private jet before the end of their shift. The flight would take just under three hours and two rooms at the Marbella were ready for them. Lisa was excited by this surprise visit by her father, although she knew it was work for him, not a vacation. She hoped they would have at least a little time together. It would be nice to see Mia as well, as the two had buried the hatchet at the wedding a few weeks earlier.

Peter sent a Marbella's limo to the airport to pick them up. It was close to nine by the time they were in the lobby of the hotel. Both Lisa and Peter were there to greet them.

"Hey, honey, it's so great to see you."

Jack held his daughter in a long embrace, then turned to Peter and shook his hand.

"Thanks for doing this, Peter. We really appreciate it."

"No problem, Jack. Happy to help. Sounds like this guy is a bad dude. Hope you snag him."

"If he's down here, we'll find him."

Mia smiled at Lisa and the two shared a quick hug. Mia nodded at Peter.

"Thanks so much, Peter. Like Jack said, we really appreciate this."

"Just let me know if there's anything I can do to help."

"Actually, Peter, there is something that I'm hoping you can do for us."

"What's that, Jack?"

"We believe our subject is working on a fishing charter in San Martin. Do you have any contacts there that might be willing to talk to us off the record?"

"I do know the owner there. He's a good friend."

"Could you give him a call in the morning?"

"Sure, no problem."

"We need to find out if they've hired anybody in the last couple of days. Our boy's name is Jed Nixon, but he's probably not using that name."

"Do you have a description of the guy?"

"I can do better than that—we've got a photo."

"I'll send it to my buddy."

Jack produced the headshot of Nixon and Peter snapped a photo with his cell.

"How well do you know the owner in San Martin?"

"Pretty well."

"Can he be trusted or is he the type that might tip off our subject?"

"He won't tip him off. He's a straight shooter. Plays by the rules; something you don't often find down here."

"Okay, you talk to him first, then I'd like to talk to him. You can explain that I'm your father-in-law and that I can be trusted."

"Sure, Jack. No problem."

Mia excused herself from the group and went to her room, giving Jack and his family time to visit. They had agreed to meet up at seven thirty the next morning. Once she was settled in her room she called home. She missed CJ already.

"Hey, sweetie, how's it going?" asked Mick.

"Good. We've arrived and I'm in checked into my room. Jack and his family are downstairs visiting."

"How was the flight?"

"It was great. I could get used to flying by private jet."

"Yeah, well, remember who you're married to—not too many chances your hubby can afford you that opportunity."

"No worries, Mick. I'd rather have you and fly commercial any day."

"Ah, thanks, honey."

"So Peter know the guy who runs charters out of San Martin. He's going to reach out to him in the morning and see if they have any new hires."

"That's perfect. If that pans out you could scoop up Nixon and be home by tomorrow night."

"Ideally, that's the way it'll go down. But who knows; I just hope this guy is actually down here."

"From what Jack said this morning, the lead sounds really promising."

"So, how are Dad and CJ?"

"Both are fine. Chuck played with him for awhile after dinner and then I put him down. He's been asleep for a couple hours. Chuck is watching TV, or should I say he's asleep in front of the TV."

"God, I miss CJ already."

"I know, sweetie. But hopefully you'll be home in a day or two."

"That's the plan. Well, I'll let you go. Sleep well."

"You, too. I love you."

"Love you, too."

CHAPTER 51

The next morning, Jack and Mia met up in the Marbella coffee bar at seven thirty. Peter had agreed to meet with them for coffee at seven forty-five and make the call to Reuben Mendoza. They assumed the fishing charter owner would likely be in the office early. Charters were an early business, typically departing before sunrise.

Jack and Mia had a few minutes to talk strategy before Peter joined them.

"We're going to need a car, so last night I asked Peter if he could spare something. I don't think we should arrive in San Martin in a limo."

"Good point."

"He's got something nondescript for us."

"Perfect."

"So, how do you see this going down?"

"Well, ideally Peter talks to Mendoza and gets a positive ID on Nixon. Then we find out where he is and if he's in San Martin then we scoop him up. That's the ideal situation, but who knows."

"He could also be out on a fishing boat. I mean, that's what he's supposedly doing down here so I guess we'd have to wait till the boat comes in."

"True, that would be the easiest way. We could go out and get him but I don't see the need. It's not like he knows we're here for him. He'll come in and we'll nab him as soon as he steps foot on the dock."

"What if he's on a day off?"

Jack responded, "Then that gets a bit more problematic. We'd have to try to find him and scoop him up when the opportunity presents itself. Let's hope he's out on a charter."

"If he just arrived here he probably isn't on a day off. I'm guessing he'd be working for awhile before he gets a day off. But there is the possibility that he hasn't started yet. And if that's the case then he could be anywhere."

"True. We should know once Peter makes the call."

"Did I hear my name?"

Jack and Mia looked up and saw Peter approaching their table.

"Hey, good morning, Peter. Mia and I were just talking strategy."

Peter pulled out a chair and took a seat.

"Always a good idea. So when do you want me to make the call to Reuben?"

"ASAP. Let's get this show on the road."

Peter pulled out his cell and shuffled through his contact list. He found Reuben Mendoza and dialed the number. Reuben picked up on the first ring.

"Peter, my friend—how are you?"

"Hey, Reuben, doing well. How are things in San Martin?"

"Everything is good. What can I do for you?"

"I need a favor and I'm hoping you can help me."

"I'll do what I can. What's up?"

"What I'm going to ask you needs to be in strict confidence. You okay with that?"

"Sure, Peter. What's going on?"

"Have you hired anybody new the past couple of days to work your charters?"

"I did. Brought on a cousin of one of my regular guys. Why do you ask?"

"What's the guy's name?"

"Butch something."

"What's he look like?"

"I don't know. Maybe thirty years old. Tall and thin."

"If I send you a photo can you tell me if it's him?"

"Sure, I can do that. Should I be concerned about this guy, Peter?"

"No, we're just trying to track someone down and we think this may be the guy."

"Sounds ominous."

Peter ignored the comment and sent the photo to Reuben's phone. A few seconds later Reuben replied, "Yeah, that's him."

Jack whispered to Peter, "Ask Reuben if our boy is working today."

Peter put his phone on speaker and placed it on the table.

"Is the guy working today?"

"Yes, he went out late last night. He's on the *Dolorosa*."

"When is the boat due back?"

"Should be back here around three."

Jack and Mia nodded at Peter and Jack flashed him a thumbs up.

Jack suggested, "Ask him if he has a photo of Pauley Nixon."

"Reuben, I believe you have another crew member named Pauley Nixon. Does that ring a bell?"

"Yeah, Pauley's been working with us for awhile. Geez, Peter, do I need to be concerned about him, too? He's been a good employee."

"Can you send me his photo?"

"Sure, hold on. I'm sure it's in his personnel file."

A minute later Peter's phone pinged and Pauley's photo appeared on the screen.

"Perfect," whispered Jack. "Ask him if Pauley's on the same boat this morning."

"One last question—is Pauley Nixon on the same charter this morning?"

"Let me check the schedule . . . Yes, they're both on the *Dolorosa* today."

"Okay, thanks, Reuben. I appreciate the help. I owe you one."

"Are you going to fill me in on any of this, Peter?"

"I will, my friend. Next time I see you I'll tell you the whole story. Gotta go. Thanks again."

Peter ended the call.

Mia looked at Jack. "Wow, that was almost too easy—"

"Sometimes the fish just jump into the boat."

Mia continued, "So we just scoop him up when he steps off the boat and hustle his ass back to Colorado."

"Peter, can we use the jet again this afternoon?"

"Of course, Jack. It's at your service."

"Excellent, now can you forward those photos to my cell?"

CHAPTER 52

"I've got news, LaNiece!"

It took a few seconds for LaNiece to realize the voice on the phone belonged to her attorney, Aquarius Morales. She hadn't heard from her since their meeting a few weeks earlier.

"Oh, hey. You've got news?"

"I do indeed. I heard back from the bigwigs in Rocklin County and evidently my letter threatening a lawsuit did the trick. They've made an offer."

"Oh, my God. That's great. What's the offer?"

"Fifty grand. How do you like that?"

"Just like that? They're willing to pay me that much money just because you threatened them with a lawsuit?"

"Yep, I told you I was good. I do this all the time, LaNiece."

"I don't know what to say. I didn't think it would be this easy."

"Sometimes government agencies drag their feet and take forever. But I got the sense they just want this to go away. There is one condition."

LaNiece grew concerned. There was always a catch, she thought.

"And what's that?" she asked cautiously.

"It's a gag order, basically. If we take the money we can never discuss the case publicly. We can't go to the media and tell them about it. The county just wants it to go away and so we have to agree to that.

Otherwise, no deal."

"So, I can't tell everyone what they did to my Jaquon?"

"No. But LaNiece, everyone already knows what they did to Jaquon. It was in all the papers."

LaNiece was quiet. One of the reasons she brought the lawsuit was to publicize the case. Her poor Jaquon had been murdered and she wanted the world to know about it. If the county was willing to write her a check then it was like admitting they were wrong.

Morales picked up on the vibe from LaNiece. She stood to make a quick twenty grand and she wasn't going to let this grieving mom stand in her way.

"Look, this is a good settlement. I strongly encourage you to accept it. These offers are usually good only for a short period of time. If they sense we are waffling at all then they could withdraw the offer. We don't want that to happen, LaNiece. You could be left with nothing."

"So, how much will I get after you take your cut?"

"Our agreement was forty percent. So you'll get thirty thousand and I'll get twenty."

"You'll get twenty thousand dollars for writing a letter?"

Morales had been down this road many times. Her work got the settlement offer but then her client questioned whether or not she had really earned it. The client never questioned things when a case dragged on for years.

"It's a lot more than that, LaNiece. I have decades of experience doing this. I know how to write the letter with just the right words. The county knows me, and knows the reputation I have in the legal community. They don't want to deal with me, so they make the offer. That's really what you're paying me for. Not just a letter but for everything that comes with it. They know not to mess with me. That's what you're paying for, LaNiece."

"I don't know, it seems like twenty thousand dollars is a lot of money. Can we make it ten?"

"No, LaNiece, we cannot make it ten. We have an agreement, in writing, signed by both of us. It's a legal document and it doesn't allow for after-settlement negotiation. The deal we made was for forty percent and that's what needs to happen."

"What if I say no to the deal? What happens then?'"

"Take the deal, LaNiece. Let me ask you a question. How much money do you have in your purse right now? How much money is in your bank account right now?"

"Not very much."

"Well, through my efforts you're about to have thirty thousand dollars handed to you, tax free. Think about what you could do with that kind of money. It could change your life! Jaquon is smiling down from heaven right now, so pleased that his mother is getting this money. Let's make this happen."

LaNiece thought carefully. Maybe it was time to move on. The money was unexpected. She hadn't really thought she'd ever get anything from the county. The twenty thousand Morales was getting really bothered her, but she would be getting thirty thousand and that was what she needed to focus on.

"Okay, I'll take the deal."

"Excellent, LaNiece. You're making the right decision."

"So, when will I get my money?"

CHAPTER 53

Butch Coleman was having a hard time learning the ropes of his new career. The fact that he was queasy didn't help. He had never been seasick before but his experience on boats was fairly minimal. He constantly fought back the urge to vomit; he didn't need his crew mates seeing him leaning over the rail losing his breakfast. This was his third day on the *Dolorosa* and things weren't getting any easier. He was starting to wonder if coming to Mexico was a mistake; maybe he should just take his chances being on the run in the US. At least he'd be on dry land.

He had been given the task of rigging up the fishing poles for the guests, something he managed to learn fairly quickly. It was the simplest of tasks, but he knew that over time he'd be given other, more challenging duties. His fellow crew members called him *greenhorn*, a term commonly assigned to new crew members.

"You don't look so good, Butch."

He looked at his cousin Pauley.

"I've felt better."

"Did you take the Dramamine I gave you?"

"Yeah, but I don't think it's working. I feel like crap."

"I can get you something stronger. Just hang in there. You'll get used to it."

Cresencio Valenzuela was closing in on Jed Nixon. Through his network of friends in the underworld he had learned that Jed had fled Colorado and was in the Tucson area with his cousin Pauley. But by the time he had scoped out the place there was no sign of Jed or his cousin.

"Mark, you outdid yourself this time. The sea bass was out of this world."

"You like it? I found the recipe online."

"Look at you—becoming quite the chef."

Mark and Angela were clearing the dishes, spending their third evening in a row together.

"Can I interest you in a brandy?"

"Sounds great."

Mark poured brandy into a couple of snifters.

"Let's move to the living room. I'll start a fire."

Angela took a seat on the sofa and watched as Mark lit a fire in the fireplace. The room took on an orange glow. He turned out all the other lights.

"This is perfect, Mark."

He smiled at her and took a seat close to her on the sofa. The two had settled back into a nice routine following their heart-to-heart a couple of weeks earlier. The sins of the past had been forgiven and the two were back to where they were before all the ugliness surrounding the bombing of the Channel 8 studios months earlier.

"It's nice to sit and relax. Been a crazy week for me," added Mark.

"It's always a crazy week for you. Have you ever had a boring day?"

"Not really. Always something going on."

"Speaking of work, what's new in the skull case?"

"On the record or off?"

"Off the record, for now anyway. What can you tell me about it?"

"Off the record I can tell you that we think we've located our subject and are hopeful to arrest him very soon."

Mark had been briefed by the sheriff a few hours earlier. He knew Jack and Mia were on their way to Mexico to track down Jed Nixon.

"So, your subject has gone from a person of interest to the prime suspect?"

"Yes, but that's not for publication."

Angela pushed on. "That sounds promising. Any chance I could have a video crew present when the arrest goes down?"

"No, that would be problematic."

Angela looked at Mark, trying to get a read on him.

"Why would that be a problem?"

"Because we've found him out of state."

"It could still be worth Channel Eight sending a news crew to cover it. Especially if we had an exclusive on it."

Mark looked at Angela. She never stopped working. She was so driven. It was one of the things he liked most about her, but sometimes it was over the top. Now was one of those times.

"Geez, Angela. Tap the brakes."

"I'm just saying, if you want some great coverage of the arrest, then I'm your gal."

"I'll keep that in mind."

"Nice little perp walk—the RCSO would look mighty good."

"Duly noted. How's your brandy?" Mark asked, changing the subject.

"It's good, and the fire makes it perfect."

Angela moved closer to Mark and tucked her arm in his.

"Yeah, this is a nice end to the day."

Angela squeezed his arm and replied, "Hmmm, I wonder what could make it even better?"

"Well, I can think of a couple of things . . . "
Mark turned and kissed Angela lightly on the lips.
"There you go . . . "

CHAPTER 54

Jack and Mia decided they would travel to San Martin well in advance of the expected three o'clock arrival of the *Dolorosa*. They didn't want to find the boat had come in early and Nixon had already disembarked. Peter had explained that once the clients had caught their limits the boats would return to shore. It didn't happen all that often, but Jack and Mia didn't want to take any chances.

The town of San Martin was small compared to Puerto Peñasco, just a sprinkling of homes on the hillside overlooking the Sea of Cortez and one small hotel a block up from the beach. There was certainly no Marbella in San Martin; the hotel and the fishing charters in the tiny town catered to lower- and middle-class tourists. If you wanted to spend a grand on an upscale fishing experience then the Marbella was your place, but if you wanted to spend a couple hundred bucks you went to San Martin.

With the town being so small, Jack and Mia were a bit concerned about being noticed by the locals. No one knew why they were there, of course, but both felt uneasy. They had dressed down, trying to look more like tourists than law enforcement personnel on official police business. After driving through the town, which took all of three minutes, they located the only pier in San Martin. Confident that the *Dolorosa* would be docking there, they headed out of town and drove up the hillside to the residential area of San Martin.

Jack looked at Mia. "The view up here will give us plenty of time to see the *Dolorosa* returning to port. The problem is we stand out like a sore thumb around here. The residents might be wondering why we're up here staring down at the sea."

"I think we look like tourists enjoying the view."

"Yeah, but for how long?"

"Good point. Maybe we can just keep moving. Maybe find another road we can access."

Jack looked at his watch. It was a little past noon.

"Are you hungry? We can go down and grab some lunch. There was a little taco shop on the beach. We can keep an eye on the pier from there."

"Sure, that works."

Jack drove back to town and found a little hole-in-the-wall place called Tito's Tacos. It was less than a hundred yards from the pier and afforded a perfect view. Jack and Mia ordered taco plates from the woman at the counter and sat down at a table by the window. The place was nearly deserted.

Jack turned to Mia. "So, when Nixon comes off the boat we'll take him into custody. But we need to be ready to deal with his cousin as well. He may not take kindly to Jed being placed under arrest."

Mia replied, "Ideally, they'll come off the boat together—that would make things easier. We don't want to have Nixon come off and his cousin lagging behind. We need to keep a visual on him if at all possible. The guy has a history."

"If they come off together, then I'll handle Nixon and you cover his cousin."

"Do you want to do this in a nice, quiet way or just draw down and tell 'em 'hands up'?"

"Ideally, this goes down nice and easy. Keep in mind, there could be others on the boat. We can't have this thing get all western."

Mia continued, "I don't know a lot about how fishing charters work, but I'm thinking that the crew probably doesn't come off the boat at the same time as the clients. Wouldn't they stay behind and clean up? Or get ready for the next charter? If that's the case then things will be much simpler. Just wait till all the customers are off and it's just the crew on board. Then we go on and nab Nixon and be on our way."

"That's an excellent point. Let me call Peter and confirm that's how things work."

Jack grabbed his cell and made the call. Peter confirmed that crew members always stayed late and cleaned up. Typically an hour or more would be required to get the boat ready for the next charter.

Jack ran things down to Mia.

"That makes things a lot simpler. We make sure the boat is clear and then we board. We still need to be careful with Pauley but at least we won't have a crowd on a pier to contend with."

The counter girl brought over their tacos and they dug in.

Butch Coleman managed to keep his food down, but it had been a struggle all day. They were heading back to shore, having caught their limit. Twelve customers on board and every one of them had maxed out. It was a happy group and the alcohol was flowing. The trip back to San Martin would take about ninety minutes, giving Butch and Pauley enough time to clean all the fish that had been caught.

Pauley was working next to him.

"How you holding up?"

"I gotta up the Dramamine for tomorrow's charter. It ain't doing the trick."

"Good idea. It'll get easier over time. Your body will adjust."

"God, I hope so."

Pauley looked at the fish his cousin had cleaned.

"You're leaving too much meat on the bone. Work the knife closer to the backbone. You wanna get all the meat you can."

Butch focused on the fish in front of him. He worked a bit more slowly but was able to carve a larger fillet, coming close to but not hitting the backbone.

"Much better, Butch. Remember, our tips come from these customers and if they see a good job with the fish they caught then the tips are larger. I got a fifty dollar bill yesterday from one guy."

Butch nodded at his cousin. The largest tip he had received so far was a twenty. Still, the money was decent, at least for the first couple days. With tips and the small salary he was paid he was making about two hundred American dollars each day. After paying for his room, board, and other miscellaneous items, he was coming out well ahead. But still, he just wasn't sure how long he could live this type of life. He missed the United States and he missed his girlfriend, Marina.

Jack and Mia finished their lunch—the fish tacos were fantastic. Then they did their best to look like tourists. There wasn't a lot to see or do in the little town but they did visit the few shops that were there. Mia tried on several things while Jack kept an eye on the shoreline. They were still close to the pier, so if the boat came in they could be there in less than a minute. He checked his watch—it was a few minutes before three. Peter had learned from Reuben that the charters typically came back around three, so the time was drawing near. Jack reached under his coat and felt for his weapon. Doing so was second nature to him, much like a man subconsciously reaching to his back pocket to check for his wallet.

Mia commented, "I really like some of their stuff."

"Well, maybe you could buy yourself a whole new wardrobe. We could stash it in the car for now and then when we take Nixon back to Colorado you could have all your bags on your arm. Kind of sashay into the station."

"Don't be a smartass, Jack."

"Sorry, it just comes naturally."

Mia smiled at her partner.

"Yeah, no kidding."

Mia heard her phone ping. She grabbed it from her purse and checked the screen.

"It's Mick."

Jack nodded and Mia answered the call.

"Hey, Mick."

"How're you doing down there?"

"It's going well. We're in San Martin just waiting for the boat to come in. Should be here anytime."

"Were you able to confirm Nixon is on board?"

"Yes, Peter called his friend who owns the charter business and he confirmed it. So we have a plan for taking him into custody, and now we're just waiting."

"Is his cousin with him?"

"Yeah, they're both on board."

"Okay, just be really careful. We don't know what they're capable of doing."

"We will, Mick. We're going to wait till all the customers are off the boat and then take Nixon down."

"And Peter's going to give you the jet to fly him back to Colorado?"

"Yes, he's been great. Anything we need, he says."

"Okay, be sure and call me as soon as you have him in custody."

"I will, Mick. Stop worrying. It'll be fine."

"I'll stop worrying once we have him in an RCSO holding cell."

"I understand."

"Okay, I'll let you go. I love you, Mia."

"Love you too, Mick."

CHAPTER 55

"**I**'ll have your taco plate."

"Anything to drink with it?"

"Yeah, give me a Diet Coke, large."

"Be up in a few minutes."

The big man took a seat near the window, one with a clear view of the pier nearby. He ran through the plan for the umpteenth time. A simple job, really. Everything was in place. Now he just needed to complete the mission. He took out his cell and typed out a text: In Mexico, will let you know when job is done.

He pressed send.

The ride back to San Martin was smooth, something Butch was happy about. It was a beautiful, clear day and the water was glassy. The captain had taken the *Dolorosa* out more than twenty miles, a bit farther than usual. The fish-finding radar had shown there wasn't much happening close to shore so he went out to a favorite spot just south of San Martin. The ride back was longer but the customers were happy to have caught their limits.

Jack peered out at the Sea of Cortez. Off to the south he could see a boat coming toward them. He estimated it was a couple miles off shore, but with no other boats on the horizon he felt confident that the boat was most likely the *Dolorosa*.

Mia was still in one of the shops, so he ducked inside.

"Mia, I think our ship is coming in. It's maybe ten minutes away."

Mia stepped outside and peered out to sea.

"Yeah, I can see it. No other boats around and it's a little after three. It's gotta be our boy."

"Let's walk down there and do the tourist thing. I don't anticipate Nixon will be first off, but we can't take any chances. It'll probably be another hour or more before he comes to shore."

The two casually walked down toward the pier. As the boat came into clear view, the name on the side was visible.

Dolorosa.

Jack raised his eyebrows. "Bingo."

The big man finished up his taco plate. They weren't quite as good as his mama's, but for a small little cafe they were better than average. He left a five on the table, walked out, and headed for the pier not a hundred yards away. He reached in and checked his jacket pocket; everything was in its place. There were very few people around, just a handful of locals and what appeared to be a couple walking along the shoreline near the pier. What he had to do, he would do quickly. By the time people figured out what had happened he'd be back in his car headed off to the little-known dirt runway a few miles inland. A small turbo prop was standing by, ready to go at a moment's notice. It hadn't come cheap but he was being paid handsomely for this job and he sure didn't want to screw up and somehow get detained in Mexico. He had heard the horror stories.

CHAPTER 56

The *Dolorosa* docked and tied up at the pier. A minute later a dozen or so customers, all sunburned and carrying burlap sacks, came off the boat. Jack and Mia watched carefully as the men were helped onto the pier by a crew member. They peered at the scene unfolding not fifty yards away. The crew member helping people off the boat looked like the photo of Pauley they had received from Reuben. They kept an eye on the *Dolorosa*, doing their best to appear to be nothing more than semi-interested tourists.

While they were watching the *Dolorosa*, Jack noticed another man near the pier, also looking at the boat. He was large and Latino; probably a local, Jack thought. Perhaps there to pick up a friend who had spent the day fishing.

Jack motioned toward the man discreetly. "Mia, what do you think of that guy?"

"Doesn't look like anything to me," Mia replied.

Jack shifted his attention back to the *Dolorosa*. It appeared that all the paying customers had disembarked and now a second crew member had emerged on deck. Jack instantly recognized the second man as Nixon; there was no mistake about it. He had a large bucket and a mop. Pauley had a burlap sack and was busy collecting trash left behind by the fishermen.

Jack whispered to Mia, "The guy with the bucket and mop—that's our boy."

"Yeah, that's definitely Nixon. And the other guy is Pauley."

"Shall we head over?"

"It's showtime."

Jack and Mia walked to the pier and headed toward the *Dolorosa*.

"You take the lead, Mia. I'm sure they'll see you before they see me."

"Got it."

As they approached the boat, both Jed and Pauley looked up and noticed Mia.

She took her cue.

"Hi, I was wondering if you could help me?"

Both men stopped what they were doing and walked over to Mia and Jack.

"Sure, what can we do for you, miss?"

"My dad and I were interested in doing some fishing. We're only here for a couple of days and, well . . . I've never been."

Pauley took the lead while Jed stood a few feet away. Both were trying not to stare at Mia.

"We run charters every day. We'd be happy to have you aboard."

"I'm a little concerned about being out on a boat. How far offshore do you go?"

"Usually just a few miles, but we go where the fish are. We have some pretty sophisticated fish-finding radar equipment—we always find something to catch."

"Would you mind if we came on board? Could you show us around? I just want to make sure I'd be comfortable."

"Sure, no problem at all."

Pauley held out his hand for Mia, helping her onto the *Dolorosa*.

Neither Jed nor Pauley made any effort to help Jack. He shrugged and came aboard.

"Come on, this way. We'll give you a little tour."

As they turned to follow Jed and Pauley, a loud *crack* rang out. Jack and Mia instantly knew what the sound was, and both dropped down to take cover. In that moment neither knew exactly what was happening or why. But the answer to that question came a second later as they saw Jed Nixon fall to the ground. Jack crawled to him and saw a gaping hole in the man's chest, blood pouring freely from the wound.

"He's been hit, Mia. Stay down," Jack shouted.

Mia was flat on her stomach, trying her best to see what was happening. She felt like a sitting duck, unsure of where the shot came from, worried more gunfire would follow. It was a frightening and bewildering situation.

Jack kept low as he tended to Nixon. Pauley was also on the ground, but having heard only one gunshot, Jack was confident he was uninjured.

"Stay down, Pauley."

Pauley didn't respond, puzzled that the man knew his name. He stayed low, trembling and covering his head.

After ten or fifteen seconds, Mia poked her head up and took a quick peek toward the shore. She saw the large Latino man they had seen minutes before, running from the scene. Given there were no other people visible to her, it seemed very likely he was the shooter. He was too far away for Mia to return fire, so she turned her attention back to Jack and Jed.

"That big guy we saw earlier is running away. Likely he was the shooter. He's out of range."

"We're losing Nixon. He's lost a lot of blood and there's no way to stop it."

Mia looked at Jack. His hands were covered in blood as he applied pressure to Nixon's chest. Pauley stayed where he was, too afraid to move.

"He's not going to make it, Mia. Goddamnit! What the hell happened here?"

"I have no idea, Jack. Shit!"

A few seconds later a short, powerfully built man appeared. "I'm Jeremiah Kubilos, captain of this boat. What the hell is going on here?"

In a firm and authoritative voice, Mia said "We're police officers from the United States, here on official business. You have a crew member with a gunshot wound to the chest. Get help immediately! And call the local police authorities. San Martin PD if they have one."

Pauley raised his head, looked at Jack and Mia, then put his head back down. He didn't want to see his cousin. This was all his fault, he thought.

"Well, I'm the captain of this boat and I'm in charge. What the fuck are you doing here?"

Jack responded, "Right now we just need to get help for Nixon."

"Nixon? His name is Coleman—Butch Coleman. Jesus, you got the wrong guy there, detectives?"

"Coleman is an alias. His name is Jed Nixon and he's wanted for murder back in Colorado. We're here to make the arrest but someone just shot him. That's about all I can tell you, captain."

"So, you come onto my boat unannounced and cause this clusterfuck?"

Mia jumped in. "Sorry to ruin your day, captain, but we have a dying man here and you're not helping the situation any. Now go back inside and call for help!"

"You got some kinda attitude, lady."

Jack interrupted. "You got any clean towels?"

"Yeah, I'll get some."

Kubilos left, seemingly in no hurry to get the towels. A minute later he returned tossed some towels to Jack.

"I've called the authorities. But from the looks of it, he ain't going to need any medical attention."

Jack put the fresh towels on Nixon's chest, but he knew it was hopeless at this point. Nixon's breathing had stopped and his chest was still.

"He's gone."

A stifled sob came from Pauley. He slowly raised his head and looked around. Believing it was safe, he got to his feet and stared down at this dead cousin.

"Keep an eye on him, Mia. I'm guessing an aiding and abetting charge will be forthcoming for Mr. Nixon."

Mia drew her weapon and pointed it at Pauley.

"Until we get all this sorted out, you're not to move. Got it?"

Pauley continued to stare at his dead cousin. Tears began to flow.

Mia looked at him, feeling almost sorry for the man.

"Can I sit down?" Pauley asked Mia, pointing at a bench next to the bait tank just a few feet away.

"Yeah, go ahead. But if you make any moves at all, I'll take you out."

Jack jumped in, "And she ain't kidding Pauley. She's done it before."

"Okay, understood," he responded, his voice trembling.

Jack wiped his bloody hands with the towel Kubilos had brought.

Jack looked at Mia. "What a fucking mess. This is going to be a nightmare. Maybe you should call the sheriff and fill him in. The last thing we want is for this to become some sort of international incident. We're going to need a lot of help on this."

Mia replied, "Let's call Peter—he may have some ideas. And who knows, maybe he can pull some strings with the Mexican authorities."

"Good idea. Keep an eye on Pauley. I don't want him overhearing the conversation."

Jack walked to the other side of the bait tank, out of earshot.

"Peter, this is Jack. We're down in San Martin and we have a problem."

Jack ran the story down and Peter said he'd be there in thirty minutes.

As he ended the call, Jack looked up and saw a police car pulling up at the pier. Two uniformed officers were moving quickly toward the boat, each with their hands on their belts ready to draw their sidearms. As they reached the boat, Jack spoke up.

"Do you speak English?"

One of the two officers, the taller and younger of the two, responded, "I do."

"Okay, my name is Jack Keller and this is my partner, Mia Serrano. We're police detectives from Colorado and here on official business. We have one man down, deceased, shot by an unknown person. The shooter has fled and his whereabouts are unknown at this time. The dead man is a suspect in a Colorado homicide."

The officers stepped aboard the *Dolorosa* and took a quick look at Nixon. His eyes were wide open as if he'd seen a ghost. The hole in his chest was huge, but the blood had pooled and was no longer pouring from the wound. He was a bluish color.

The English-speaking officer turned to Captain Kubilos and said, "We can call off the medical help. No need for them now."

Kubilos nodded and left to make the call. Both Jack and Mia thought it was odd the officer wanted to cancel the request for the medical team.

The English-speaking officer looked over and said something in Spanish to his partner. Jack didn't follow what was being said, but Mia caught a little of it. Her late mother was Latina and Mia had picked up some Spanish as a little girl. She played dumb, hoping the two men would continue their conversation, unaware that she was able to follow it at all. Jack looked at her and saw what she was doing. He kept quiet, allowing the two men to converse.

As Mia continued to listen to the two men, her face started to show concern. Jack picked up on it and suspected that the discussion between the two men was about trying to get some kind of bribe from them. Mia looked over at him and could see what he was thinking. She gave him a little nod.

Hell, he thought. The situation was growing shittier every second. He looked back toward the beach, hoping Peter might be arriving. He would know what to do—he was a powerful man in Puerto Peñasco and would be familiar with a culture where bribes were commonplace. But there was no Peter.

"Detective Keller, may we have a word with you?"

Jack looked at the English-speaking officer. Here it comes, he thought. Jack stepped toward the man, getting a little closer than what was comfortable. He wanted to intimidate the young man, or at least send a message that he was no pushover.

"What is it?" he asked in a firm voice.

The officer took a small step backward, then spoke. "We have a very serious situation here. It seems that your actions have led to the death of this man. It could prove to be a very difficult situation for you and your partner."

"We had nothing to do with this man's death. He was murdered by someone else; we were just present when it happened."

"So you say. Were there any witnesses to this murder?"

"What are you getting at?"

"We are just seeking the truth. We have a dead man and we really don't know what happened. There will need to be an official investigation by the *federales* and that could take considerable time. I suspect that neither of you will be allowed to return to the United States until this is all sorted out. As law enforcement officials, I'm sure you understand."

The conversation had caught Pauley's interest—he was sitting near the bait tank, listening intently. Captain Kubilos was also there, standing off to the side with his arms folded, listening to every word.

Jack responded, "We're not going to be intimidated by a couple of San Martin PD flunkies. We'll take our chances with the *federales*."

Mia cringed at Jack's comments. Insulting these two wasn't likely to help the situation.

The officer remained surprisingly calm and let the insult slide. He turned to his Spanish-speaking partner and said something that included the word *federales*.

"I've asked my partner to notify the *federales* immediately. He can place that call right now. Unless . . . "

Jack was struggling to contain his anger; it was a shakedown, plain and simple.

"So what is it you're proposing here?"

"That is an excellent question, sir. This is a very troublesome situation—one that has many complications."

"It's not really that complicated. We have a man, now deceased, wanted in the United States. We plan on taking him back. We can have him out of here within the hour. You can wash your hands of the situation and be on your way like none of this ever happened."

"Oh, no, no, no. This man was killed on Mexican soil. As I mentioned, there will be an inquest and this could take some period of time. We need to determine exactly what happened to him, to ensure he didn't die at the hands of a couple of trigger-happy American cops."

"Fuck you."

Mia stepped in. "Gentlemen, I'm sure we can work this out."

The officer turned toward Mia. "Ah, finally. Someone who makes some sense."

"So, as Detective Keller asked, what is it you want?"

"I believe we can simplify this unfortunate situation with a donation to the San Martin police department. And an additional donation to the captain of this boat and this crew member who has obviously been traumatized by what has happened on this boat."

So there it was—a bribe would take care of things. Before Jack could respond, Mia spoke up.

"Jack, we have a visitor."

He turned his attention to the pier and saw Peter walking quickly toward them.

The officers saw Peter and both pointed at him.

"Stop right there."

Peter stopped in his tracks, twenty feet from the *Dolorosa*. Jack grew concerned. If the San Martin officers somehow learned that Peter was the owner of the Marbella in nearby Puerto Peñasco, the price of the bribe would certainly go up. He needed to tread very carefully.

"John, give us a few minutes here. Maybe wait for us on the beach."

Peter looked at his father-in-law. Obviously something was amiss, so Peter just nodded and turned back toward the beach.

The younger officer asked, "Who is that man?"

"He's part of our investigative team. No need to involve him at this point. He doesn't have the authority to act on the behalf of our police agency."

"And do you, Detective Keller?"

"Perhaps, but first I need to meet with my team privately to discuss the situation. What kind of 'donation' are we talking about?"

The officer turned toward his partner and spoke in Spanish. After half a minute he turned toward Jack and said, "Five thousand American dollars to the San Martin PD and a thousand dollars each to the captain and his crew member. All in cash."

Kubilos grinned. Pauley's eyes widened.

"Of course," Jack replied, disgusted.

"Take a few minutes to talk to your team."

Jack called out to Peter, who had nearly reached the beach. "John, come on back."

Peter turned and began walking back to the boat.

"We'll need some privacy."

It wasn't a question; it was a demand. The officer nodded.

"Stay on the pier."

The younger officer turned to his partner and said something in Spanish, pointing to the beach. He was telling him to block the way in the unlikely event the American officers tried to make a run for it. He left the boat and made his way to the beach.

Jack looked at Peter, who had reached the boat.

"We need to talk, John."

Jack motioned to Mia. The two climbed from the boat, joined Peter, and strode thirty yards down the pier.

Once out of earshot, Peter whispered "What the hell is going on, Jack?"

"It's a shakedown. They want seven grand to make this all go away."

"That's bullshit! I can put an end to this with a phone call."

"No, hold on Peter. Let's talk this through."

Mia looked at Jack, not sure where he was going with all this. She couldn't believe he would agree to be extorted.

"There's nothing to talk about, Jack. These people are scum; you don't give in to their demands."

"I normally would agree with you, but this is a really complicated situation."

"You tell them to fuck off, I make a phone call, and you're back on the plane by dinner time."

"And what do we do with the body?"

"You take it back to Colorado. Obviously this isn't how you wanted to take him back, but the guy is dead and your case is cleared."

"Just wrap it in Saran wrap and toss it on your jet?"

"We can make it work, Jack," responded Peter, sensing Jack's growing frustration.

"And you think you can make a call and these two idiots will stand down and let us take the body back to Colorado?"

"I'm confident I can do that."

"How confident? Because if we start down that road and it doesn't go so well, I'm guessing the cost of doing business will go up dramatically. Listen, Peter—these guys don't know who you are. They think you're one of us. If they figure out you have financial resources, this could get real ugly, real fast."

"I don't do much business in San Martin but my business associates in Puerto Peñasco will know the people here who are in power. It's just a matter of getting everyone lined up."

"So, what are the odds you can get all this done, and done in a hurry? These guys aren't going to give us a couple of days to get the money together."

"They will if we tell them it will take that long."

"No, they won't, Peter. We aren't all going to stand on this boat with Nixon starting to stink, waiting for money to get wired or whatever. So, how confident are you? Give me a number."

"I'd say eighty percent."

"Not high enough. I say we pay them the seven grand and get on the plane."

Mia spoke up, "Jack, we can't give in to extortion. That's not the way we do things. I'm with Peter. Let him pull some strings so we can do this right."

Jack turned to Mia. "So if we do it your way, how do we explain all this when we get home? And what the hell do we do with Nixon's body?"

Mia answered, "We don't really have to explain anything; Mick is the only one who knows we're here. We return to Colorado and let the search for Nixon just fade away. It'll just remain an open investigation and over time everyone will forget about it. The coroner can deal with the body. Mick is pretty tight with Dr. Mora—we can just list Nixon as a John Doe."

"You're assuming we can get on that plane with Nixon. Peter's only eighty percent confident he can make this all go away. If we can't pull it all together, then we're screwed. Word here will be out as to who Peter is, and things could get very unpleasant for him. He doesn't need some coverup bullshit hanging over his head."

"Don't worry about me, Jack."

"You shouldn't have to deal with our mess. I say we pay them the seven grand and get the hell out of here. Peter, can we get the money from you and then pay you back?"

"Yes, that's no problem."

"How quick can you have it here?"

"Within the hour."

"Mia, call the sheriff. Run all this down to him and see what he says. If he says no to the seven grand, let me speak to him."

Mia looked at her partner. There was no changing his mind. "Okay."

Mia walked further down the pier and made the call.

Jack turned back to Peter. "Call your people and get the seven grand here. If we opt for doing things the other way then we won't need it, but if the sheriff gives us the go ahead then the sooner we get it done the better. Time is of the essence."

"Okay, I'll make the call."

Peter got on his phone and made the arrangements. He asked that the person delivering the money come in a nondescript vehicle. He didn't need a limo from the Marbella pulling up to the pier.

Several minutes passed before Mia finished her call with Mick. She walked back to Jack and Peter standing near the boat.

"He said pay them the money."

Jack let out a sigh of relief.

"Smart man. Let's go tell Dumb and Dumber the news."

The three walked back to the boat.

"If we get you the money, then you take possession of the body. That's part of the deal—we don't want it."

"Not a problem," replied the officer.

Captain Kubilos turned to Pauley and said something in Spanish. Pauley responded angrily. Jack looked to Mia and she just shook her head.

"We'll have the money here within the hour."

"Very good, my friend. Now we wait."

CHAPTER 57

Mick was furious about what had transpired in Mexico. He didn't like giving in to extortion, but seven thousand dollars, in the grand scheme of things, was cheap. From a purely financial perspective the RCSO would have incurred probably ten times that in investigative costs bringing back the body. There would need to be an official investigation into what had happened in Mexico and that could prove to be nightmarish. The press would have a field day—*RCSO Involved in Shootout in Mexico*—the damn story would likely go national. The feds would get involved, and it would quickly turn into a total and complete fiasco.

One thing he had learned in his nearly four years as sheriff was that were times to be practical and this was certainly one of those times. Jack and Mia would soon be back in Colorado and they could all wipe their hands of this mess. The search for Nixon would no longer be a priority and over time he'd be forgotten. And, Mick reminded himself, justice had been served. Nixon was dead. Granted there was no due process but there was no doubt he had killed Tracey Thompson and then inexplicably sent the man's skull to the RCSO. Why he did that would never be known.

Mick picked up his phone and texted Mark Archer. He needed to brief him on what had transpired in Mexico. He would be the only other person to ever hear about this mess. As the media guy he would need to be prepared if, God forbid, word ever got out about Nixon.

Archer appeared at Mick's office a minute later.

"What's up, boss?"

"Come in and close the door."

Uh oh, thought Mark. That was never good.

"What's going on?" he asked, taking a seat across from Mick.

"As you know, Mia and Jack are in Mexico, there to scoop up Jed Nixon."

"Yeah . . . ?"

"I just heard from Mia and there have been some complications."

"Like what?"

"Nixon is dead. He was shot to death in front of Jack and Mia, just as they were about to take him into custody."

"What?"

"They found Nixon and his cousin working on a fishing boat down there. They tracked him and had just boarded the boat to make the arrest. They were talking to him and someone shot Nixon and he went down. They didn't get a good look at the shooter, but they saw someone running from the area seconds later."

"Good God. That's crazy."

"Wait—there's more. So Jack administers first aid to Nixon, but it's useless. He got center punched and there's a gaping hole in his chest. A few minutes later the local police show up."

"Uh oh . . . "

"Yeah, *uh oh* is right. They're demanding a payoff from Jack and Mia."

"A payoff for what, exactly? They didn't shoot the guy."

"At first Jack and Mia were thinking they'd bring Nixon's body back to Colorado. They have Jack's son-in-law's jet at their disposal and they were going to fly back tonight with the body. When the Mexican police figured that out, they saw an opportunity and they're demanding a payoff."

"How much are they asking for?"

"Seven grand total."

217

"And if they pay it, and I'm guessing that's the plan, where will they get their hands on seven thousand dollars?"

"Jack's son-in-law. He's got the resources and he's right there."

"So, they pay off the authorities and bring Nixon back? That's what's going to happen?"

"Not exactly."

"Okay, so what 'exactly' will happen?"

"Part of the deal with the Mexican cops is that they keep the body. Jack and Mia will return to Colorado empty-handed."

Mark looked at his boss. He didn't like this at all. "Who all knows they're down there to make this arrest?"

"Nobody but you, me, Jack and Mia."

"No other investigators?"

"Nope. We kept it quiet . . . didn't really want people knowing we're out nabbing people in other countries."

Mark considered what he was hearing. The RCSO hadn't done anything illegal, per se. Nixon wasn't a Mexican national, he was a US citizen. So there was no reason the RCSO couldn't travel to Mexico, arrest him, and bring him back to Colorado. Typically, a courtesy call was made to authorities in the other country informing them of what was happening, but that clearly hadn't been done here. This was a stealth operation. The question was whether it could remain a stealth operation. If word ever got out about what happened, it could blow up in a big way. He suddenly remembered that he had shared with Angela that Jack and Mia were "out of state" to arrest Nixon. But, he thought, that could be explained away—they struck out, it was a dead end—and he had not mentioned anything about Mexico.

"Well, in theory this all works, but I have to tell you—it makes me very uneasy. If this is ever discovered there will be hell to pay. It could get real ugly."

"I know that, but it seems like the best course of action. I mean, we could bring Nixon's body back, but then we'd have one hell of a mess to deal with, and I sure as hell don't need some international incident blowing up in my face. I've got a re-election campaign to launch here soon."

Mark looked at his boss. In three short years he had become a politician. That wasn't all bad—you needed to understand the political side of the job to survive, but now it looked like that might be his primary purpose for choosing this course of action.

"So, this is going to happen? The wheels are in motion?"

"Yes, I'm just waiting on a call from Mia letting me know it's taken care of."

"Okay, just keep me posted."

An unmarked white Ford SUV pulled up to the pier and Roberto Salazar climbed out. Peter waved to him, motioning for him to approach them.

"Do you have the money, Roberto?" Peter asked as Salazar reached him.

"Yes, boss, it's in my coat pocket. Would you like me to take it out?"

Roberto was being very careful; he didn't know exactly what was happening.

"Yes."

Peter took the envelope with the cash, dismissed Salazar, and stepped onto the boat. Jack and Mia were right behind him.

"We have your money. Let's make this happen so we can be on our way."

The two officers stepped toward Peter. Jack moved his hand closer to his side so his weapon was just inches away. He knew this was the moment of truth, and that if the crooked cops were going to try something, now would be the time.

"Very well. Let's see the cash."

Peter took the cash from the envelope and showed it to the officers.

Kubilos and Pauley moved closer to see. Jed lay just a few feet away, covered with several towels. The blood had seeped through the towels, turning them crimson.

Jack spoke, "So, do we have a deal?"

"Yes, sir."

"We're going to leave now. The body is yours, gentlemen."

"Very well."

The officer took the cash and Jack, Mia, and Peter walked quickly to their respective cars. Thirty minutes later they were safely back at the Marbella.

Once the Americans left, the officer divvied up the cash. Pauley thought about refusing his thousand dollars. It felt like blood money to him, but ultimately he took the cash. Jed would have wanted him to have it, he reasoned. Kubilos took his share and stuffed it into his pocket. The officer who had done all the negotiating kept three grand and gave his partner the remaining two.

The officer turned to Captain Kubilos and said, "We'll be on our way, then."

"What do you want me to do with the body?"

"I don't care. Do what you wish. Toss it to the fishies if that makes you happy."

Hearing the comment, Pauley started to look sick to his stomach again.

"Okay, we'll take care of it," Kubilos replied.

The two officers left the boat and headed down the pier to their vehicle. Once they had driven away, Kubilos pulled out his cell phone and began taking photos of Jed's body. He removed the towels and zoomed in on the chest wound.

"What the hell are you doing?"

"Never you mind."

Kubilos finished taking photos and turned back to Pauley.

"We need to dispose of the body."

"He needs a proper burial, cap."

"I agree, we'll give him a burial at sea. He was a fisherman, after all."

"He was hardly that, cap. He's worked on this boat for three days. We need to bury him properly."

Pauley was angry, not liking what Kubilos was planning to do.

"I'm the captain and you'll do what I say."

"Fuck you. How's that, cap?"

Pauley stormed off the boat and headed down the pier toward the beach.

"Very well," Kubilos yelled out. "You're fired, asshole."

Now alone, Kubilos fired up the *Dolorosa*'s engine and headed back out to sea.

CHAPTER 58

It was nearly midnight by the time Mia returned home. She was exhausted from the trip, but still very keyed up. She had been unable to sleep on the plane; Jack, on the other hand, slept almost the entire flight.

"Welcome home, Mia."

Mick embraced his wife and held her close for several seconds.

"It's great to be home. I feel like I've been gone a month."

"It's over, sweetie. Just forget what happened down there and we can get back to our lives."

"I want to see CJ."

The two walked together to CJ's room and peered in. He was sound asleep, so Mia, while tempted to pick him up, let him be. She and Mick stood and watched their son for a couple of minutes, listening to his rhythmic breathing.

"He's just perfect, isn't he?" she whispered.

"Yeah. We did good, Mia. We did good. Always focus on what's important in our lives, nothing else."

"So, did Jack and Mia arrest Jed Nixon?"

Angela and Mark were laying in bed, exhausted from an extended lovemaking session.

Angela was cuddled against Mark, her head resting on his chest. She could hear his heart beating, still rapid and strong from the exertion.

"What? You're asking me that now?"

"Yeah, I guess so. Just making conversation."

"Yeah, right. You're never just making conversation. Do you ever stop working, Angela?"

Angela knew she needed to proceed carefully. She didn't want to upset Mark; things were finally going well again between the two. Her obsession with work had always been a sore subject between them.

"Hey, I stopped working for an hour or so . . . " she responded, playfully kissing his chest. "And you know, you didn't seem to mind too much."

"That's true, and no, I didn't mind it at all. And no, we didn't make the arrest. Things didn't pan out like we'd hoped."

It was the truth, just with a whole lot of details left out. Lies of omission.

"So, Nixon is still on the loose?"

"We don't know where he is. Hopefully he surfaces at some point."

Again, the truth. The comment about Nixon "surfacing at some point" was unintended, and he closed his eyes for a second after he said it. He didn't know what had been done with Nixon's body, but being disposed of at sea was a likely possibility.

"Where exactly were Jack and Mia looking? You said they were out of state?"

"Does it matter, Angela? It didn't pan out and so they'll refocus their search elsewhere."

"No, it doesn't matter. I was just curious."

"Okay, enough said. It's Saturday and we're both off. What do you want to do today?" asked Mark, moving the conversation away from Jed Nixon.

Pauley Nixon hadn't been able to sleep much since his cousin's murder two days earlier. He was out of a job, but had the thousand dollars in cash from the bribe. With his final paycheck from the *Dolorosa* he had enough to stay in Mexico for a few weeks, but his taste for the place had soured. For two nights he had experienced vivid and frightening nightmares. Each ended the same way, with Jed looking at him with hopeless eyes that looked like they were asking, "Why have you done this to me?" Pauley would sit up in bed, covered in sweat.

The truth was that Jed had brought on his demise all on his own. Granted, Pauley had brought him to Mexico, but his intentions were good. The odds of Jed eluding capture in the States were slim at best—Jed wasn't the sharpest knife in the drawer. The fact that he had texted his girlfriend while on the run was proof of that. And, Pauley suspected, those trackable texts were likely what led not only the Colorado authorities to San Martin, but brought Jed's killer as well. He considered the possibility that the killer was someone who lived in San Martin, but Jed had only been in town a few days, hardly enough time to create that kind of enemy.

Pauley had not seen the person who shot his cousin. He heard the shot and a second later saw Jed drop. His focus immediately went to his cousin; he paid no attention to where the shot had come from. It had all happened so quickly. But now that he'd had some time to reflect on things, he suspected that Jed had been killed by a professional. It was all very efficient and not in any way personal.

But who would want him dead? Upon his arrival in Tucson, Jed had told him that he had killed someone, a snitch, and that he had been ordered to do so by his superiors in the drug ring. He said the police were onto him and had put his photo on the news, which is why he had to make a quick departure from Colorado.

It was possible that the family of the man Jed killed could have hired someone to take him out, but Pauley thought that was unlikely. Another possibility was that the person who had ordered Jed to take out the snitch had also ordered the hit on Jed. Maybe when his photo appeared on the news the shot caller got nervous and ordered Jed's death. If Jed had been arrested by the police then the possibility of Jed turning state's evidence in exchange for a lesser punishment was a real possibility—something the head of the meth trade in Colorado wouldn't stand for. Take out Jed before he got caught and squealed to police.

Pauley knew he'd likely never know exactly what had happened. Maybe it didn't matter anymore—his cousin was gone and now he needed to decide his own future. Stay in Mexico or return to Tucson? He liked Mexico and the charter fishing business had been good to him, but now he was without a job. There were plenty of other charters based along the Sea of Cortez; maybe he could land a job with one of them. Puerto Peñasco was close by and he knew there were several charters operating out of the scenic port.

Maybe he'd try his hand at the Marbella—it was a top-of-the-line charter operating out of a very high-end hotel. He had a few years experience under his belt, who knows, he thought . . . maybe that would be a good fit for him.

"So, who killed Jed Nixon? Or do we even care?"

Mia asked Jack the question as the two were sitting alone in the RCSO break room having coffee. She got the answer she expected.

"I don't give a shit. Do you?"

"I don't know. I guess I do. It may not be our problem but it is somewhat intriguing, don't you think?"

"It's like taking out the trash. As long as it gets done, who cares who does it?"

"Geez, Jack. A bit cynical, are we?"

"Nixon got what he deserved. Remember, he killed Tracey Thompson, beheaded him, and sent us a real nice memento of the killing."

Mia contemplated what Jack was saying. He was right, but she still felt some compassion for Jed Nixon. It prompted another thought.

"And, of course, we can't tell Tracey Thompson's mom that her son's killer is dead."

"Nope, Chookie will just have to live with that."

"Doesn't seem right, Jack."

Jack thought about Chookie. He had taken advantage of her, getting her to give up her son, which ultimately led to the young man's death.

"Yeah, but a lot of life isn't fair. I just don't see any way to tell her that her son's killer is dead without spilling the beans about what happened in Mexico. I mean, I'd like her to know but we'd be putting ourselves at risk by telling her. And we just can't have that. Best to let it go, Mia. Just forget about all of it."

CHAPTER 59

Three days after the episode on the *Dolorosa*, Pauley Nixon walked into the Marbella resort asking for an employment application. He filled out the form and returned it to the HR person. She told him that someone would contact him soon about a possible job on one of the Marbella's many charters. Pauley thanked the young lady and returned to San Martin.

Cresencio Valenzuela returned to Colorado without being detected. The contract had been carried out and now it was time to get paid. He had contacted Reginald Gray soon after the job was done, letting him know Nixon was dead. They agreed to meet at Reggie's home in Castle Springs.

After getting that initial call from Valenzuela, Reggie had kept a close eye on media reports, waiting for news of Nixon's death. But three days had passed and there was no mention of it. The hit had been carried out in Mexico but he was sure there would still be some media coverage. Nixon was someone the RCSO had in its crosshairs and surely they would tout that they had their man, even if he was brought back in a body bag. Reggie was growing concerned about the situation and wondered if Valenzuela was being straight with him. Without proof of Nixon's death all he had was Valenzuela's word that the job had been carried out. It would be foolish, even deadly, for Valenzuela to lie to Reggie. He couldn't imagine he would do that. But what happened down in Mexico and why no news of Nixon's death?

Valenzuela arrived at Gray's home a few minutes early so he sat in his parked car. He contemplated what the meeting with Reggie Gray might bring—he, too, was concerned about the lack of media reports about Nixon. He had left in such a hurry he didn't know what happened in the minutes following the shooting. But he knew there was no way Nixon could have survived the blast—he hit him dead center, probably blowing a hole in his heart the size of a half dollar.

He checked the time on his phone. It was showtime. He walked up to Reggie's door, rang the bell, and waited. A half minute later the door opened.

"Come in."

Reggie led Valenzuela through the foyer to a large sofa in the living room.

"So, why haven't there been any media reports about Nixon's death?"

Reggie didn't waste any time, Valenzuela thought.

"I don't know, boss. I've been wondering that myself."

"If an American, wanted for murder, is shot to death in Mexico in front of police detectives, it makes the damn news."

"I don't know what to say, Reggie. I took him out, no doubt about it. I center punched him and he went down like a sack of potatoes. Blew his fucking heart out of his chest."

"Yeah, that's what you told me. But do you see my predicament here?"

"Look, Reggie. Nixon's dead and that's the job you hired me to do. I got nothing as to why it didn't make the six o'clock news. But I guarantee that Jed Nixon will not be a problem to you—that snitch is history."

"I paid you five grand up front and promised another fifteen when the job was complete. Now I have a situation where I don't know if the job is done or not. So, I'm inclined not to pay you the other fifteen."

Valenzuela shifted uneasily on the sofa. He wasn't about to get screwed out of money he was due, but this was Reggie Gray and he knew he couldn't push too hard. He didn't want to have Gray green-light him.

"With all due respect, boss, I think I deserve the rest of the money. We had a deal, Nixon's dead, and your problems been solved. Nixon ain't going to be spilling his guts to no cops."

"That's what you say, but if somehow Nixon is still alive it could cause me some serious problems."

"He's dead, boss. Guaranteed."

Reggie looked at Valenzuela. He leaned toward believing him—it would be a big mistake to be lying about this, but he had to be sure.

"Okay, I'll tell you what. I'll give you another five. If you want the other ten then provide some proof that Nixon's dead. You do that and I'll be happy to pay you the rest of the money."

"You don't believe me, do you? You really think I'd come in here and lie about this? That would be major-league stupid, boss."

"I agree with you there. And I don't think you're lying, but without proof I'm afraid the original terms of our deal need to be modified. I've told you what I'm willing to do. Take it or leave it."

"Boss, it was an expensive job. Ten grand barely covers my expenses. I did your fucking dirty work for free, essentially."

Valenzuela knew he was pushing his luck talking to Reggie that way, but he was upset and felt he was being taken advantage of. Reggie remained cool, realizing it was understandable that Valenzuela was upset.

He responded calmly, "I've given you another option—get me proof and there's another ten in it for you. Frankly, I think I'm being generous giving you ten without any proof Nixon's dead. Good thing I'm in a giving mood today, Cresencio."

Valenzuela didn't see much choice so he accepted the deal and took the five thousand dollars. He vowed to Reggie to get proof of Nixon's death and return to collect the other ten. He wasn't sure how he'd do that, but ten grand gave him plenty of incentive to figure out something.

Pauley received a call from the Marbella less than twenty-four hours after putting in his application. They wanted him to come in for an interview with Gil Mendoza, the manager of the Marbella's charter operation. Pauley was still unsure if he wanted to stay in Mexico or return to Arizona, but given the interest from the Marbella he figured there wasn't any harm in seeing what they could offer him. He told the woman on the phone he could be there within the hour and the interview was set.

CHAPTER 60

Mark Archer knew what he had to do. It wouldn't be pleasant and he certainly didn't want to hurt her feelings but he needed to tell Rachel that he couldn't see her any longer. He liked Rachel but things with Angela were back on track and he wanted to commit to her again. He texted Rachel and they were set to meet at Bean Crazy.

He arrived a few minutes early and ordered himself a large black coffee. He found a seat near the back, a bit out of the way of the other tables. He checked his phone for messages. There was nothing—a rare occurrence. A couple of days had passed since Jed Nixon's murder in Mexico and Mark was growing slightly less concerned. If things were going to be discovered it would likely have happened by now. Maybe, just maybe, they were in the clear.

"Hi there."

Mark jumped a bit at the words.

"Oh, hey, Rachel."

"Sorry to startle you. You looked like you were a million miles away."

"Yeah, I was. Just thinking about a work case."

Rachel took a seat at the table, coffee in hand. "It never stops, does it? Can you ever just free your mind from your work and forget about stuff?"

Mark chuckled. "Sometimes, but it's difficult. I need to learn how to do that but at this stage in my career it probably isn't going to happen. So, how are you doing?"

"I'm okay. I heard from Kendra this morning. She called to check in—something she doesn't do often enough."

"How are things going for her at college?"

"She seems to be doing well. She's made some friends and she and her roommate have grown close, so that's good. I still worry about her every day, but I think she's gotten past what happened to her at school."

"That's great, Rachel. She's a strong girl. She's going to be fine."

"Well, I hope so. So, how have you been doing?"

"Me? I've been good. Lots going on at work but otherwise good."

"Good."

"Look, thanks for meeting me. I wanted to talk to you."

Rachel saw the look on Mark's face and knew instantly what was coming. The two hadn't really connected for a few weeks and the texts and phone calls had been less and less frequent. She had strong feelings for him but knew, deep down, that those feelings weren't reciprocated. She had hoped for more but he seemed hung up on Angela. Their relationship had just never really gained any traction.

"Sure, what's on your mind?" she asked, her eyes drifting downward. She didn't want to look him in the eye. She focused on the napkin holder sitting on the table.

"You know, you're very special to me. I think you're a wonderful person and I consider you a good friend—"

"Yes, but . . . "

"Over the past couple of weeks I've reconnected with Angela. As I've mentioned to you before, she and I had a previous long-term relationship that ended several months ago. Anyway, we've started seeing each other again and I wanted to tell you in person."

"Is this an exclusive relationship you're having with Angela?"

"Yes, we've been talking the last few days and we both feel like we should give it another try. And that's what I wanted to tell you today."

"I see."

"Look, this is never easy, and you're an incredible person. It's been great getting to know you and I'm just sorry things have turned out this way."

Rachel had heard enough. There was no reason to sit and have some deep discussion with Mark about him and Angela. He had made up his mind. His loss, she thought.

"No need to explain things further. Thanks for being honest with me." She stood to leave.

"I'm sorry, Rachel. I wish you all the best."

She didn't respond, just turned and headed for the door.

Mark sat quietly and finished his coffee, feeling terrible he had caused Rachel any hurt.

Fifteen minutes into his interview with the HR person at the Marbella, Pauley Nixon was offered a job. It was a constant battle to find good, experienced deckhands for the many charters offered at the Marbella and with his experience in San Martin, Pauley was a prized catch. He was asked to start the very next day and he agreed.

Cresencio Valenzuela was determined to find a way to collect the ten grand Reginald Gray owed him. He was upset he had been screwed out of money he felt was owed to him. He had killed Jed Nixon fair and square and deserved the money. He was puzzled that there was no media coverage of Nixon's death—the sheriff's department people were there when he shot him. How could that not get reported? The more he thought about it the angrier he became. But he knew he couldn't cross Gray—that would be a certain death sentence.

So he hatched another plan.

CHAPTER 61

"Channel eight news, this is Martha Cvijanovich. How can I help you?"

"Yeah, I have a tip for you guys. Am I calling the right number?"

"Sure, what would you like to report, sir?"

"A murder."

Martha paused for a beat before responding and activated the record button on the phone. "Okay, go ahead and tell me about it."

"A few days ago there was a murder in Mexico. The victim was Jed Nixon, someone the police have been looking for. I've been following the story in the news and I recognized him from his photo you guys are always showing. They killed him."

"Who killed him?"

"The cops."

"The police killed him? And how do you know this, sir?"

"Because I witnessed it."

"You saw the police kill this man?"

"Yes, ma'am. They shot him in the chest. Detective Keller with the Rocklin County Sheriff's Office killed him in cold blood. It was horrible. The poor guy never had a chance."

"How do you know it was this particular officer?"

"I've seen him plenty of times on the news. I couldn't believe he was down there, at the same place as me and my family. Figured he was just on vacation. He was with a woman—a younger woman."

"Where exactly did this happen?"

"On a fishing boat in San Martin, Mexico. Like I said, I was there on vacation with my family and I saw it go down. It was horrible. I haven't been able to sleep since it happened."

"Have you told anyone else about this?"

"No, I didn't know what to do. I was afraid if I go public with this the cops would come after me and my family."

"Tell me more about what you saw."

Cresencio Valenzuela proceeded to tell Cvijanovich about Jed Nixon's death, putting the blame solely on Detective Keller. Once he finished his story, she pushed him for his name and contact information, even saying there could be a Channel 8 reward in it for him, but Cresencio declined the offer. Once he said what he needed to say, he hung up. The wheels were in motion.

Pauley arrived at the Marbella at four thirty in the morning, half an hour before the start of his shift. It was his first day and he wanted to make a good impression. It took a few minutes for the clerk at the front desk to find someone who could direct him to the boat dock. He was told to ask for PJ Watson, the captain of the *Top Shelf*. Pauley made his way to the dock and found the captain. After a quick introduction, Pauley was told to board the *Top Shelf* and prepare for the guests.

As soon as Cresencio ended the call with Channel 8, Cvijanovich walked to the office of Bette Alburtis, the assignment editor on duty.

"Hey, I just got an interesting call on the tip line."

"Yeah, whatcha got?"

"The caller reported seeing a murder go down."

"What?"

"Happened in Mexico, he said, while he and his family were down there on vacation. And get this—he said the cops killed the guy."

Alburtis was dubious. "The cops killed a guy in Mexico? I suspect that happens with some regularity down there. Why is he calling a television station in Denver?"

"Because he said the cops who killed the guy were Rocklin County Sheriff's Department detectives, and the guy they killed was Jed Nixon—the wanted subject they've been searching for."

"The RCSO was down in Mexico and they killed Jed Nixon?"

"That's what he's saying. And get this, he said the officer that did the deed was none other than Jack Keller. Happened on a fishing boat, he claims."

"What the hell? Did he sound credible?"

"He did to me. I recorded the call if you want to hear it."

"Yeah, send it to me. Go, do that now."

Cvijanovich left the office. Alburtis sat at her desk contemplating what she had just heard. The RCSO killing Jed Nixon in Mexico? Sounded too crazy to be true. She picked up her phone and made a call.

"Angela, can you come to my office? I've got something for you."

"Be right there."

Angela made the trek across the large newsroom, her curiosity growing as she approached Alburtis's office. The door was open so she walked in.

"What's up, Bette?"

"Martha Cvijanovich just took a bizarre call from the tip line. The caller reported that Jack Keller of the RCSO was down in Mexico a few days go and that he killed Jed Nixon—the guy they've been looking for."

"What?" Angela asked incredulously.

"The guy said he was there with a younger woman and that he shot and killed Nixon on a fishing boat."

"That sounds crazy. How credible is the caller?"

"Martha says he sounded credible. She's pulling the recording now. I told her to send it to me ASAP."

"Look, I know Jack Keller. He's got his quirks and has a long history of troubles with the RCSO, but I can't believe he's capable of doing something like this. The caller must be mistaken. Keller's no killer."

"I know you're tight with the RCSO, so I'm assigning the story to you. Go find out what, if anything, is going on here."

It was no secret that Angela had a personal relationship with Mark Archer. Alburtis knew that if anyone could get to the bottom of this bizarre story, it was Angela.

"Okay, I can make some calls. I want to hear that recording first, though. I need to make sure the guy is credible before I go making any crazy accusations."

"I'll forward it to you as soon as I get it from Martha."

"Okay, I'll get on it."

"Thanks, Angela. And keep me posted, will you?"

Angela rushed back to her office, her mind racing. Mark had told her that Jack and Mia were pursuing Jed Nixon somewhere "out of state" a few days earlier. Could it be that by "out of state" he was referring to Mexico? And the fact that the tipster was reporting Keller was with a younger woman fit the story as well. Could he have been in Mexico with Mia looking for Nixon? People on the run often fled to Mexico, so it wasn't outside the realm of possibility. But Keller went down there and killed Nixon? Why not take him into custody and bring him back to Colorado? She told herself to slow down, to think this through. She wanted to hear the audiotape of the call and judge for herself how credible the guy sounded. There was no way Keller could have done this, but if somehow he did and if Mia was with him and saw it go down ... what a story this would be. The wife of the sitting sheriff being part of a murder in Mexico.

She went to her computer, put in her password, and heard the familiar chime. There it was—a new email from Bette Alburtis. She opened it and listened carefully. Once the audio was finished she listened to it a second time and then a third. Martha was right—the guy sounded credible.

She contemplated how a conversation with Mark might go. He often became irritated with her when she went into reporter mode. She knew she needed to be careful with this; the two had just gotten back together and things were going well. She didn't need to bring back all the negative feelings from the bombing at Channel 8. They were past that now and on a good track.

She checked the time and noted she had four hours until she was scheduled to anchor the five o'clock newscast. The conversation she needed to have with Mark would go much better in person. She didn't like talking to him about serious matters on the phone. She needed to see his facial expressions and that required a face-to-face meeting.

She picked up her cell and dialed his number. He picked up right away.

"Hey, Angela. What's up?"

""Hi, Mark, I was wondering if you had a few minutes for a cup of coffee?"

"Really? Everything okay?" It was a bit unusual for her to call him in the middle of a work day.

"Yes, everything's fine. I'm going to be down in Castle Springs this afternoon covering a story and thought we could see each other while I'm there."

It was a lie, but she knew he wouldn't buy that she was driving forty minutes to Castle Springs just to have coffee with him.

"Yeah, I think I could shake loose. What time are you thinking?"

"I'm leaving now, so let's say two o'clock at Bean Crazy on Fifth Street?"

"Okay, see you then."

Pauley was a quick study on board the *Top Shelf*. While the boat was considerably larger and much more modern than the *Dolorosa*, things operated basically the same way. The other crew members were all welcoming to him and the captain seemed to run a tight ship. The clients were definitely a higher class of people than what he was accustomed to on the *Dolorosa*, which was understandable given the high-end nature of the Marbella guests.

He thought about his cousin Jed constantly. He had wanted a proper burial for his cousin but that wasn't to be. A burial at sea, the captain had said—that's what he was going to do with the body. Jed had been with the *Dolorosa* for just a couple of days and now he was to spend eternity at the bottom of the ocean. It just didn't seem right to Pauley.

CHAPTER 62

The lunch crowd had thinned out at Bean Crazy and there were only a handful of customers when Angela and Mark found a table in a corner. Angela didn't want anyone overhearing their conversation so it had been her, not Mark, who suggested the out-of-the-way table. Mark was concerned about her interest in being so private.

"So, what's going on, Angela?"

"Look, I'm not going to beat around the bush. A couple hours ago we got a call to the newsroom from an anonymous caller with some very disturbing news."

Mark was dubious of anonymous callers; the RCSO had seen plenty of false stuff called in over the years.

"Okay, so you got a call from some anonymous caller, and . . . ?"

"The guy said he had been in Mexico a few days ago and that he witnessed a murder."

Mark's stomach did a little churn. He shifted uneasily in his chair.

"So why is the guy calling Channel Eight?"

Mark hoped he wouldn't hear the answer he expected. He braced for Angela's response.

"Because the guy who was murdered was Jed Nixon and the person committing the one-eighty-seven was none other than Jack Keller."

"What the hell?"

Mark did his best to act incredulous at Angela's comments while his stomach went into free fall.

"That's what the guy's saying. I listened to the audio of the call and he sounds pretty credible. He's no fifty-one-fifty."

"Angela, that's ludicrous. You know Jack. There's no way he'd do that."

"I do know him and I find it pretty hard to believe myself. But there's more—the caller said Jack was with a younger woman. And I'm thinking maybe that's Mia. You said they were out of state the other day trying to track down Nixon, and, well . . . the pieces fit."

"I said they were out of state, not out of the country."

Mark was trying his best to lie his way out of the conversation, but Angela was having no part of it.

"Well, out of state doesn't exclude out of the country. You're nit-picking, Mark."

"This is total bullshit, Angela. You can't take this anonymous caller seriously. Come on, this is ridiculous!"

Mark felt confident with his words in one respect—Keller hadn't killed Nixon. Jack and Mia were just witnesses, and ultimately took part in a bribery and cover up. They weren't exactly innocent third parties, but they certainly weren't responsible for a murder.

"So, were Jack and Mia in Mexico looking for Nixon? You have to tell me, Mark. I need to hear the truth."

He looked at Angela. She had kept secrets for the RCSO in the past, and it looked to Mark like he might need to level with her about what had happened in Mexico. He felt like he could trust her, but if this story ever got out he knew it would destroy a lot of careers.

"Okay, I'll tell you what happened, but I need your assurances this is off the record and won't be on your five o'clock newscast."

"You know I can't do that, Mark. I mean, I'll do everything within my power to be fair about this, but I need to hear the truth."

"The last time we kept secrets it led to big problems in our relationship. I don't want that to happen again, Angela."

It was a veiled threat, one that didn't get past Angela. She knew what he was saying; he'd tell her what was going on but if she didn't keep it a secret, their relationship would once again be seriously damaged or be over for good.

She was willing to take that chance.

"I understand, Mark. What happened in Mexico?"

"Okay, off the record, correct?"

"Like I said, I'll do my best, you know that. But I need to know what happened down there, so if necessary I can protect you and the RCSO. You don't want some other reporter covering this. I know this isn't an ideal situation but at least it's me and not someone from another news agency who won't work with you."

Mark knew that what Angela was saying was true. If the story was going to come out it was best if she was the reporter.

"Okay, I'm going to trust you here, Angela."

He paused and looked her in the eye. Another subtle threat, she thought. Understandable.

"It's true, Jack and Mia were in Mexico looking for Jed Nixon. They were able to track him down working on some fishing boat in a small town on the Sea of Cortez. So they went down to make the arrest and bring him back to Colorado. That much is true."

"And then . . . ?"

"They find him working on the boat and they go aboard to grab him. He doesn't know who they are or why they're there, so things are going as planned. Just as they're about to make the arrest, someone shoots Nixon. The shooter was somewhere onshore. Neither Jack or Mia got a good look at him. Jack tried his best to administer first aid, but it was hopeless and Nixon died right there on the boat."

A stunned Angela slowly shook her head.

"Unbelievable. So they have no idea who shot him or why?"

"Nope. I mean, they have their theories but we have nothing solid."

"There must have been others on the boat—witnesses to what happened?"

"Yeah, a couple, including Nixon's cousin. He's the one who got him the job on the charter."

"So this guy sees his cousin shot to death?"

"Yeah, and there was one other person on board as well. The captain, I believe."

"Okay, so there are witnesses who can testify Nixon was shot and killed by some random person, not by Jack or Mia."

"Yeah, that's true. But I'm not sure they'd be cooperative. His cousin probably blames the RCSO for Nixon's death. He has a checkered past himself, so I'm sure he has a tainted view of reality. And I can't speak for the captain."

"Yeah, but in a pinch they could clear the RCSO."

"Ideally, yes, but I really hope it never gets that far. Frankly, we'd just like all this to go away."

"Why? You guys did nothing wrong."

"Well, there's more . . . "

Here it comes, thought Angela. There's always more.

"After Nixon went down, the captain called the local authorities. A couple of cops showed up and once they figured out what had happened they saw a golden opportunity."

"Oh, God. A shakedown?"

"Yep. So there are Jack and Mia, in another country, a thousand miles from home, and they're being extorted."

"But they didn't do anything wrong."

Mark was pleased to hear Angela say that. She was seeing things his way.

"Exactly, but here's where the rubber hits the road and the reality of the situation really sets in. Jack and Mia have a decision to make. Either pay off these yahoos and be back in Colorado by nightfall or tell them to shove it and face an unknown future at the hands of the Mexican authorities."

Angela shuddered at the thought. She had heard all the stories of what could be, at times, a corrupt Mexican government.

"So they paid the guys off and went on their way?"

"Yep."

"How much?"

"Seven grand."

Both sat in silence for a few seconds contemplating the situation Jack and Mia had faced.

"So, I'm sure you can understand why they did what they did."

"Yes, I can see that. But who killed Nixon? And why?"

"We have some ideas about that. We never released the backstory about Nixon, always just saying he was a person of interest. There's a lot more to the story."

"Tell me about it."

"Nixon was involved in the meth trade. He was a relatively low-level guy in the organization, but we believe he was asked by the higher-ups to take someone out. That someone was a snitch and, as you know, snitches don't last long in that world. So, Nixon kills the guy a few months back, and for some reason the higher-ups aren't happy with him. No idea why they're unhappy—who the hell knows—but they green-light him."

"Green-light him?" asked Angela.

"Put a hit out on him."

"And so the guy who shot him in Mexico was just following orders?"

"Yeah, that's what we think probably happened. We don't know for sure, but all the pieces fit."

"So, the RCSO's vague description about the victim's dismembered body—what was all that about?"

"Well, the story gets weirder. Evidently, Nixon not only killed the snitch, but he dismembered the body. We recovered only the victim's skull."

"He was beheaded?"

"Yeah, and there's more. Might as well tell you the whole story. But remember, I'm trusting you right now, Angela."

"I know."

"So the head was discovered in a UPS box."

"What?"

"And the box was mailed to the RCSO."

"Oh . . . my . . . . God."

"It was mailed a few months ago, and once we determined who the victim was the case kind of came together. We put out Nixon's photo on the news and he immediately fled. Went to his cousin's place in Arizona and then the two hightailed it down to Mexico."

Mark left out the details about the box being on the top shelf of the RCSO property room, undiscovered for weeks. Angela didn't need that part of the story.

"Why would Nixon send the box to the RCSO? I mean, that's seriously stupid."

"Good question. We can only surmise that it was some kind of effort to taunt us. But that's just speculation on my part. And yes, the guy was a moron."

"So, what happened to Nixon's body?"

"Part of the deal was that the Mexican authorities would keep the body. Jack and Mia wanted no part of it. They couldn't exactly load the guy on a plane and fly him back. So they paid the seven grand and came home."

"So, Jack and Mia committed no crime—they were just in the wrong place at the wrong time."

"Pretty much, and they were left in quite the predicament. So they made the decision they felt was best and now we just hope it all goes away."

Mark looked at Angela, trying to get a read.

"This is a lot to process. But I understand why they did what they did."

Mark summarized, trying to seal the deal. "Basically we have a crime that happened on foreign soil, a murder—one that Jack and Mia were simply witnesses to, nothing more. They were extorted by the

Mexican police, making them victims in all this, and they paid the money to free themselves from a very untenable position. If they had refused to cooperate they would likely still be in Mexico, possibly in jail, and I don't want to even think of what that would have been like for them. In my mind, they had no choice but to pay the money."

It made sense, Angela thought. But God, what a story!

"Yeah, I get it."

"So, can you just sit on this thing? Make it go away?"

Angela paused for several seconds, weighing her options. She thought it would be best to kill the story but she wanted to milk it a bit and earn some brownie points with Mark.

"Well, I'm inclined to do that, but I have an assignment editor asking me to investigate what happened. And we have this eyewitness calling our tip line. It might be more difficult than you think to kill the story. If I don't do it, they could easily assign someone else to do it. And then all bets are off."

"This story can't get out, Angela. No good can come from it."

"I understand all that. I'm just looking at this from a realistic standpoint. If the story got reported in the right way, highlighting Jack and Mia getting extorted-—victimized, really—then maybe it wouldn't show the RCSO in such a bad light. I'm just thinking out loud here, Mark."

"No, that wouldn't look very good and could open up all kinds of issues and questions. We don't need some federal investigation. My boss is up for reelection in a few months. He doesn't need this coming out."

As soon as he mentioned Mick and his election campaign, Mark regretted saying it. It was a mistake and made it seem like this whole thing was about Mick.

"Oh, come on, Mark. You know I don't care about that part of it. I like Mick but his reelection issues are none of my concern. Not a good reason at all to kill the story."

"I know that, Angela," he replied, trying to do damage control. "It's just another consideration in all this. Obviously, Jack and Mia are my primary concern here. This could really do a lot of damage to their careers. And I just don't see anything good coming from any of this."

"I agree. I'm just trying to figure out how best to proceed. I have to tell my assignment editor something when I get back."

"Tell her we talked and there's nothing to the story. Tell her Jack and Mia have been at work and couldn't have been in Mexico the other day."

"Well, that's a lie and I'm not comfortable doing that."

"But it's my lie, Angela, not yours. I'm the one lying to you, telling you they weren't there."

"Boy, that's some convoluted logic there, Mark."

"Yeah, but that's on me, not you. I'll fall on my sword on this one."

"I guess I can try that. I'm going to have to really sell it. Bette Alburtis is not stupid. She's going to look at me sideways, I'm sure."

"You can do it, Angela.'"

"All right."

With nothing else to say the two left Bean Crazy and walked to the parking lot. When they reached Angela's car, Mark leaned in and gave her a long hug.

"I love you, Angela."

Angela looked at Mark. She hadn't heard him say that in a long time.

"I love you, too."

On the drive back to Denver, Angela rehearsed in her mind what she'd say to Alburtis. She didn't like lying to her editor, but in this case she felt it was justified. She tried her best to concentrate on the task before her, but her mind kept going back to those four words she had just heard from Mark . . . *I love you, Angela.*

On the way back to the RCSO Mark thought about the conversation with Angela. She seemed on board with killing the story, but, as she said, her assignment editor would ultimately make the decision. He hoped Angela would be able to convince her it was a non-starter. He considered whether or not he should tell the sheriff about the Channel 8 anonymous caller and the subsequent meeting with Angela. He decided to hold off for now, at least until he heard back from Angela about the future of the story. No need to concern his boss with something that might not even happen.

CHAPTER 63

Angela walked into Bette Alburtis's office as soon as she returned to the station.

"Whatcha got for me, Angela?"

"I met with Mark Archer. He said both Keller and Serrano-McCallister have been at work for the past several days. There's no way they went to Mexico. And if they had, he said he would have been briefed about it. Looks like our anonymous caller is a crackpot."

"Shit. I thought we had a great story here."

"Yeah, me too. But it just doesn't pan out."

"So what motivates our caller to make up such an elaborate and detailed story?"

"Who knows, but it happens. There are always crazies out there looking for their fifteen minutes of fame, I guess."

"Yeah, but this guy didn't fit that bill. You heard the audio—he sounded awfully credible to me. And to have the details down so pat . . . it really makes me wonder."

Alburtis wasn't letting go.

"But if Jack and Mia have been in Colorado all this time then there's no way they were in Mexico. They have an alibi. The guy's story is bogus. Who knows, maybe he's got a beef with the RCSO. Maybe popped for a DUI or whatever—could be anything."

"Yeah, I know that happens, but this guy was so specific. It wasn't like the callers we get sometimes who are obviously just interested in slandering someone. This feels different."

"There's nothing to this, Bette. We just need to let it go."

Alburtis sat at her desk after Angela left, contemplating what she had learned from her best reporter. Would Mark Archer lie to cover up the actions of RCSO detectives? She didn't know Archer very well, having only met him a few times at social gatherings. He seemed like a straight shooter, and he had an excellent reputation as an honest media guy for the department. But if he was faced with something explosive, like a detective covering up a murder, would he still be honest and forthcoming?

She did a quick Google search on Mick McCallister and found half a dozen listings with a home address and phone number for the sheriff. She wasn't surprised at the ease with which she was able to learn this information—the Internet made virtually anything findable. There were no secrets anymore, she thought. She jotted down the phone number and left her office.

Six blocks from the Channel Eight studios was a Stop & Shop, a small market with a pay phone out front. It was the only pay phone in town, or at least the only one Alburtis knew about. She and her reporters would often use the phone when they needed to make a call that couldn't be traced.

She grabbed some quarters from her purse and dialed the number listed for Mick McCallister. She was hoping it was a landline and not McCallister's cell number.

Alburtis waited anxiously as the call went through.

"Hello."

A man's voice.

"Hello, my name is Susan Rivera and I'm calling from the Hacienda Hotel in San Martin, Mexico. May I please speak to Mia Serrano-McCallister?"

"She's not here. Can I take a message?"

"Yes, I'm calling to let her know she left her credit card here at the hotel the other day. A Visa card, and I just wanted to let her know in case she discovered the card was missing. She can either cancel the card or I'd be happy to mail it back to her."

"Oh, okay. I can let her know."

"That would be great. And tell her we look forward to seeing her again soon."

"I'll do that."

"Ummm, before you go, would you mind if I asked you a quick question?"

"Sure, what is it?"

"Here at the Hacienda we mostly cater to business guests. Do you know if she was here on business or pleasure? We are always interested in improving upon the customer experience."

"She was there on business. But I thought she stayed at the Marbella Resort in Puerto Peñasco. I didn't know she was at your hotel."

"Look, I'll get you go, I'm sure you're busy. Thanks so much for your time."

Chuck hung up the phone, puzzled by the call.

"Angela, please come back to my office."

Angela was busy reading the script for the five o'clock newscast. She wished she hadn't answered her phone; she didn't have time for Bette Alburtis.

"Can I come after the cast? I'm just going over the final script."

"It'll just take a minute. Come on back."

Angela was both frustrated and concerned by the call. She walked quickly to Alburtis's office, hoping she wanted to see her about something other than the anonymous caller. She held her breath and walked in.

Alburtis cut to the chase. "Mark Archer is not being straight with you. I know that at a minimum Mia was in Mexico a few days ago. Not sure about Keller, but given the caller's story, I'm pretty sure they were both there. We need to jump on this story, so as soon as you finish with the five, let's sit down and strategize. Amber can handle your anchor duties for the six and the ten."

"How do you know for sure?"

"I called the McCallisters' home and spoke to someone there who essentially confirmed that Mia was in Mexico."

"What? You called her? And she admitted it?"

"No, I said I was with some hotel and that Mia had left her credit card there. The guy I spoke with didn't act surprised at all, in fact he mentioned the hotel she did stay at when she was down there. That's enough confirmation for me."

Angela thought about the McCallisters. She remembered that Mia's father lived with them—he had been badly injured months earlier when a bomb was tossed into their home by Jaquon Jackson's associates. It all made sense. Alburtis had gotten lucky—she managed to reach someone other than Jack or Mia who could confirm the trip to Mexico. Angela had to give her assignment editor credit—it was genius.

"Okay, I'll get on it when I finish the five. Nice work, Bette. I'm impressed."

She replied with a wide smile. "Yeah, I took a stab at it and got lucky. What can I say?"

CHAPTER 64

Angela could barely keep her mind on the five o'clock cast; her mind was reeling with the news Bette had shared with her. She needed to let Mark know and maybe give him some time to come up with something. She didn't see any easy way out for the RCSO; the focus would need to shift to damage control for Mark and the sheriff. Jack and Mia weren't responsible for Nixon's death, they were just witnesses to it. The extortion was the sticky part—paying off Mexican authorities would definitely be an issue. But did they really have any choice in the matter? It would take a masterful job by the RCSO to get through the mess, but she knew Mark Archer was the one guy who might be able to pull it off.

As soon as she finished with the newscast, she placed a quick call to Mark to give him a heads up. She told him what had happened and that she'd be calling him again soon for an official on-the-record comment. He was stunned by what Angela told him and immediately made a beeline for Mia's office.

"Mia, you need to call your dad. I think someone called your home and had a conversation with him about your trip to Mexico."

"What? What are you talking about?"

Mark explained what Angela had told him. She made the call and put it on speaker so Mark could hear.

"Dad, it's me. Listen, did you get a call today from someone saying they were from Mexico and wanting to speak to me?"

"Yeah, you left your credit card at the hotel. She asked if you wanted it mailed back to you."

Mia and Mark looked at each other.

"What else did she say?"

"Not that much. She asked if you were there for business or pleasure. That's about all."

"What did you say?'

"I told her there you were there on business. Was I wrong to say that? Am I getting you in trouble?" Chuck asked, growing concerned.

"No, it's okay, Dad. I just needed to know exactly what was said. Anything else you can remember?"

"Yeah. She said the name of the hotel she was with down there and I said I thought you stayed at the Marbella. You did, didn't you?"

"Yeah, we did."

"Oh, God, Mia. I hope I didn't do anything to get you in trouble. I should've kept my mouth shut."

"You didn't know, Dad."

"So, who was this woman?"

"I think she was a reporter digging for information about our case."

"Oh, that doesn't sound good."

"Okay, I have to run. I'll see you when I get home."

She ended the call.

Mark sighed. "We need to brief Mick."

As the two made their way to Mick's office Mark's cell rang. He pulled it out of his pocket and saw it was Angela calling. He needed to meet with Mick before he could offer an official comment for Angela, so he let the call go to voicemail.

Mick's door was open and the two walked in. Just looking at their faces Mick knew something was up, especially when Mark closed the door behind them.

"Sit down. What's going on?"

Mark started in, "A couple hours ago I was contacted by Angela Bell telling me that Channel Eight had received an anonymous call from someone reporting that Jack Keller had murdered a man in Mexico. The story was handed to Angela and she called me to let me know."

"Oh, shit."

"So, I met with Angela and told her about the whole mess in Mexico—I really had no choice and I felt I could trust her. She understood our situation and said she'd kill the story."

"So we're in the clear?"

"I thought we were, but then Angela's assignment editor made a call to your house and spoke to Chuck. He didn't know any better and essentially confirmed that Jack and Mia were in Mexico the other day. The assignment editor has now asked Angela to pursue the story. It's going to come out, Mick. We just need to figure out how best to couch all this."

Mia said, "Dad didn't know. I'm sorry, Mick."

"Not his fault, I guess. We just need to figure out how to proceed."

"Angela said she'd need to interview me. She called me a few minutes ago but I didn't answer. I'm going to need to call her back."

"Okay, you're the media guy. What would you suggest we do?"

"This editor isn't going to let this go, so we need to respond. I think we need to come clean. Go ugly early. If we try to cover it up or dodge the questions, it'll only make it worse."

"What kind of legs will this story have?"

"If it's a slow news day, it'll go national. And probably hit CNN International because of the Mexico connection. If it's a busy news day then we could contain it somewhat, but either way we're looking at substantial coverage. Certainly statewide, at least."

"Could we delay things a day at least?"

"Yeah, I can make that happen. It's already past six so I can get Angela to stall it till tomorrow. But one way or the other we're going to have to pay the piper. It won't be any better tomorrow."

"Yeah, I know, but it'll give us a little bit of time to strategize."

"Okay, I'll call back Angela and tell her we'll have a lot more tomorrow. She'll agree to stall it in exchange for an inside angle to the story. We'll have to give her a little more than we give the other media outlets."

Mick replied, "Okay, go call her now and get that commitment from her. Then come back in here so we can figure out how the hell we're going to proceed with this thing."

Mark left the office to make the call.

"I'm really sorry, Mick. I'm sure Dad meant no harm."

"I know, Mia. It's just one of those things."

"Should we get Jack in here for the discussion on how to handle this tomorrow?"

"Yeah, I suppose so. But I sure as hell don't want him talking to any reporters. This thing will be handled by Mark and me and no one else. We gotta keep a tight lid on it."

"Well, I can't imagine anyone else here would want to talk to the media about this. I don't envy you and Mark."

"Part of the job. Not a fun part, that's for sure, but a necessary one. Text Jack and tell him we need to see him right away. I'm guessing he hasn't left for the day."

Mia sent a text to her partner and a minute later he was standing in Mick's office doorway.

"You wanted to see me, boss?"

"Yeah, come on in and close the door."

"Angela, it's me. I just spoke with the sheriff and we want to stall the story until tomorrow."

"I can do that, but tomorrow I'll have to do a full-court press. Alburtis is on my ass about this, calling me every ten minutes."

"Tell her you couldn't reach me. It's almost seven, it wouldn't be unusual for me to have left the office at this hour."

"Yeah, but she knows we have a relationship and she'll tell me to reach out to you anyway."

"Well, sometimes I don't answer my phone or reply to texts. Tonight is one of those nights."

"Gotcha. I'll check in with you in the morning then."

"Okay, thanks Angela."

Mick filled Jack in on what was happening. His response was predictable. "Screw 'em, Mick. Don't say anything to the press."

If it were only that easy, Mick thought. Keller was the best investigator he had ever known, but press relations were certainly not his thing.

As that discussion was taking place Mark returned to Mick's office.

"Angela is on board. She'll hold off on the story until tomorrow. But she's going to hit it hard in the morning."

Jack shifted in his chair and rolled his eyes. Mick noticed.

"Jack, tomorrow is going to be very unpleasant and you're going to be in the crosshairs of a lot of it. Maybe you should take some time off and go somewhere. Just get out of town for a few days."

"Why? I did nothing wrong."

"I agree, but there will be people who don't look kindly on the extortion component of this story."

"Sheriff, with all due respect, may I remind you that your wife and I were the ones being extorted. We just extricated ourselves from an impossible position. I would do the exact same thing if faced with the same situation again."

"I know that, Jack. But we'll be attacked by some in the community for how it was handled. That's just the reality of it and we—or I, actually—need to figure out how best to handle the situation."

"Here's how you handle it, sheriff. Tell them to fuck off."

Mick ignored the comment and turned back to Mark.

"So, how shall we handle this, Mr. Spokesman?"

"We need to control the message and I think the best way to do that is to create a webcast outlining what exactly happened, starting with Tracey Thompson's murder. We can leave out the skull being found in our property room, but everything else is fair game."

"Can you write up a script for me so we can record it tonight?"

"Yeah, give me an hour or so and I can get it done. I'll need to get our video team together. It'll cost some overtime."

"That's fine. Call them in."

"Okay, how about if we meet back here at nine. I can have the script ready by then and have it on the teleprompter for you."

"Do you think this webcast will deflect some of the questions reporters would ask otherwise?"

"It will if we do it right. We need to be thorough, essentially answering any and all questions they would want to ask. The local reporters will want more. They're always looking for a unique angle. But the national media will be appreciative of the webcast—it saves them time and money. They don't have to send a reporter out here to cover the story. They can just lift whatever they want from our video."

"That all works. Let's meet back here at nine, then. Jack, you're welcome to join us then or you can head on home. It's up to you. But taking a few days off might be a good idea. Just a suggestion."

"Maybe I'll do that, sheriff."

CHAPTER 65

M ark locked himself in his office and began working on the script. He organized the information chronologically, starting with Tracey Thompson's murder but leaving out the details of the skull discovered at the RCSO. He outlined the excellent investigative work that led to Jed Nixon being identified as the killer and the subsequent search that led investigators to Mexico where they found him working on a fishing boat. Mark carefully explained Nixon's murder by an unknown assailant and the extortion demands made by Mexican authorities. He hit hard the difficult position RCSO detectives found themselves in and how and why they made the decision to pay the money. He knew they would be asked about Nixon's body so he hit that head on, saying that because the murder had happened on Mexican soil the RCSO had no authority to claim the body. It was essentially true, but the fact that Jack and Mia wanted no part of dealing with Nixon's body was left out.

He went back over the script, polishing it and reading it out loud. He always found it important to hear what the words sounded like when spoken. Sometimes they came out a lot differently than he had intended on paper. A lot of it was the tone in which the words were said, but Mark had no concerns about Mick. He was a pro and understood the importance of a well-placed pause or using inflection in certain places for emphasis.

As read by Mark, the script ran a little over four minutes. A bit long, but there was a lot to say. Overall, Mark was happy with it, feeling confident that he said what needed to be said without going down any paths that would lead to unwanted questions.

He made his way back to Mick's office.

The RCSO video team was made up of four RCSO employees, all with other jobs within the department, but who had an interest in video production. When Mark Archer had seen the need for department webcasts about ten years earlier, he had cobbled together the team. The four individuals were utilized when necessary and were excited at being called in after hours. They knew something major was happening and felt like an important part of the RCSO team. And seeing their video work featured on local and national news stories was always a thrill.

The team had set up in the large conference room upstairs. They had a large green screen that gave them the capabilities to put any kind of background behind the person who was on camera. Typically this was Mark, but on occasion it was the sheriff himself. The video team had been told that Mick McCallister would be doing this video.

Mark arrived at Mick's office and found him sharing a sandwich with Mia at his desk.

"I've got your script, sheriff. You want to go over it now?"

"Yeah, send it to me so I can get it up on my laptop. What's it time out at?"

"Just over four minutes for me, probably a bit longer for you— maybe four and a half."

"Can we condense it a bit? I don't like going that long."

260

"I made it as concise as possible. If we cut anything else out I think we'll lose some of the message. But take a look at it and see what you think."

Mick got the script up on his screen and began reading aloud. He liked to read a script two or three times just to get comfortable with it. He didn't like to over-rehearse because he felt it didn't come across naturally if it was too polished. Mark timed it as Mick read.

"Four minutes, fifteen seconds. Not bad."

Mia jumped in, "I like it. It sounds great, Mark."

"Thanks. I think we cover what we need to cover. Nothing more, nothing less."

After reading it aloud one more time, Mick said he was ready to go. The three made their way to the conference room and got busy. By ten o'clock they were done and left the video team to edit it all together.

On his way home, Jack grabbed some takeout at his favorite Castle Springs Chinese restaurant. His mood was dour. He was unhappy that the media had gotten wind of the story. Fucking reporters, he thought. He drove past the local Stop & Shop and for a moment considered picking up a bottle of Southern Comfort. But he thought better of it and accelerated quickly past the store. He had been sober for more than a year and wasn't going to blow his sobriety because of this story.

The sheriff had suggested a couple days off and he considered what he might do with the time. He knew sitting home alone wasn't a good idea. The weekend was a couple of days away, so with his days off, he could stretch things to four or five days. He grabbed his cell phone and called Lisa.

It was nearly one in the morning by the time Jack arrived at the airport in Puerto Peñasco. Peter had sent the jet to Colorado to pick him up after Jack had explained what was going down in Rocklin County. Jack not only needed to get out of town, he felt obliged to let Peter know that what had played out a few days earlier in San Martin was about to be made very public. He didn't see any path that would lead to Peter's involvement being disclosed, but wanted to make sure he was aware of everything before the news hit the next day. He was hopeful that the story wouldn't make it south of the border, but as Archer had explained earlier, the Mexico connection could give it at least limited international coverage. Peter had helped Jack and Mia that day and he didn't want anything coming back on his son-in-law.

Peter was waiting in the lobby of the Marbella when Jack walked in.

"How was your flight, Jack?"

"Great. Thanks again for sending the jet. The earliest commercial flight would have me arriving late tomorrow afternoon and I just didn't want to wait that long to get down here."

"Anytime, Jack. You know that."

"Where's Lisa? She turn in already?"

"Yes, a few hours ago. She's been under the weather the past few days."

"Nothing serious, I hope."

"No, just really tired and a little stomach thing going on. Just a touch of the flu, I think."

"Sorry to hear that. Hope she's better in the morning."

"I'm sure she'll be fine. So let's chat a bit about what you told me about on the phone earlier. It sounds like it could be serious for your department."

"Yeah, I guess. The proverbial shit will hit the fan tomorrow."

CHAPTER 66

Neither Mick or Mia slept well, and by five they were both sitting in the kitchen. There was a large pot of coffee on the counter and they were on their second cups.

"Well, it should be an interesting day, huh?"

Mia looked at her husband. She was always impressed with his ability to remain calm no matter what was happening.

"That's putting it mildly. What time does Mark want to put out the webcast?"

"He said late afternoon. That forces the reporters' hands—they're more inclined to just go with what we have in the video because they're up against hard deadlines. If they get the story at four or five o'clock they know they can't put if off till tomorrow—they'll have to do something with it or run the risk of getting beat on the story by their competitors. Ideally they'll watch the video, get what they need, and do their stories without adding anything in. That way we control the message."

"So, when they call you or Mark for further comment, you guys just dodge the calls?"

"Well, it doesn't sound very nice when you put it that way, but yes, essentially that's what we'll do. But we're not really dodging anything—with the webcast we're giving them four and a half minutes of information that covers the story efficiently. That's a lot more than most agencies would offer in this kind of scenario."

"But what about Angela? She's been very cooperative with us on this."

"Mark will work with her privately and give her a little more than the other news organizations are getting. She'll come out of this looking good."

"And the other news organizations don't get upset by this?"

"They may not like it much, but that's just the way it goes. Some reporters are more aggressive than others. Angela has a reputation for being very aggressive—someone who often gets more out of a story than others."

"I know having a personal relationship with Mark helps her in these kinds of situations, but it doesn't always seem very fair to me. I mean, I appreciate what Angela does for us, but is it right?"

"I've had that conversation more than once with Mark. He says that when a big story breaks he might get fifteen or twenty calls from reporters. Maybe more if it's a national story. He has a duty as the department spokesman to return every one of those calls. But he can only return one call at a time so someone is first and someone is last. He looks at who is calling and determines the order in which he returns the calls. If you're last on the list then it could take a few hours to hear back. Angela tends to be his first callback. He trusts her and she's been more than fair with the RCSO. If there's a reporter who, in Mark's opinion, hasn't been fair to the RCSO on previous stories, then that person is the last one he calls back. Make sense?"

"Yeah, I guess so. It's a weird game."

"I agree, and I'm thankful we have a guy like Mark who handles all this for us."

Chuck walked into the kitchen carrying CJ.

"Good morning, guys. You're up nice and early."

"Good morning, Dad. Here, let me have that little bundle of joy."

Mia took CJ into her arms and lightly kissed the top of his head.

"God, I miss this little guy."

Mick looked at his wife and son and reminded himself to remember what was important. He would keep that thought in his mind as a difficult day unfolded.

Pauley had received a phone message from the HR department at the Marbella telling him he had a few more forms to fill out. His first day had gone well; Captain Watson had been accommodating and the other crew members all seemed capable. It was a much different vibe than the one on the *Dolorosa*—more upscale and much more relaxed.

He arrived in the Marbella lobby at seven hoping to find someone who could help him with the forms. There was a short line at the front desk and he took his place behind the guests. As he waited he glanced around the lobby of the hotel, taking in the expansive use of marble and glass. The place was beautiful, far nicer than any hotel he had ever been in. As he looked around he saw two men walking through the lobby toward the hotel restaurant. He did a double take, shocked by what he was seeing. As he watched the men disappear through the doors of the restaurant, he tried to process the scene. Why were the two detectives he encountered on the *Dolorosa* days earlier here at the Marbella?

He stepped out of line and walked to the restaurant. He peered through the doors, careful to stay out of the line of sight of the two men. A few moments later a waiter walked by and Pauley pointed into the restaurant, asking, "Who are those two men?"

The waiter looked at Pauley and saw that he was wearing a polo shirt with the Marbella emblem.

"That's Peter Donnelly and his father-in-law."

The waiter saw a puzzled look on Pauley's face.

"Mr. Donnelly owns the Marbella."

"Oh."

"You must be a new hire."

"Yeah, it's my second day. I work on the fishing charters."

"Well, you'll get to know Mr. Donnelly soon enough. He's a wonderful boss; very nice and friendly to everyone here."

"Okay, good to know."

Pauley headed back to his car. The forms would wait till another day.

Mark Archer arrived at work a few minutes before eight, armed with a double espresso. He checked his computer to see what kind of news day it was shaping up to be, hoping something big was breaking somewhere to away any some of the interest in the soon-to-be-released RCSO story. That would be the perfect scenario—have a major story break around four that afternoon and then put out the news release and webcast a few minutes later.

He thought about Angela and how he would handle Channel 8 on the story. He owed Angela, but he wasn't sure what new or additional information he could really offer her. The sheriff said about all that could be said in the video. The best he could do for Angela would be to give her the webcast earlier than everyone else, giving her an opportunity to put together a much more in-depth story. If he released the video at five, the other media outlets would scramble to get something for their six and ten o'clock newscasts. Angela would have her story ready to go and might even get it into the five o'clock cast, creating a breaking news splash. He'd have to have Angela agree to holding it till at least five thirty. He felt confident she'd be happy with the arrangement.

Pauley was still reeling from his cousin's death. He had no idea who had fired the fatal shot but he suspected that Jed's involvement in the killing of the snitch had something to do with it.

And now it turned out that two of the three people on the *Dolorosa* that day weren't even law enforcement? One was the owner of the fancy resort he was now working at and the other guy was his father-in-law. It made no sense—what were they doing that day coming aboard the *Dolorosa*? And who was the third person, the pretty woman who had accompanied the older guy on the boat?

He tried to make sense of it all but things just weren't adding up. He thought back to how things had transpired that day. The older guy and the woman were first to board the boat. The third person, Peter Donnelly, didn't come until later, and he was the one that brought the cash for the payoff. The couple had obviously called him and it didn't take long for him to arrive. So why would the owner of the Marbella come down and provide the money for a payoff?

Why did these three not want Jed's death to be discovered? They hadn't killed him. The older man and woman were merely witnesses, just like Pauley was. What were they hiding?

The more interesting question was if the owner of the Marbella resort was willing to pay off the police, wouldn't he be inclined to pay even more if faced with the threat of the murder becoming public? Seven thousand dollar seemed like a lot of money that day, but to a guy like Peter Donnelly it was probably chump change. And besides, Pauley had only received a thousand bucks in the deal. And it was his cousin who had been killed!

Maybe Peter Donnelly needed to pay up again to keep the murder quiet. Pauley began contemplating how exactly this could be accomplished.

CHAPTER 67

The day was largely uneventful at the RCSO. Mick, Mia, and Mark all went about their normal business waiting for the late afternoon to arrive. Mark had sent the webcast to Angela so she could put together her story in advance of the official release at five o'clock. She had pushed him for more but he'd held firm and she was eventually satisfied with the arrangement. She would have a lengthy and detailed story ready to go for the breaking news segment that would come midway through the five o'clock newscast.

Bette Alburtis knew nothing about Angela's arrangement with Mark and was constantly badgering Angela to get on the story. Angela assured her she was doing everything she could, but that the RCSO was holding firm to its story that their two detectives were not in Mexico and had no knowledge of Jed Nixon's death. She told Bette she was working a couple of different angles on the story and was confident she would have something by the end of the day. Bette pushed her hard for details but Angela was keeping her at bay.

Initially, Angela had considered letting Bette in on the secret arrangement she had made with Mark but thought better of it. Bette would likely order her to go public with the story well before the five o'clock agreement, enabling Channel 8 to get a huge leg up on the competition. But that would certainly anger Mark and she wasn't willing to take that risk. And if Angela refused to cooperate, Alburtis would simply hand the story off to another reporter. Angela didn't want that to happen; losing control over how the story would be presented was one issue, but losing the story for herself was another.

She had watched the webcast three times, trying to find a unique angle that would tell the story and, at the same time, let the RCSO come out looking okay. She kept reminding herself that Jack and Mia were not responsible for Nixon's death. An unknown assailant had murdered him. And that, she decided, would be the angle she'd pursue. Who killed Jed Nixon? She could make that work.

She texted Mark and within a minute had a return call from him.

"What's up, Angela?'

"Hey, I'm working the story and I think I have the angle I want to pursue."

"Okay, what's your angle?" Mark asked hesitantly.

"Obviously, I need to explain what happened in Mexico, but once I do, I want to totally shift the focus onto who killed Jed Nixon. I mean, there's a killer on the loose, and who knows—he could certainly have ties to Colorado."

"That sounds great, Angela," replied Mark, relieved.

"But I need to know more about the murder. Some details that no one else would know, and any RCSO theories on what might have happened."

Mark considered what Angela was saying. She was being more than fair with him and he felt he could deliver what she was asking.

"Okay, I can do that, provided it'll shift the focus off Jack and Mia."

"So what can you tell me?"

Mark thought for a moment.

"You could also play up the outstanding detective work that led us to Mexico. That might be of interest to your viewers as well."

"Absolutely, I can do that. So, whatcha got?"

Mark spent the next fifteen minutes outlining the case for Angela.

Pauley considered blowing off work and calling in sick. But he thought better of it and decided to work his shift. He was developing a plan and if things went well he would no longer need to work on any Mexican fishing charters. He could return to his home in Tucson and figure out the next steps in his life.

He knew that demanding more extortion money from a powerful man like Peter Donnelly was a dangerous game, but he was willing to take the risk. Donnelly had gotten off cheap. Pauley needed to extract a much larger sum. Not a crazy amount, but something that would allow him to return home.

But how to proceed? A letter to Donnelly outlining his demands? A face-to-face meeting where he presented those demands in person?

If Pauley sent a letter, Donnelly could choose to ignore it although it would certainly get his attention. A guy like that wasn't used to being pushed around. But an in-person meeting would be tough to ignore. And he could get a read from Donnelly if they met in person. But how did a deckhand on a Marbella fishing boat get a face-to-face meeting with the owner of the place?

He didn't, was the logical conclusion. It would need to be a chance meeting. And he wouldn't wait—the meeting would happen at the end of his shift.

Jack was in the Marbella dining room enjoying his first cup of coffee.

"Good morning, Dad! How're you doing?"

Jack looked up to see his daughter, Lisa, standing at the table. He stood and embraced her.

"I didn't even see you come in!"

"You looked deep in thought. Everything okay?"

"Yes, of course. Just thinking about some work stuff."

"Well, you're at the Marbella now. Work thoughts are not allowed."

"Got it. So, Peter tells me you've been a bit under the weather?"

"Oh, I'm fine. Just a little tired and fighting a stomach bug. Nothing serious."

"Well, get plenty of rest and drink a lot of fluids."

"Thanks, doc. Geez, you sound just like my husband."

"Sit down. Have a cup of coffee with your old man."

Lisa took a seat at the table.

"So, I was a little surprised by your visit. Don't get me wrong—I love it, but it was unplanned."

Jack considered sharing with Lisa about what could be coming—the publicity about Nixon's murder and the coverup. But there was no guarantee the news would reach Mexico so he didn't see the benefit of worrying his daughter needlessly.

"Yeah, just some work stuff. Following up on what Mia and I were doing down here the other day."

"How long will you be here?"

"Probably until Sunday. I need to get back to work on Monday."

"That's great, Dad. I wish you'd visit more often."

"Well, you've got me now, at least for the next few days."

"So, what are your plans today? You said you have work to do?"

"I do, but it can wait a bit. I may want to do a little fishing today."

"Oh, you should. Just let the concierge know and Marcie will take care of everything."

CHAPTER 68

Mick tried his best to stay focused on his workday, but thoughts of what would be transpiring later that afternoon crowded his mind. The idea that his detectives, including his wife, could somehow be accused of murder was ludicrous. He hoped the public agreed with him but he knew that those with an axe to grind with the RCSO, or with law enforcement in general, would have a field day with it. He had seen it all before.

He picked up his phone and dialed Ron Calkins. He needed to alert the chairman of his re-election campaign committee about the news that was about to break.

"Hey, sheriff, how you doing today?"

Calkins was a wealthy Colorado rancher who lived in the western portion of Rocklin County. There were more cattle than people and Calkins liked it that way. He was a quiet, thoughtful man who had met Mick and Mia at a charity dinner years earlier. He had seen something special in Mick and the two had become fast friends. Four years earlier, when Mick had confided in Calkins that he was considering a run for sheriff, Calkins had committed both his time and considerable financial resources to the effort.

"Doing fine, Ron. How's the family?"

"Just got news that grandchild number three is on the way. Janis is thrilled."

"I'm sure she is, but I'm guessing Ron is pretty tickled as well."

"Yeah, I am. Nothing better than grandchildren. You should try it, Mick."

"I figure I'm at least a couple decades from those days. But it'll be great, no doubt."

"So, what can I do for you, sheriff?"

Mick told Calkins what had happened in Mexico, giving him a heads up about would likely be a big story by the end of the day. Calkins offered his unwavering support and said he'd personally call each of the other members of Mick's re-election committee to let them know. Mick thanked him, hung up, and tried his best to get back to work.

Jack boarded the *Top Shelf* just after nine and introduced himself to Captain PJ Watson. Watson knew who Jack was but played it like he was unaware of the connection between Jack and Peter. Jack would be given top-notch treatment on board the *Top Shelf*, but Watson didn't want it to seem like he and his crew were doing that because of the connection to the owner of the Marbella. He prided himself on treating every customer like royalty.

After the introduction, Jack walked into the galley, took a seat at the counter, and ordered himself a large coffee.

The woman behind the counter stuck out her hand and introduced herself.

"Hi, I'm Catrina Schambra. Welcome aboard."

"Hi, Catrina. I'm Jack."

"Is this your first time onboard the *Top Shelf*?" she asked.

"No, I've been on a couple of trips with you guys. But it's been awhile."

"Well, I hope you catch your limit today. Fishing's been good."

"That's good to hear, but to tell you the truth I just enjoy being out here. If I catch something, that's a bonus."

"I totally get it. And not the first time I've heard that."

"There's something about being on the water. I know we're not that far from shore, but it seems like a different world out here."

"Yep, my sentiments exactly."

Jack looked at the woman behind the counter. She was attractive and had a soulful quality about her. He felt a little stirring.

"How long have you been working on the *Top Shelf*?"

"Just a few months. Moved down here from northern Nevada."

"Nice. I'm from Colorado."

"Denver?"

"Near Denver. Castle Springs, just a little south."

"I've heard of it. Did some skiing a few years back at Breckenridge. It's beautiful there."

"It is. Most of the major ski resorts are a couple hours west of me."

"Do you ski?"

"I used to, but haven't in awhile."

"You should get out there again and give it a try."

Jack thought about the bullet still in his hip. Skiing was probably not in his future, but he didn't want to explain any of that to the pretty woman behind the counter.

"Maybe I will."

Catrina smiled at him.

Jack returned the smile and took a quick glance at her hand.

No wedding ring.

CHAPTER 69

Angela spent the morning putting things together for her five o'clock breaking news story. It was long, running nearly three minutes, but most of it covered the good detective work that led Jack and Mia to Mexico. She downplayed, as best she could, Jed Nixon's murder. She felt confident that the RCSO, and more importantly, Mark would be happy with her story.

Mark Archer spent his morning drafting a press release outlining the series of events in Mexico and referencing the webcast that he'd attach to the release. His plan was to send it out at 5:05 pm; he hoped that many of the television news stations might miss it as it came in. Their attention would be on their live five o'clock newscasts and the release might sit in email inboxes for a while before being noticed. Channel Eight would be the exception.

Jack finished his coffee, bid Catrina a good day, and made his way to the back of the *Top Shelf*. The boat was already a few miles off shore and it was a beautiful day, perfect for fishing. But as he had told Catrina, it was just nice to be out on the ocean away from everything. He had heard from Mia via text message, letting him know that the news release would be going out around five o'clock Colorado time.

That made it four o'clock in Mexico, just about the time the *Top Shelf* would be coming in for the day.

He took a seat at the back of the boat and stared out at the shoreline. There were a handful of other guests aboard, eight in total. A couple of young men were sitting at the back of the boat and they offered Jack a quick introduction. After brief pleasantries, Jack settled back into his thoughts, staring back at the land as it got further and further away. Those thoughts were interrupted when a crew member came by, asking the two young men what kind of fishing they would like to do. Both said they were interested in catching a sailfish, so the crew member handed off the proper gear. Then the deckhand turned to Jack and asked him the same question.

Jack looked up, making eye contact with the young man.

"Nothing right now, I'm just enjoying the ride. Maybe a little later."

"Okay, just let me or Pauley know and we'll fix you up."

Jack did a double take at the man. "Did you say 'Pauley'?"

"Yeah, he's the other deckhand working today. Either one of us can set you up with anything you need. Just let us know."

"Okay, thanks," Jack replied.

Pauley? What were the odds, he asked himself. How many Pauleys could there be working fishing charters in Mexico? His mind raced through what it could mean if the Pauley on board the *Top Shelf* was Jed Nixon's cousin.

Jack got up from his seat and began walking around the boat. He needed to get a look at the other deckhand to see if it was indeed Pauley. He moved carefully, determined to see Pauley before Pauley saw him. He glanced around as he moved toward the bow of the boat. He passed by the other guests, nodding at each as he went by. As he went by the galley he looked in and saw Catrina. She gave him a little smile and a wave. He returned the wave, then moved on. As he reached the bow he saw the other deckhand. His back was to Jack so he couldn't be sure if it was Pauley or not. Jack stopped, moved as close to a side wall as possible, and waited for the man to turn around.

Several seconds passed before the deckhand turned toward a customer to answer a question.

Shit, thought Jack. It was Pauley.

Jack moved quickly back toward the stern, calculating what all this meant.

From the events that occurred on the *Dolorosa* days earlier, Pauley knew Jack was a detective from Colorado. Pauley knew he had nothing to do with Jed's death. He knew about the extortion demands made by the local police and had personally benefited from them, pocketing a thousand dollars. So, as far as Pauley was concerned, maybe Jack was just doing a little fishing while in Mexico. But Jed Nixon's murder had occurred several days earlier so why was Jack still in Mexico? Maybe he took advantage of the situation and stayed down there to enjoy some vacation time? It was feasible but sounded a little far-fetched to Jack. But then again, Pauley wasn't the sharpest. Maybe Pauley wouldn't remember him and there was nothing to worry about. But if he did remember him, so what? If anyone had a reason to be worried it was Pauley; he had taken a thousand dollar bribe in exchange for his silence. When the news about what had occurred broke later in the day would it reach Mexico? Would Pauley even hear the news? He was a deckhand on a fishing boat—was he really tuned in to world events courtesy of CNN International? And if he did happen to see the news what would he learn? The fact that Jack and Mia were cops down in Mexico looking for Jed would be confirmed. The bribe would become public, but that reflected poorly on Pauley more than Jack or Mia. The worst part would be that Peter's role in everything could become public, opening him up for criticism and possibly more extortion attempts.

Jack considered his next move. There was no doubt that Pauley would eventually see him; it was a relatively small boat with only eight customers. Given that, he decided to get the jump on Pauley. Maybe the element of surprise would give him some clue as to what the day might hold. He walked back to the bow of the boat and saw Pauley helping another customer with his gear.

"Excuse me, can you give me a hand when you're done there?"

"Sure, I'll be with—"

Pauley froze mid-sentence as he looked up at Jack.

"Hi there, Pauley. How are you doing today?"

"I'm . . . uhhh . . . I'm good."

Pauley clearly remembered him.

Jack continued animatedly, "Great day for some fishing, huh?"

"Yeah, it should be good . . . "

"Looking forward to it. Maybe you can get me set up with my gear when you get a second."

"Ummm, sure. Be with you in a few minutes."

"Okay, I'll be back at the stern. Great to see you, man."

Pauley walked into the galley before going to meet Jack at the back of the boat. He needed some coffee and wanted a few minutes to gather his thoughts.

"Black coffee, Pauley?" asked Catrina.

"Yeah, thanks."

Catrina poured him a large cup and handed it to him. She looked at Pauley and noticed the concerned expression on his face.

"Everything okay? You look a little spooked."

"I'm fine."

"You don't look so fine."

"I'm okay, damnit. Mind your own business!"

"Geez, Pauley. Sorry I asked."

Pauley looked at Catrina and regretted snapping at her.

"I'm sorry, it's just that one of the customers . . . I sorta know the guy."

"Okay, and?"

Pauley realized he was probably saying too much. "It's nothing. Forget it. No big deal."

"Okay, no worries," Catrina said, wiping down the counter.

Pauley sat at the counter and drank his coffee in silence. He had just a few minutes before he needed to find the Colorado cop and set up his gear.

He tried to sort things out in his head. The Colorado cop was on board the *Dolorosa*. He was also reportedly the father-in-law of the owner of the Marbella. So, was he really a cop? If not, why did he come aboard the *Dolorosa* moments before Jed was killed? Was he really Peter Donnelly's father-in-law? The employee he had met earlier that day had told him he was, so there was really no reason to doubt it. But if he wasn't a cop, why was he onboard the *Dolorosa* that day saying he was? And why did he allow himself to be extorted?

The only reason he could think of for going along with the extortion demands would be that he was a cop and wanted to free himself from a bad situation. He and the woman he was with hadn't done anything wrong but Pauley knew the Mexican authorities could have caused some big problems for the two of them. So, maybe he was both a cop and Donnelly's father-in-law. He thought back to the *Dolorosa* and remembered that the cop and his female partner had made a phone call and soon after Donnelly showed up with the money. They identified Donnelly as another cop. But thinking about it now, he realized that it was odd that another cop could be called and show up with seven grand in cash a half hour later.

So, Pauley theorized, the two cops needed money to get out of a bad situation and called Donnelly, the guy's son-in-law. Donnelly delivered the goods and the three walked away, seemingly free of the situation. This theory lent itself well to Pauley's plan to further extort Peter Donnelly. If he had been part of all this, then he was probably good for more money.

So was there any risk to him with the cop being onboard the *Top Shelf*? Like the Colorado cops, Pauley hadn't done anything wrong that day as far as the murder. Granted he had benefited from the extortion, but that wasn't on his initiative. He was a witness to his cousin's death, a murder that he still didn't fully understand with respect to motive.

Pauley finished his coffee and made his way to the back of the boat to find the cop.

Jack stood at the stern staring out at the shoreline, which was now barely visible. He heard someone walking toward him, glanced over, and saw Pauley approaching.

He stuck out his hand and said, "I don't think we've officially met. My name is Jack Keller."

The two shook hands.

"I'm Pauley," he replied weakly.

"So, you've changed boats? No more *Dolorosa*?"

"Yeah, I started here yesterday. After what happened . . . "

Pauley stopped, thinking he didn't need to bring up the events on the *Dolorosa*.

Jack pushed a little more. "I understand. Sorry about your cousin."

"How do you know he was my cousin?"

"The reason my partner and I came aboard the boat that day was to take him into custody. As we explained that day, we're detectives from Colorado. We knew a lot about your cousin."

Pauley looked around, making sure he was out of earshot of the other anglers.

"Do you know who killed him?"

"I have a pretty good idea. I think he was taken out for being a snitch."

Pauley looked at Jack; their theories matched up.

"So, you're investigating Jed's death?"

"Of course."

Pauley was surprised by the direction of the conversation. Jack could see a softening in Pauley and took it as an opportunity to make some inroads with him. Jack wasn't sure what, if anything, might come with the possible publicity about Nixon's death, but it couldn't hurt if he made peace with Pauley.

He continued, "Pauley, we don't judge people; if someone gets murdered then it becomes a top priority to find the killer. Your cousin's death is no exception."

Pauley didn't say anything. He got Jack's gear set up and handed him the pole.

"Let me know if you need anything."

"I will, Pauley. Thanks for the help."

As the afternoon hours passed, Mark Archer began to imagine various scenarios. It was his practice to anticipate, as best he could, the questions he would likely be asked in difficult media situations. Generally, he closed the door to his office and practice his responses out loud. He practiced not only the words he'd use, but the inflection as well. The way he said things was just as important as the words he used.

After thirty minutes of practice, he felt ready to address reporters. He checked his watch; it was just past four thirty. He gathered up his notes and with a printed copy of the press release he'd be sending and made his way to Mick's office.

CHAPTER 70

The fishing on board the *Top Shelf* was brisk; the passengers had landed two sailfish along with quite a few sea bass and yellowtail—more than two dozen fish in total. Jack had three yellowtail to his credit and was enjoying the day. He had a few more brief exchanges with Pauley, all of which were pleasant.

Around three o'clock the captain came on the loudspeaker and asked everyone to pull up their lines; they were returning to shore. Each angler did as asked and then headed to the galley for some drinks. Catrina was waiting for the eight men with an assortment of Mexican beers and pitchers of margaritas.

Pauley got busy cleaning fish and thought more about all that had transpired between him and Jack Keller. Their conversation had shed light on what had happened on the *Dolorosa* that day and it all made sense. But their conversation had not covered anything about Peter Donnelly. Pauley considered asking Keller about the man who brought the money to the boat that day, but thought better of it. Bringing Donnelly into the mix could mean trouble, he thought.

He thought more about the extortion demand he planned to make of Donnelly once they returned to the Marbella. Now, knowing Keller was indeed a cop and had ties to Donnelly, he began rethinking the idea of extorting his boss. Perhaps it wasn't the best idea. He had a pretty good gig with the Marbella, the first couple days had been easy and if the tips he received his first day were any indication, he'd do pretty well financially.

If he did go through with his plans to extort Donnelly, Keller would certainly get involved. But beyond that, Pauley worried that a man like Donnelly was very likely connected with powerful people, including the local police. If the extortion demands were rejected and Donnelly told the local cops what happened, Pauley could quickly find himself in hot water. He didn't want to see the inside of a Mexican prison.

Keller avoided the galley as he had no reason to be around alcohol. He thought about Catrina and hoped he'd have a chance to speak to her again before departing the *Top Shelf*. She was attractive, fun, and interesting—definitely someone he'd talk to Peter about when the time was right.

He walked to the stern and found Pauley cleaning fish.

"Pretty good day, huh, Pauley?"

"Yeah, yesterday was about the same. This boat seems to have better luck than the *Dolorosa*."

"Those sailfish were a nice score for those guys. God, they were excited."

"Like a couple of little kids."

"Yeah, that's cool, though. Made their whole trip."

Pauley continued working on cleaning the yellowtail, sea bass, and grouper.

"Do you want your yellowtail cut in fillets?"

"Yeah, that'll be great. Probably grill 'em up tonight for dinner."

Pauley saw an opening to bring up Peter Donnelly, but thought better of it. He continued working.

Jack looked at the shore, which was coming into clearer focus now. Wouldn't be long before they were back to the pier. As he looked at the smooth water, he noticed something. He stepped toward the railing for a better look.

"Oh, shit. You'd better call the captain."

Pauley looked over at Jack. "Why, what is it?"

Jack motioned toward the water. Pauley stepped to the railing and looked out. Not forty yards away, on the port side of the *Top Shelf*, was a very bloated body bobbing in the water.

"You ready, boss?"

The sheriff looked up and saw Mark standing in the doorway to his office. Mick was at his desk working on budget reports but hadn't had much success focusing on the numbers. His mind was consumed with the news that was about to hit—an accusation that his top detective had committed murder in Mexico.

Mick felt confident that he and Mark had put together a good strategy for addressing the issue, but with the media you just never knew. A rogue reporter looking to make a name for himself could wreak havoc on a story. The facts could be clear as day but if a reporter was determined to make a story go a certain way, it was a difficult thing to combat.

He thought back to an incident from a few years earlier. The RCSO had been part of a deadly officer-involved shooting and a particular Denver reporter was determined to make the department look bad. The facts were that an individual had run over several people in his truck and was about to hit many more in a busy fast food restaurant parking lot when he was shot and killed by deputies. They had no choice but to stop him as he sped toward the crowd. They opened fire, killing the driver, and the truck rolled to a stop before hitting anyone.

A reporter interviewed Mark Archer at the scene and asked him why the deputies had killed an "unarmed" man. Mark explained that the truck the man was using to run people down was in fact a deadly weapon under the law and that the deputies had acted properly.

The reporter insisted that because the driver didn't have a gun, he was unarmed. Archer patiently explained over and over that her thinking was flawed, and that a six-thousand-pound truck, when used to run people over, was indeed a weapon, but she wouldn't budge. Sure enough, the story led with "Deputies kill unarmed man" and the department got some grief from those who only read headlines. The department was able to get past the reporter's biased reporting but it was something that Mark Archer had to deal with.

"Yeah, come on in."

Archer stepped in and took a seat. Mick looked at his watch and said, "It's a little past five. We ready to go?"

"Yep, I can send the press release and webcast from my phone. Shall we let it rip?"

"Yeah, go ahead. You're listed as the contact, correct?"

"No, actually I put you down, with your home address and phone. That's okay, isn't it?"

"Such a smart ass. Aren't you due for a performance evaluation right about now?"

"Yes, sir, I believe I am."

"Good, I'll make sure your sarcasm is noted."

Mark smiled and grabbed his phone from his pocket.

"Ready, boss?'

"Yeah."

Mark hit *send* and the wheels were in motion.

CHAPTER 71

Captain Watson radioed the local authorities to let them know about the body in the water. Within fifteen minutes they were fishing Jed Nixon's body out of the water. The captain didn't want his passengers seeing what was going on so he kept the boat at bay, making sure the view from the galley, where everyone had gathered for an impromptu happy hour, didn't include the scene playing out forty yards away.

Watson had quietly asked Catrina to keep the men occupied, and free drinks had done the trick. While everyone was in the galley, Keller stood on the stern, watching the proceedings. It had been days since Nixon had been "buried at sea," and Jack knew that bodies seldom stayed at the bottom of a body of water. People often thought that as long as the body was weighed down, it would never surface, but Jack knew better. When bodies decomposed, the gasses produced would cause the body to bloat. And when bodies got bloated, they became very buoyant.

Jack looked at Nixon's body as they brought it onboard the small police boat. The body was at least double its normal size and there were pieces missing. Jack was surprised the sharks hadn't finished it off, but from the looks of it, some had tried. He thought about what the discovery of Nixon's body might mean. It was the local police who had extorted money for the coverup and so Jack figured Nixon's body would be disposed of quietly and efficiently. No need to make a big deal of it, he thought. The less said, the better.

In any event, he thought he should let Mark Archer know. He sent him a quick text. A minute later his cell rang; Archer's number popped up on the screen.

"Keller."

"That's a helluva a text message to get, Jack."

"Yeah, thought I should pass it along."

"So Nixon's body just popped up? And you saw it?"

Jack chuckled, "Yep, about forty feet from the fishing charter I'm on right now. Crazy, right?"

"That's unbelievable."

"I don't think it's anything to worry about. The Mexican cops took it away, and it's not like they want to draw any attention to it. They'll dispose of it and that'll be the end of it. But I thought you should know in the unlikely event the media gets wind of it."

Archer considered what Jack was saying. He agreed that there was little chance the discovery of Nixon's body would be publicized.

"Yeah, I think we'll be fine. But thanks for letting me know. How's the fishing down there today?"

"Caught a couple of nice yellowtail. Should make for a nice dinner."

"That sounds good. Oh, before I let you go, if by chance the Nixon murder makes the news down there, would you let me know? I need to keep my eye on things."

"Sure, I'll keep you posted. See you next week."

"Thanks."

Within ten minutes of sending the release, Mark Archer's cell began to ring. He let the calls go to voicemail, determined to give Angela and Channel 8 a decent head start. She already had the story and would do her breaking news at five thirty, but Mark saw no reason to give other reporters any kind of break. The timing of it all was critical.

Channel 8 news was in a commercial break when Angela took her spot in the newsroom. The backdrop of reporters and editors working hard at their desks was the look she wanted. Soon, the anchor would breathlessly announce they had breaking news and would throw it to Angela.

"Coming back to Brett in thirty, Angela."

She nodded at the floor director as she did a quick check of her makeup using a small compact she always kept close by. A fresh application of lip gloss and she was ready to go.

"Five, four . . . "

Hand signals silently provided the *three, two, one.*

The anchor looked into the camera and, with his most serious look, said, "Channel Eight has just learned of a new development in a story involving the Rocklin County Sheriff's Department. Angela Bell is in the newsroom with more. Angela, what can you tell us?"

The director cut to a full-screen shot of Angela.

"Brett, we just received word that the RCSO's search for Jed Nixon, a person of interest in the murder of Castle Springs resident Tracey Thompson, has ended. Nixon was reportedly killed in the seaside fishing village of San Martin, Mexico, a few days ago. The details of what exactly happened in Mexico are still sketchy, but Channel Eight has learned that Nixon was murdered by an unknown assailant while working on a fishing boat. The story takes a bizarre twist as RCSO detectives Jack Keller and Mia Serrano-McCallister, wife of RCSO Sheriff Mick McCallister, were present when the murder occured. The two were there to take Nixon into custody for Thompson's murder. But just seconds before they could make that arrest, Nixon was shot and killed, evidently by someone firing a weapon from a nearby pier."

Brett chimed in, "Angela, that's an incredible turn of events. So the gunman is still at large?"

"Yes, that's correct. The RCSO is busy now trying to determine who the shooter was, but with the murder happening nearly a thousand miles away, the investigation is proving to be a difficult one."

Viewers now saw both Brett and Angela on a split screen. Brett asked, "Angela, you mentioned that Jack Keller, the well-known RCSO homicide detective was, at one point, actually suspected of killing Nixon himself?"

"Yes. In fact, yesterday Channel Eight received an anonymous tip that Detective Keller had shot and killed Nixon, but there is no evidence to support that. However, Keller was there, along with Mia Serrano-McCallister. Both witnessed the murder."

"This story just gets stranger and stranger. So, what's next for the RCSO in the hunt for Nixon's killer?"

Angela answered, "Just minutes ago I was able to speak with Mark Archer, the spokesman for the RCSO. He told me that finding Nixon's killer was a top priority for the department and that they actually had personnel back in Mexico right now trying to gather evidence."

"Was the RCSO able to bring back Nixon's body?"

"No, the Mexican authorities took possession of the body, which is not unusual given that the murder happened on Mexican soil."

Brett asked, "So things such as ballistics, which can often assist detectives in murder cases, won't be available since there's no body?"

"That's correct, Brett. This case will be very challenging for the RCSO. A body can provide many clues, but in this case, with no body, the RCSO is at a distinct disadvantage."

"Okay, Angela—thanks so much for bringing this story to light. It's no doubt something that we will follow in the hours and days to come."

Mick and Mark sat in the sheriff's office watching the Channel 8 report.

"That went pretty well, I'd say," commented Mick. "No cringeworthy moments."

"Yeah, Angela came through for us. Now we just need to hope the other stations and the *Denver Post* do the same."

"Yeah, the *Post* is always a wild card."

Mark responded, "It just depends on which reporter gets the story. If Sylvia Paniagua catches it I think we'll be fine. She's objective and has always given us a fair shake. If Becky Hansen gets the story, then we'll have problems. She's always had it in for law enforcement. She's a pain in the ass."

"So, how many calls have you received so far?"

Mark checked his smart watch.

"Looks like sixteen emails and five voicemails. A pretty large response given it's only been forty-five minutes since the release went out. Looks like the story is going to have legs, sheriff."

"Shit. How will you respond?"

"I'll return each call, keeping deadlines in mind. Normally I do my best to accommodate reporters' deadlines, but in this case I'll wait until just past the deadlines to return the calls."

"You're a sneaky bastard, Archer."

"Yeah, I have my moments."

CHAPTER 72

Jack was back at the Marbella by five, sitting with Lisa in her living room.

"How was the fishing, Dad?"

"It was great. Caught a couple nice yellowtail. I thought maybe we could grill 'em up for dinner."

"You know, yellowtail are typically used for sushi. I can call our sushi chef and have him prepare something for us. Does that sound good?"

"I'm not eating raw fish. Sorry, sweetie, but my preference is to grill 'em."

Lisa smiled at her father. "Okay, Dad. That's fine. We can have a nice salad, too."

"What's that I hear about yellowtail?"

Jack and Lisa turned and saw Peter coming into the room.

"Hey, honey, you're home early."

"Well, get used to it. I may soon be getting home earlier and earlier. Probably going to drive you crazy."

Jack looked at Peter, unsure of what Peter was talking about. "What's going on?"

Lisa explained. "Peter is going to hire a CEO to run the Marbella and all the other businesses. He'll still be available for consultation but the day-to-day stuff will be left to the new person."

"Really, Peter? I didn't realize you were wanting to turn the reins over to someone else."

"I've been thinking about it for awhile. In fact, I spent the afternoon interviewing potential candidates. Found a couple that could work."

Lisa looked at her husband. "Really? That's great! When can they start?"

"I still have a few others to interview, but I think within the next few weeks I could have someone on board. But there will be a transition period, probably a few months."

"Well, it sounds like we have something to celebrate tonight," responded Jack.

"That, and Dad had some success today on the *Top Shelf.*"

"Yeah, yellowtail, huh?'

"Yep, hoping to grill tonight. Sound okay?"

"Of course. How about you and I handle the fish and Lisa can prepare whatever else she wants to serve it with? Something healthy, I'm guessing."

"That'll work."

"Let me grab something to drink and then maybe you and I can get busy out on the patio."

Lisa left the two men and went to the kitchen to figure out what to serve with fish. Peter grabbed a beer and handed Jack an iced tea. The two went out onto the patio where Peter turned on the large television mounted on the wall.

"Any word on the events in Colorado today?"

"I haven't heard anything yet."

"Let's check if it's getting any coverage."

"The news release went out about ninety minutes ago. At least, that's what they had planned. Might be too early still."

"Let's put it on and keep an eye on things."

Peter found CNN International and both men took a look. The screen was filled with footage of a hurricane that had hit the Caribbean earlier that day.

Jack said, "Maybe they'll be busy with that and not cover our stuff. That would be ideal, huh?"

"We can only hope."

CHAPTER 73

Sylvia Paniagua sat at her desk at the *Denver Post* reading a very detailed story on the Channel 8 website about Jed Nixon's murder. The *Post* had received a press release and video from the RCSO outlining a series of bizarre events that had occurred a few days earlier in Mexico. Paniagua barely had enough time to read the release and watch the video and now she was reading an article that was easily twelve hundred words. She wondered how they could have put something together so quickly. Either some very good reporting or Channel 8 had an in with someone at the RCSO. She had heard rumors about Angela Bell and Mark Archer. It looked to Paniagua that maybe Channel 8 had gotten a little heads up in advance of the story. There was no way they could put this story together so quickly otherwise.

Reading through the story a second time she could see that the focus of the article was centered on the search for Jed Nixon's killer. The actual murder of Nixon on a Mexican fishing boat, with two RCSO detectives present, wasn't mentioned until the fourth paragraph. To Paniagua, it was a clear case of Channel 8 burying the lead. It could be a rookie error by a Channel 8 reporter or it was something done intentionally. The lead in this story was obvious—the murder of a man wanted by police in front of two RCSO detectives. She scrolled back to the top of the article and saw it had been written by Angela Bell. It was no rookie error, she thought. This was an effort by one of the most experienced reporters in Denver to intentionally draw attention away from the RCSO being present when the murder had occurred. But why?

The only answer she could come up with was the cozy relationship between Channel 8 and the RCSO, specifically between Archer and Bell. She checked the websites of the *Post*'s other media competitors and saw that no one else had the story up yet.

Paniagua sat at her desk and pondered the events on the fishing boat, allowing the scene to play out in her head. Nixon had been shot and killed by an unknown assailant in front of Jack Keller and Mia Serrano-McCallister. The two detectives returned to Colorado, case closed. Their primary suspect in the murder of Tracey Thompson was dead. How convenient, she thought. But where was the body?

She picked up her cell and scrolled through her contact list looking for a number for Mark Archer. She had had many conversations with the RCSO spokesman during her time reporting for the *Post*. Archer's name popped up quickly and she hit dial. The call went to voicemail so she left a message.

"Hello, Lieutenant Archer, this is Sylvia Paniagua from the *Denver Post*. I received your press release and video this afternoon and I have a couple of quick questions for you. Specifically, I'm wondering what happened to Jed Nixon's body. Did the RCSO take possession of it? Also, I'd like to talk a little bit about your detectives being down in Mexico, essentially the mechanics of being in another country on an investigation for a crime that happened on American soil. If you could give me a call back at your earliest convenience I'd greatly appreciate it. I'm on a tight deadline. Again, my name is Sylvia Paniagua from the *Post*. My number is 303-555-6412."

It was a little past eight when Mark Archer checked his voicemails. Since five o'clock when the release had gone out, he had been inundated with texts and emails, which over the years had become the most common forms of communication between him and reporters. He liked putting his responses to reporters' questions in writing to reduce the chance of being misquoted. He found that any reporter under the age of thirty-five was comfortable with this approach, but the older, more seasoned reporters didn't like it at all. They preferred a real conversation, one where they could pick and choose the quotes they liked best. There was a flow to those exchanges, giving reporters more of a chance to steer the conversation the way they wanted. Mark, of course, preferred it the other way—written responses led to far fewer problems.

Most of the voicemails were fairly routine and he felt he could direct the reporters back to the webcasts for the answers they were seeking. But as he went through the messages, he grew a little concerned about one from Sylvia Paniagua at the *Denver Post*. In her message she asked about Nixon's body and this worried him. He just didn't want to start down a path that could lead to more questions about Jack and Mia's role onboard the *Dolorosa*. Seven grand of taxpayers money to pay off extortion demands would take this story to a whole new level.

Paniagua said she was on a tight deadline. He considered calling her back but given the late hour he felt it was not unreasonable that he would have left for the day. A return call would have to wait until morning. She'd be forced to do her story without the benefit of a conversation with the RCSO spokesman. She, like everyone else, would need to rely on the sheriff's words in the webcast.

CHAPTER 74

"This yellowtail came out perfect, Dad."

"Yeah, I have it admit, it's pretty damn good."

Jack looked at Lisa's plate and saw she had hardly touched her food.

"You still not feeling a hundred percent?"

"I'll be fine. It's just my stomach."

Peter jumped on. "If you aren't better by tomorrow maybe you should see Doctor Chadwick."

"Yeah, maybe I will."

"Good, let's give her a call first thing in the morning."

Peter shifted the conversation. "How were things aboard the *Top Shelf*?"

"It was great. The crew was helpful and the accommodations were first class."

"Good to hear. I should have you go out more often and report back to me. I only hear the good things; it would be great to have an objective opinion of how we're doing."

"Any time you want to send me out, I'm game."

"How many anglers did we have today?"

"I think about seven or eight. It was a small group—that's one of the things that makes it so great. I've been on fishing boats where they cram forty or fifty people onboard and it's a frickin' mess. Lines get tangled, tempers flare . . . no thanks. I'll take the *Top Shelf* any day."

"We cap the number of customers at a dozen so we should never have those issues. Glad it was a good experience for you, Jack."

"I did chat a little bit with the women who runs the galley. Catrina was her name, I believe. She was terrific, great with all the customers."

Jack's comments caught Lisa's attention. She looked at her father, getting a read on him.

"I don't think I know Catrina. Tell me more about her, Dad."

"Oh, I'm not sure there's any more to tell. She was just really fun and I enjoyed talking to her."

Lisa raised her eyebrow at her dad.

"Geez, Lisa, can't I speak about a woman without your radar going up?"

"My radar isn't going up, I'm just curious. Like I said, I don't believe I know her. Peter, do you know Catrina?"

"No, I don't think I do. What's she look like, Jack?" Peter replied with a smile.

Great, Jack thought. Peter was egging him on now. He figured he'd come clean; they weren't in junior high.

"She's probably mid forties, with dark hair and dark eyes. Very pretty."

"Oooh, I think my Dad has a little crush."

Jack looked at his daughter.

"So what if I do?"

"Nothing, Dad. I think it's great. You've been single a long time."

"Oh for God's sake, Lisa. I'm not proposing marriage to the woman. I just found her kind of interesting, that's all."

"Well, is she single?"

"I don't know, it didn't come up in our conversation. But I did notice she wasn't wearing a ring."

"Peter, you need to check tomorrow. Look at her personnel file and see if she lists a husband."

"Lisa, I'm not sure that's really appropriate."

"An innocent peek, that's all. Come on Peter, it's no big deal. You could be doing Catrina a favor. You never know."

Jack didn't say anything. Both Lisa and Peter noticed Jack didn't seem opposed to the idea.

"Okay, I'll check tomorrow."

"Thanks, honey."

A few moments of silence followed until Peter pointed at the television screen. He grabbed the remote and raised the volume level. Jack and Lisa turned their attention to what was playing on CNN International.

"Ah, crap," Jack said.

Cresencio Valenzuela was sitting in his living room channel surfing. At ten o'clock he cued up the Channel Eight news. His eyes got big when an image of Jed Nixon filled the screen; he quickly upped the volume and watched closely as anchor Angela Bell outlined the story of Nixon's death.

His anonymous call to the station two days earlier had worked. The story confirmed Nixon's death in Mexico and Valenzuela's mind went straight to the ten grand that Reggie Gray would have to pay him. But the story on the news wasn't all good in that it referenced the interest the RCSO had in finding Nixon's killer. He considered how the hit had gone down—it was clean, he thought. They'd have one hell of a time tracking him down. He had more than a dozen hits under his belt and the cops had never been able to touch him. He was good at his craft, and the hit on Nixon was one of his better efforts.

He thought about picking up the phone and calling Reggie, demanding his money. But he thought better of it. The hour was late and the call would wait till morning.

The story on CNN International was short and lacked details. There was no mention of the extortion component of the story, just a thirty-second rundown of Jed Nixon's murder and the fact that he was being pursued in Mexico by Colorado authorities. They specifically named the RCSO and used a few seconds of video from the webcast, but there was no specific mention of Jack, Mia, Peter, or the Marbella.

"What was that all about?" asked Lisa, concerned, staring at the television.

Jack looked at his daughter. "When Mia and I came down here the other day we witnessed something on the fishing charter out of San Martin. The media got wind of it and I was concerned about how the story might be reported."

"What did you see?"

Jack told his daughter what had happened, leaving out the extortion part and Peter's role in delivering the seven thousand dollars.

"Oh, my God, that's horrible. So why is this making the news all the way down here? I mean, this is a Colorado case, right?"

"Because someone made an anonymous call to a television station in Denver and said I was the one who killed the guy on the boat."

Lisa raised her hand to her mouth, "What?"

"I didn't do it, obviously. But Mia and I were there and we saw the whole thing go down. We have no idea who killed the guy. The shot was fired from a distance."

"So why would someone say you did it?"

"Who knows? Maybe someone with a beef with the RCSO, or me specifically. It happens, sweetie. Don't worry about it."

Lisa got angry. "Someone accuses my father of murder and you don't want me to worry about it?"

Peter jumped in, "Lisa, it doesn't look like Jack being accused is even being reported on. This thing will blow over and in a day or two the media will be onto their next big story."

"I should have been told! I'm finding out about this on CNN?"

"We didn't tell you because we weren't even sure it would make the news. Frankly, it must be a slow news day for CNN or they wouldn't have done anything with it."

Lisa folded her arms. "I should have been told."

"Okay, I apologize for that. That's on me," Peter responded.

Jack jumped in, "No, I should have told you. I guess I didn't want to worry you."

"No more secrets. Do you both understand that?"

Jack and Peter both nodded.

"I'm sorry."

"Sorry, sweetie."

Jack left the room and walked onto the patio. He dialed Mark Archer to let him know about the CNN story.

CHAPTER 75

It was nine thirty by the time Mick and Mia arrived home. They had waited out several newscasts, monitoring the coverage with Mark Archer. Nothing too inflammatory had popped up in any of the stories; it seemed the webcast and their efforts to soft pedal the part of the story about Jack and Mia being on board the *Dolorosa* at the time of Jed Nixon's murder had worked.

Mark went home planning to relax and go to bed early, but he had an uneasy feeling about the call from Sylvia Paniagia at the *Post*. He made a mental note to call her first thing in the morning. He had talked to Mick about her call, and the two had decided to just say they didn't know what happened to Nixon's body—that after the murder the Mexican authorities had stepped in and handled everything and Jack and Mia had returned to Colorado. And, technically speaking, this was the truth. Mexican authorities had taken over after the murder. That just left out the part about the extortion. And, truth be told, they didn't know that happened to Nixon's body, although Jack had expressed a strong suspicion that the body was dumped at sea. And now, with Jack's phone call about Nixon's body surfacing, his suspicions had been confirmed.

Mark woke early and was in his office a little before six. He wanted to keep an eye on the news coverage coming from the East Coast and with the two-hour time difference between Eastern and Mountain time, he needed to be in early. Jack's call the night before telling him that CNN International had run a brief story on Nixon's murder had him somewhat concerned, but he hoped it was a one-and-done kind of thing. If some big story broke, he was confident the media would quickly lose interest in Jed Nixon. Come on, hurricane, he thought to himself. Or maybe a big earthquake.

He checked all the local media websites and saw no damning coverage. Maybe they had dodged the bullet, he thought. But then he remembered the call he'd soon be making to Sylvia Paniagua. The fact that no other reporters were pursuing the angle that she mentioned in her message could be a good sign. That, or it could make her even more determined Reporters liked finding something that no one else was doing with the story.

Mick and Mia drove in together, arriving at the office at seven thirty. They checked in with Archer first thing, and he told them about the CNN International story from the night before. Archer also let them know that the overall coverage had been largely benign, and that just maybe there was a light at the end of the tunnel.

Lisa slept in a bit while Peter got ready for work. Jack was in one of the Marbella suites and had expressed some interest in doing some more fishing aboard the *Top Shelf.* Peter suspected he might be looking for a little more time with Catrina, which was fine with him. Jack had been single a long time and if he found someone he liked, then more power to him. Peter scribbled himself a note to check Catrina's personnel file when he got to the office. It was a little sketchy in terms of the ethics, but his intentions were good. Maybe Catrina was looking for someone, too.

He left Lisa a note on the kitchen table reminding her to make an appointment with Dr. Chadwick.

CHAPTER 76

M ark picked up the phone and dialed the number for Sylvia Paniagua. It was a bit early for a newspaper reporter to be in the office, so his hope was to leave a quick message and then maybe dodge her for a good part of the day. Those hopes evaporated when she picked up on the first ring.

Damn it, he thought.

"Hi, Sylvia, this is Mark Archer returning your call from last night."

"Good morning, lieutenant. Thanks for the call back. I had a couple questions for you about the Jed Nixon case."

"Sure, what can I do for you?"

"I'm curious—what happened to Mr. Nixon's body?"

She didn't waste any time, he thought.

"To be honest, we don't really know. The murder took place on Mexican soil and the authorities there had jurisdiction. So, that's probably a better question for them."

Mark knew he was taking a chance suggesting she call down to San Martin. If she did and she found someone willing to talk, then things could unravel rather quickly. But the odds of her making the call and finding someone willing to spill the beans was pretty remote. And suggesting it got him off the hook.

"Yeah, maybe I'll do that."

It was a-less-than-enthusiastic reply. He knew she wouldn't make the call. His gamble had worked.

"What else can I help you with?"

Paniagua asked him a few more questions that he easily deflected. He reminded her that the webcast the sheriff had done answered virtually all the questions she had, and that she was welcome to take quotes from the video. The call ended after a few minutes. Mark breathed a sigh of relief and got busy with his day.

Paniagua sat at her desk and considered where she was with the story. The call that had prompted the story had come in to the Channel 8 newsroom anonymously. She knew they wouldn't share anything more with her about the call, and since it was anonymous she had no way of contacting the person making the call.

She considered the possibility of having the *Post* offer a reward if the anonymous caller would contact them directly. If she had an opportunity to talk to the person maybe she could shake loose some additional information on what happened in Mexico. But offering a reward to an anonymous caller was new territory for her—she had never seen a news agency do such a thing. It might not even prompt a call from the person and there was a risk the *Post* would get a flood of calls from people wishing to insert themselves in the story or just looking to make a quick buck.

She was frustrated. She sensed there was more to the story, but she didn't see a way to move forward.

Catrina Schambra was indeed single. She was forty-six years old, divorced, and didn't appear to have any children. She was from Minden, Nevada, rented a room in Puerto Peñasco and had been employed at the Marbella for just a few months. Peter recognized her employee photo, he had just never attached a name to the face. There was more than a twenty-year age difference between Jack and Catrina, but who knew? Love worked in mysterious ways.

CHAPTER 77

"So, how long have you been feeling crummy, Lisa?"

"Three or four days, I guess."

"It's mostly your stomach? Just queasy?"

"Yeah, and I just feel off."

"Hmmm. When was your last period?"

"About a month ago. I'm due about now."

"Are you using birth control?"

Lisa looked at Dr. Chadwick. The thought of being pregnant had crossed her mind. She and Peter had been using birth control, but she remembered the afternoon a couple weeks earlier when he had come home frustrated and they had sex. It had all happened so quickly that they had not used any form of protection.

"Almost always."

Dr. Chadwick smiled. "If I had a dollar for every time I'd heard that . . ."

"Do you think I'm pregnant?"

"There's only one way to find out. We'll do a quick pregnancy test. Should have the results within the hour."

Lisa surprised her husband with a drop-in visit to his office at the Marbella. She rarely bothered him at work, but today was special. And there was no way she could wait to deliver the news to him. After talking with her husband she approached Juan Manuel, the head chef at the Marbella. She asked him for a favor and he was more than happy to accommodate her request.

Jack boarded the *Top Shelf* and made his way to the galley.

"You're back!"

"Yeah, I just couldn't get enough yesterday . . . had to come back for more."

Catrina smiled at the handsome man taking a seat at the counter in front of her.

"Coffee?"

"Yes, please, as large a cup as you've got."

"Coming right up. Hey, how'd you do yesterday? I didn't have a chance to ask."

"A couple of nice yellowtail. Grilled one of them up last night. It was great."

"Sweet! Hey, I noticed you didn't come in for cocktails on the ride back to the Marbella. You a loner, Jack?" she replied, smiling.

"No, an alcoholic, actually. A recovering alcoholic, I should say."

Catrina grew serious. "Oh, I'm sorry for teasing you. My mistake."

"No worries. I've been sober for more than fifteen years," he replied, leaving out his one misstep a year or so earlier.

"Good for you. I'm impressed. It's a tough road, sobriety."

"Yes, it is. But everyone has their struggles, you know?"

"True enough."

Catrina looked at Jack and felt the stirrings of a strong attraction to him. He was quite a bit older than she was, but he was nice and he was certainly honest. He pulled no punches and she liked that. He was different than most men she knew. She handed him his coffee and made sure their fingers touched.

Peter spent his day interviewing more people for the CEO position. He settled on two possible candidates and decided he'd take a few days to think about it. He arrived home a little before six and found Jack and Lisa sitting on the patio.

"Join us, Peter. We're just discussing dinner plans," Jack said.

"Let me get a drink first and I'll be right with you."

"I'll get it for you, Peter. Sit down."

Lisa left and Peter took a seat at the table.

"How was your day, Jack? Did you do some more fishing?"

"I did, sort of. Just spent the day onboard the *Top Shelf* but never actually put a line in the water. Just enjoyed the ocean."

"Ah, sounds nice. And I'm guessing Catrina was working today?"

"She was."

"Well, for the record, I took a quick peek at her personnel file today."

"Peter, you didn't have to do that."

"Yeah, I know. So do you want to know what I learned?" he asked, smiling.

"Learned about what?" Lisa asked, coming back to the conversation. She placed a drink in front of her husband.

"I did a little snooping on Catrina today."

"Oh, really?" replied Lisa.

"Geez, you two. I feel like I'm back in junior high."

"Come on, Dad. Just a little harmless fun."

"You guys are blowing this all out of proportion."

"So, do you want to know what I learned, Jack?"

Jack looked at Peter and then at Lisa.

"Yeah, okay. What have you got?"

Lisa smiled at her Dad. She liked seeing him interested in a woman.

"Well, she's forty-six years old, lives in town, and came from Northern Nevada. Been with us just a few months."

"Peter, you're leaving out the most important part. Don't leave us in suspense!"

"Oh, yeah . . . I almost forgot."

Peter was laughing now. "She's single."

"I knew it!" responded Lisa.

Jack felt outnumbered. "Okay, that's good to know."

Lisa looked at her Dad. "Yes, that is good to know. I just think you need to do a little more fishing when you're down here. And you need to come down more often."

"Well, I'd like to, but I do have a job in Colorado."

"Have you given any thoughts to retirement, Jack?" Peter asked.

"Retiring? Not really, as long as I am able to do the job, I'll probably stick with it."

"What if you had a reason to be down here more?"

"You mean, like a woman?"

"Well that, and . . . "

"What?"

"Hold on just a minute. Peter can you join me for a minute in the kitchen?"

"Sure."

"What's going on with you two?"

Neither answered as they stood and left the room, leaving Jack to wonder.

A minute later Lisa and Peter walked back in the room, each holding something behind their backs.

"What the hell is going on? You two are acting all mysterious."

Lisa looked at her husband and he nodded. They brought their arms forward and placed what they had been hiding in front of Jack.

"What's all this?"

Neither spoke, they just broke into wide smiles.

Jack looked down at two cupcakes on the table—one pink and one blue.

Lisa looked at Jack. "Hey, Granddad. "

"What? Oh, my God. Are you kidding me?"

Lisa wrapped her arms around her father's neck and hugged him tightly.

"You are going to be a wonderful grandfather, Dad."

"I can't believe this. When did you find out?'

"This afternoon. I told Peter right after my appointment with Dr. Chadwick."

"This is incredible. I am so happy for you both."

"I guess it wasn't the flu after all," Peter added.

"No, evidently not! Any idea of a due date?"

"About eight months from now, she said."

Jack thought for a moment. "Maybe retirement isn't that far off after all."

The three shared the cupcakes.

"Here's to the future," Jack said.

"I love you, Dad."

"I love you, too, sweetie."

ACKNOWLEDGMENTS

This book was a little bit of a struggle; sometimes life gets in the way. In August 2018 we lost my mother-in-law, Rose, and the loss set us back a little bit. But, over time I was able to get back on track and finish *Top Shelf.*

I have so many people to thank for helping me write my fourth novel. First and foremost my beautiful wife and best friend, Giselle, who read each section as I wrote it and offered me feedback.

As always, I thank Dara Murphy for keeping me on track with the mechanics of the story. Dara reviewed every word I wrote and corrected grammar and punctuation. Knowing she was there to back me up enabled me to write what I was feeling and not worry too much about the technical stuff. She is simply one of the brightest people I know and her attention to detail saves me every time!

One of the byproducts of writing these stories is the discovery of the many book clubs that have read my novels. Being invited to participate in a fun evening of discussion of how I wrote the book has been a blast! And having an intimate gathering of people offering feedback has been hugely beneficial to me. I'm flattered by the interest and their support. Please contact me if you would like me to come out to speak to your book club.

There are several characters in the book named for winners of charity auctions. It has been fun for me to see the excitement people have when they see their name in print. I'm happy to support these charities.

I also appreciate the continuing support of Kevin Bernzott of Bernzott Capital Advisors. He has generously provided me the opportunity to share my novels with his many friends and business associates. Interestingly, Kevin finds himself portrayed as a Rocklin County detective in *Top Shelf*!

A special thank you to my good friend Dan Green of OMG Media in Monterey - his assistance is greatly appreciated.